Sticks And Stone

GRACE MCGINTY

Also by Grace McGinty

Hell's Redemption Series: The Redeemable / The Unrepentant / The Fallen

Damnation MC Duet: Serendipity / Providence

The Azar Nazemi Trilogy : Smoke and Smolder / Burn and Blaze / Rage and Ruin

Dark River Days Series: Newly Undead In Dark River / Happily Undead In Dark River / Pleasantly Undead in Dark River

Black Mountain Mates: Hunting Isla

Eden Academy Series: The Lost and the Hunted (Prequel) / Heart of the Hounded (Prequel) / Rebels and Runaways (Book 1) / Sweethearts and Savages (Book 2)

Shadow Bred Series: Manix / Frenzy / Feral

Stand Alone Novels and Novellas: Bright Lights From A Hurricane / The Last Note / Inside The Maelstrom Part 1 and 2 / Sticks and Stone

Omega Lottery: Tryst In The Dark

Sticks And Stone

For Pascal, who patiently answered all my questions so the hockey scenes were authentic.

For Amy Jo and Robert, who heard my call out and didn't hesitate to help.

For Raewyn, gold medalist in badassery during the Covid Olympics. Thank you for being the best damn tortoise in the editing game.

CHAPTER
One

NOVA

IT HAD TAKEN me three months not to have an anxiety attack every time the front doorbell rang. I'd tried everything: therapy, deep breathing—hell, I'd even changed the doorbell tone, and later took it away altogether. My friends knew not to ring it; they just called when they were out the front. Even the food delivery guys didn't ring anymore.

Maybe I should have tried desensitizing myself to the doorbell instead, because apparently, someone knocking had roughly the same effect anyway.

Breathing in and out, I walked toward the front door.

It hadn't always been this way, obviously. No one is born with an aversion to doorbells. No, my brain—the wonderful and complex piece of equipment that it was —now associated the doorbell with the worst day of my life.

Even as I walked toward it now, the present was overlaid with memories of three months ago. Opening the door, smiling. Feeling the expression fall from my face as I took in the two policemen in front of me, their faces solemn. Collapsing on the ground, wailing, as they told me that my parents had crashed on the freeway and died instantly. Continuing to wail until one of the officers stood me up, holding me in his arms until the neighbors appeared.

Then Rita, my neighbor and one of my mother's best friends, held me as I cried for the next six hours. Her daughter Chloe—my best friend—arrived hours later and took over, so her mother could properly grieve without trying to hold me together too.

Rita took care of the funeral arrangements. Oscar, her husband, ensured I ate, using that Dad tone that I'd never again hear from my own father to make sure I swallowed every single bite.

Since then, it'd been the worst twelve weeks of my life, but I was moving through life, existing. It was getting easier. Not better, but easier.

Except for the fucking front door.

Sucking deep breaths in through my nose and out through my mouth, I dragged myself back to the present. *Open the door. It's okay. It's probably just Mormons or something.*

My stomach dropped when I saw it wasn't Mormons. I definitely would have preferred that to the sight of my father's lawyer and an unknown woman.

"Miss Stone. It's good to see you." Mr. Lief, my dad's lawyer, didn't say I looked well, because I really didn't. I looked tired, exhausted both physically and emotionally.

"It's nice to see you too, Mr. Lief. I'm surprised, though?"

We'd done the reading of my parents' wills. They'd left me everything, but as their only child, it was pretty standard. I'd sold my father's partnership in his chiropractic firm back to his business partners. My mom had been a customer service clerk at the DMV. They didn't have much except this house and their 401(k)s, so the whole process had been reasonably simple, especially as we didn't have any close extended family. All my grandparents were gone, as well as my Uncle Jerry. My dad had been an only child.

"Not as surprised as I am. May I introduce Mrs. Janette Fischer? She's from Child Protective Services."

Well, now I was super confused.

Mrs. Fischer leaned forward and shook my hand. "Nice to meet you, Miss Stone."

Smiling tightly, I returned the gesture. "Please, call me Nova."

She nodded, the shadow of a smile passing over her face. "May we come in?"

I frowned but nodded, standing to the side as they stepped through the doorway. I was kind of glad I'd just been floating through life like a ghost, because the house was still clean from the last time Chloe had come over and baked me cookies, hovering like a mother hen as she tidied my house for me.

Janette Fischer looked around my childhood home, still filled with my mother's knick-knacks and family pictures, as if my parents were just going to walk back in the door again. It screamed *undealt with grief,* but screw it.

I'd be ready when I was ready.

"I'm not sure what this visit is for, but I promise you, despite the baby face, I'm actually twenty-four," I joked weakly.

Mr. Lief gives me a tight smile. "Sorry for the intrusion, but after Mrs. Fischer reached out, I thought it would be best if I sat in on this meeting. A familiar face, and all that."

Mr. Lief had been my father's golfing buddy since I was ten. If he wasn't here in an official lawyer capacity…

"I'll get straight to the point, Miss Stone."

"Nova," I corrected weakly, because I could already feel my heart beginning to pound too hard in my chest.

"Nova. I'm not sure if you're aware of this, but a child has recently come into the care of the emergency foster system. An infant. His mother, unfortunately, died suddenly of a postpartum brain aneurysm two nights ago. We haven't been able to get hold of her emergency contacts." She swallowed hard. "The child's birth certificate lists your father as his parent, making you the infant's half-sister. From what we can ascertain, you're also his only living relative."

White noise rushed into my ears. Just one long, loud buzz as she continued to speak slowly, but I couldn't hear her over the sound any longer.

My father had a baby. Another child? Jesus, he was like fifty, and he'd been having an affair with someone? Having babies with them?

"Nova?" It was Mr. Lief's voice that snapped me back to the conversation.

"I'm sorry. I had no idea..." I had no idea, what? I had no idea that my dad, who'd just died, was a cheater? I had no idea who this woman was? That I had a baby something?

Mrs. Fischer's face was understanding. "I fully comprehend that this is a shock, Nova. Mr. Lief reacted much the same way when the Department reached out to him."

Mr. Lief was shaking his head, like he was still in shock. *That makes two of us, buddy.*

Mrs. Fischer, with her gray and brown hair, sucked in a deep breath. "The Department always prefers children to go with a family member. The ties of blood and belonging are important. You're the only blood family he has."

My heart felt like it was going to explode in my chest.

"But I want you to know that you aren't obligated to take him in. I understand this is a shock, especially on the heels of your parents' deaths, so take some time to think about it."

"If I don't take him, what happens?" The words tasted like poison on my tongue, but I had to know.

She nodded her head gently. "He's only six weeks old, Nova. He'll stay in foster placement and will probably—most likely—be adopted. Babies have an easier time of it than older children. Although, he does have a congenital heart defect that may make it more difficult—"

"He's sick?" I was going to throw up.

"He has a congenital heart defect, called an atrial septal defect. It's nothing to be worried about just yet, but he may need surgery in the future if it doesn't close on its own."

"And people won't want to adopt him because he's what, bruised fruit?"

Mrs. Fischer shook her head. "I don't think that will be the case at all, but adoption itself is a costly process, and most families can't take on the added burden of a medically unwell child."

I flopped back into the couch cushions, my brain reeling with the intrusive thoughts that were hammering me from all sides.

My dad had a six-week-old son.

My half-brother had a heart defect and was an orphan.

My parents were dead. Hell, *I* was an orphan.

Was this what my parents had been talking about

when they'd crashed their car into a guardrail on the freeway? The police had said they'd lost control, but had it been because my parents were fighting over his affair?

An affair with someone young enough to have a baby?

I'd thought my parents had been happy. They'd loved each other for as long as I could remember, like a true kind of love. They'd often danced together in the kitchen. My dad still used to slap my mother on the ass when she gave him coffee in the mornings.

They'd *loved* each other. But this baby was proof that maybe they hadn't, really. Maybe it had all been a lie.

"I understand this is a lot for you to take in, Nova. You don't have to give me an answer now."

I was mad at my father, which was odd, because fifteen minutes ago, I would've never thought I could picture his face without feeling grief. But now I thought about him and this orphaned baby, and I felt *angry*.

But not angry enough that I would give up a remaining piece of him. That I would set someone else adrift in the world when I could give them a past, a history. Not so mad that I'd forsake the last person in the world who shared my bloodline, let him go to a family who might not be able to pay for his heart problems, or let him sit in foster care because surgeries were too expensive and no one wanted him.

I shook my head at Janette Fischer. "I don't need to think about it. Tell me what I need to do to adopt him."

CHAPTER

Two

NOVA

PREPARING for a newborn was not an easy task. There was a reason you had to use the whole nine months pre-birth to get prepared.

Chloe had driven home after I'd called her in hysterics. We'd spent that first night drinking wine and eating ice cream, and I'd cried my eyes out. Bawled like a baby. Chloe had cried too, because she'd spent as much time at my house, with my parents, as she had her own.

The betrayal of my father cut deep, and still, I couldn't wrap my head around it. It felt like a lie, but Mr. Lief had sent me a copy of the baby's birth certificate, and right under the title of Father, was my dad's name. His date of birth. This address.

There was no mistaking it.

So I packed away my grief, and my betrayed memories, and I got to work. I bought books on babies and had them overnighted to me. I found checklists on the internet and printed them out until I had a small tree's worth of paperwork.

I went shopping. I wasn't rich by any means—and I expected I'd be even less so with a baby around—so I tried to buy what I could secondhand, hitting up thrift stores and online marketplaces to find things. Except for a car seat. I bought a state-of-the-art, top-of-the-line car seat.

A week later, Janette Fischer returned to my house to conduct a 'home study,' which I'd prepared for like I did any other test: by panicking until I was a basket case. I'd put child safety locks on literally every single door. I'd boxed up all the small things I thought a baby could put in its mouth, even if I may have gone a little overboard.

I'd cried the whole time as I boxed up Mom's things. This whole thing felt unfair to her. Like somehow, Dad's memory got to live on, but she'd be the burned party forever. That hurt. But I also knew what Mom would've done in my situation, so it helped as I packed her things away and put them in the garage.

When Janette arrived, the place looked like Alcatraz, but at least it was as baby-proof as I could get it. She walked through the house, making notes on her clipboard, while I sat on the couch and fretted.

In my head, I made more plans, more lists. I'd found a place online that would sell bulk diapers, but I thought maybe I should get reusable ones. Fuck, I'd just get a mixture of both because who had time to wash dirty diapers all the time when they were learning to take care of another human being?

Janette returned, giving me a huge, reassuring smile. *Thank god.*

"You've done a wonderful job in the last week, Nova. It must have been hard work."

You could tell she worked with children, because she had that gentle, encouraging tone of voice that may have been condescending if I'd been any less needy for reassurance.

"Thank you. I'm cramming every baby book under the sun in preparation."

She gave me a tight smile. "There's been a development that I think you should know about. A contesting petition has been filed for baby Huey's adoption."

I reared back. "What? I thought I was his only living relative."

Janette nodded. "You are, but Miss Madison—Huey's mother—was a foster child and had maintained some relationships with her previous foster siblings. These siblings wish to file for adoption."

"Will they get it?"

She shrugged. "It's my opinion, and the one that will be given in my report to the court, that you are the more stable option. But I can't guarantee what the court will do. Mr. Lief will be informed, and he'll figure it out for you, Nova. Don't panic."

The hearing was next week, and she was telling me not to panic for a whole seven days?

I gave her a tight smile and pushed down my anxiety. If Janette thought I was the better option, then that was that. Nothing would change.

I stood in the county courthouse with Mr. Lief on a random Wednesday in September. Mr. Lief was clear that family law wasn't his forte, but he thought this would be fairly cut and dried, despite the celebrity of the contesting party.

"Woah, hold up... Celebrity?"

"River Cooper, NHL defenseman."

"Football?"

Mr. Lief, bless his heart, kept his face impassive. "Ice hockey. He plays for the Ann Arbor IceCaps." Well shit, I knew nothing about ice hockey, but that sounded impressive. "Take a seat and I'll go see if they are running on schedule."

When we walked into the courtroom, there was no doubt in my mind who the hockey player was. He was huge, maybe six-four, and dressed immaculately in a suit. If nothing else about him told me he was making good money as a professional sportsperson, then his suit would do it. Behind him were two equally big guys, maybe a couple of inches shorter.

Holy shit. They all looked like they should be on the cover of *Sports Illustrated*. One of the shorter guys met my eyes and nudged the behemoth. Then all three looked at me, and I felt like an ant.

I was dressed nicely. I had a sensible dress that I'd pulled out of my mom's closet—then promptly cried for forty-five minutes after putting it on. We'd been roughly the same size and it fit perfectly. It was gray, with a pretty lace Peter Pan collar. I probably looked like a nun or a governess or something, but I wanted to make the right impression. I might only be twenty-four, but I was a responsible adult with a good job. I wasn't out here partying every weekend like I was in college. I had a job I did from home, so I was perfectly fit to look after a baby full-time.

But after seeing this well-dressed man in a suit that would've cost more than my car, combined with the quick Google search I'd done on my phone for his contract pay after Mr. Lief had name-dropped him, I wasn't sure why the old lawyer was so confident. This guy could pay for everything baby Huey would ever need. A nanny to look after him around the clock. He'd have opportunities I could never grant him. Surgeons who were top of their field. Gold-plated pacifiers.

I wasn't an idiot. I knew that financially, he had me beat. But could someone who was constantly on the road give a baby the love he deserved? My mom had read me a bedtime story every night until I was eleven and was able to read my own. She'd picked me up and dropped me off at school every day. Had attended all my ill-advised sporting attempts.

Would a nanny and a part-time dad be enough for a

kid to feel the same level of love and contentment I had?

So that's why I lifted my chin and stared back at every single one of those men, my eyes lingering on River Cooper. I wasn't here for a pissing match. I was here so that my brother could have a life filled with love and understanding. Safety and consistency.

After staring at him for a good ten seconds, I lifted my hand in a wave. We might be adversaries today, but I didn't want to be enemies. They obviously cared for Huey, and his mother, and I didn't want to cut Huey off from any family he still had, even if they weren't blood relatives.

It didn't help that they were stupidly good-looking, though. Honestly, River Cooper was gorgeous. A square-cut jaw, and light brown wavy hair that he'd styled back from his forehead. He had arms the size of my legs, and thighs the size of my whole torso.

He spun away without acknowledging my wave, as did the guy on his left. That guy was wiry, but just as tall and strong, his skin a soft tan that seemed to make the brown of his hair look even darker under the overhead lights.

It was only the last guy—a huge man with longish honey-blond hair and a clean-cut face—who lifted his hand back, his eyebrows raised.

Well, I guess he's the nice one.

I sat down at the table beside Mr. Lief, and the hearing got underway. The lawyers argued. CPS gave their report. Most of the legal jargon went over my head but it came down to this in layman's terms:

1. I could provide a home and around-the-clock care for Huey.

2. I was his actual blood relation. His sister. That counted for a lot, apparently.

3. I was financially stable and would be able to provide for all of Huey's needs.

But, on the other side, it was just as good.

1. River Cooper already knew Huey. He was his uncle in everything but blood. He had supported Alana, Huey's mother, throughout her pregnancy as he'd considered her a sister.

2. He could provide a standard of living and opportunities that Huey would never get with me.

3. He could have the best medical care money could buy.

In the end, even I was almost convinced he'd be better off with River Cooper.

I'd tried hard not to think of Huey's mother, Alana, over the last week. The woman who had seduced my dad into cheating on my mom. I mentally pulled myself up before villainizing her, though.

My dad had been a grown-ass man, not some innocent teen. He'd had a successful business and a mountain of life experience; he wasn't lured unwillingly by some Jezebel, no matter what popular media would have you believe. He had a choice and he'd chosen badly.

Alana may or may not have known he was married. The point is, *she* wasn't the one who had stood at an altar twenty-five years ago and made promises to my mom. The fault was firmly on my dad's shoulders.

Still, when I saw the grief around River Cooper's eyes, it was hard to hide from the fact that she'd been special to someone. Several someones, if the palpable sadness of their small group was anything to go by.

After a long hearing, the judge granted me full legal custody of Huey. My heart thundered, and my eyes misted over. Now it was real. I was the parent of a six-week-old baby.

What the hell had I done?

CHAPTER
Three

RIVER

MY HANDS CURLED into fists where they rested on my thighs as the judge ruled in favor of the girl. My heart twisted in my chest as I failed Alana one more time. I'd promised her that I'd take care of the baby if anything ever happened to her, and I'd lost him before I even had him.

I spun to look at Nova Stone as the judge finished his closing speech. She was looking at him as he spoke, absolute terror on her face. It was like she didn't even *want* Huey; she was just fighting for him for the sake of it.

I squeezed my fists harder, and Rigby's hand patted me on the shoulder from where he sat behind me. Rigby was my teammate, but more than that, he was one of my best friends. We were family. He knew when I was about to blow my shit better than any other person on the planet, except perhaps Devan. And Alana.

My heart squeezed like it did every time I thought of her death, and I pushed those feelings back down. Instead, I stared at Nova again.

She wasn't what I'd expected, though I really didn't *know* what I'd been expecting. Someone who was immoral, like her father, who'd knocked up my best friend and then ghosted her?

If anything, Nova was almost angelic looking. Her hair was straight and hung just past her shoulders, like chestnut silk. She had olive skin, but freckles right across her nose, which made her seem even younger than her twenty-four years. Her curvy little body was wrapped in a severe, almost matronly dress, and she looked like she was playing dress-up in her mother's clothes.

My lawyer had told me that her parents had died in a car crash twelve weeks ago. I could almost see it in the way her body was bowing in on itself in grief. I knew that feeling all too well.

But I didn't want to feel sorry for her. Not at all.

As if she could tell I was watching her, she turned those big eyes my way. From this distance, I couldn't tell what color they were, but she looked at me, petrified, and some part of me was satisfied that she was freaking the hell out.

You reap what you sow. That's what my foster parents had always said. Didn't matter that neither Nova Stone or I had done any of the sowing in this situation.

Devan slapped my back. "Stop staring at her like

you want to eat her. We still need to get on her good side. Otherwise, we'll never see Huey again."

His words were gruff and bitter, and I looked over at my brother. Not by blood, but by bond. Me, Devan and Alana had made a pact to look after each other, and the weight of our failure sat heavy on us both.

I'd been out partying it up with puck bunnies and too much vodka, while she'd been seduced and taken advantage of by some old, married fuck. I'd been skating around, making a name for myself, and she'd been giving birth to a baby that the father refused to acknowledge. Devan had been there at the birth, but I should have been there too.

We'd both been too far away when she'd had a stroke and died, Huey beside her on the bed. It was only sheer luck that her next-door neighbor had been bringing her breakfast every morning and had found them.

Because I hadn't been there.

The doctors had told us it was a postpartum intracranial hemorrhage. They were rare, but they happened—there was nothing anyone could have done. But it happened to my best friend, while she was alone.

I should've forced her to move back to Ann Arbor with me and Devan. But she'd argued her whole life was here in Tucson. *He* was here in Tucson. Huey's father.

She hadn't known he was dead a month before

Huey was born. Would she have come home with me if she had? The endless what-ifs were killing me.

Devan nudged me with his elbow. "Let's go. I want to catch the girl before she leaves. We need to talk to her."

I nodded, giving my lawyer a quick thank you as I left. I stopped and signed a few autographs, but finally we made it out into the sweltering Tucson heat. Jesus, I wanted to go home already, but not before we got what we came for.

Devan wanted to buy Huey. I knew that. And I'd pay anything for him. But one look at Nova Stone told me that wasn't going to be an option. She looked shit scared but determined, and I knew that kind of expression. She was a do-what's-right kind of person. She wouldn't sell a baby for *any* amount of money.

So that was what we had to appeal to, but we had to do it stealthily. I wasn't known for my even-temperedness, though. I was an enforcer for the team, though I was fast and good at defense too. Gone were the days you could just be an enforcer, skating around and starting fights. So I worked hard and protected my team if they needed it.

Devan, though, was as smooth as he was dark. Rigby often joked that Devan didn't have an emotional wall around him. He had an abyss. If you stepped into it, you either sank or managed to drift across to find that soft heart he kept hidden away. Most people never made it that far.

He was a product of his upbringing, but we all were. Me with the fighting, Devan with the emotional unavailability, and Alana with her daddy issues that had gotten her knocked up by a man whose daughter was only two years younger than her.

We waited in the parking lot, and eventually, Nova Stone arrived. Her feet stilled as she saw us all, waiting around my Range Rover. I tried to put myself in her shoes as fear crossed her face. Maybe we should've waited for her in the courthouse, not out here in the parking lot like we were going to jump her.

The long silence probably didn't help as my brain scrambled around, trying to decide what to say.

As always, it was Rigby to the rescue.

"Miss Stone? My name is Rigby Engman. We just wanted to formally meet you, if we could. River you've met, of course, and this is his brother, Devan Mayson. We're in town for another day, and we'd really like to set up a meeting with you, just to discuss Huey." He gave her a soft smile—the disarming one that attracted women to him like flies to honey—before glaring at me over his shoulder. I curled my lips into something I hoped was a pleasant expression.

"If we could, Miss Stone," I grunted out, so she didn't think I was mute. Devan didn't even try.

She looked between us all, clearly steeling her spine. Taking a shaky breath, she nodded. "Sure. I know that he means something to you all; otherwise, you wouldn't be here. I don't... I would never try and cut him off from his family. I know what it's like to be alone in the world, and I don't want that for him, ever."

Something relaxed in my chest at her soft words.

Rigby nodded encouragingly. "Just name a time and place."

She dragged her eyes from Rigby to me, and swallowed hard. "CPS is dropping off Huey this afternoon, so how about tomorrow morning? At the Cheeky Javelina cafe?"

Rigby nodded, making a note of it in his phone. He pulled out his business card. "This is my number, in case you need anything beforehand. We'll see you there at about ten?"

She nodded and hopped into a rickety old Mazda. I mean, it had to be twenty years old.

That wasn't safe for Huey.

I hated this. Hated that his life and safety were going to be in the hands of a woman I didn't know. What if she was a psycho? Foster care had taught me that not all sociopaths were identifiable. Sometimes, they were sweet, motherly types on the outside.

We watched her drive away, and Rigby huffed. "You fuckers are useless. Could you be any more ominous?"

He climbed into the back seat of the Range Rover. Rigby mightn't have grown up with Alana, but he'd been my friend since we were rookies, and when we were both called up for the same team, it had felt like fate. He'd adopted her as an honorary little sister, and had been there through her pregnancy too. Had held Huey in his huge arms as a tiny newborn. Cried at her funeral only a few weeks later.

He mightn't have the same history with her as Devan and I, but he'd loved her—of that I had no doubt.

I climbed into the driver's seat, Devan sliding into the passenger seat beside me. Staring through the windshield, I asked, "So, what do we do?"

Rigby and I both looked at Devan. He was so fucking smart. To look at him, you'd think he was some kind of shady bastard. He'd seen things growing up— we all had—and it still affected him today. So he had that coldness that put people off, and the brains to make you run around in circles before you even knew what was happening. He'd been investing money since I first went pro. He'd taken half of my first contract's pay, and invested it.

Our money tripled. Then he started an investment company, with me and him having a fifty-fifty split, and he'd turned it into a multi-million-dollar profit-making machine. I had no idea how he did it. I didn't ask the hard questions; I just gave him money, and he made millions. That was the deal.

"If we can't buy Huey, we buy the girl instead," he said, his voice deadpan.

Everyone had a price. We both knew that all too well.

CHAPTER

Four

NOVA

I HAD NOT BEEN PREPARED. Honestly, *nothing* could have prepared me.

When Janette had dropped off a sleeping Huey, I'd looked down into the face of my baby brother and fallen in love. Deeply. Wholeheartedly.

I knew as she placed him in my arms that I would do absolutely anything for him. Give him anything. Raze the world for him. He was dressed in a tiny blue onesie, with a little cap on his head, his closed eyes fanning tiny blond lashes across his cheeks. He was beautiful.

I'd put him in the crib in my room, filled out all the paperwork Janette had given me while he slept, and grilled her for forty-five minutes about little things I should know. She'd given me his medical history, and that of Alana's. She'd also given me a box full of Huey's baby things, including a picture of him with his mom, and I'd held it together reasonably well, I thought.

But after Janette had left, I'd stared at that photo. The girl in it was so full of life and happiness. She was blonde, which must have been where Huey got his soft blond fuzz from, and she was smiling as she held him close, looking down at him with such love.

I'd sat on the couch and cried for her. Cried for the fact she'd never see her baby grow up. Cried that my dad—the man I'd loved and respected—had done her wrong. Cried about the unfairness of it all.

If she hadn't died, would she have ever sought me out? Would I have ever met Huey?

Then Huey had woken up and freaked out, as much as an infant could freak out. He didn't know me, but here I was, trying to give him a bottle after testing its temperature on every sensitive part of my body. I'd even dripped a little on my eyelid.

He'd finished his bottle, then continued to cry. He cried until I called Rita next door. She'd come over, burped him, put him to bed, and then held me while I sobbed. When she finally went home, Huey had cried on and off all night.

What the fuck was I thinking?

A part of me really wanted to cancel today's meeting with Huey's uncles. I'd sat through the hearing, but I still didn't really understand their dynamic with Alana. Had River Cooper dated her? Were they former lovers?

Or was it the familial relationship that River's lawyers had stated it was?

There was only one way to find out, and to discuss what was best for Huey. And that was to go down to the Cheeky Javelina.

It had taken me two hours to get Huey ready to leave the house. I'd gone through the Diaper Bag Checklist twice, as well as stumbled through the Morning Routine Checklist. I burped him the way Rita had showed me, trying to judge what he needed to wear in summer in Tucson.

I decided on a short-sleeved onesie. And then I packed a little cardigan thing in case it got cold. And a sleep sack thing in case it somehow became arctic. And his little knit cap. And sixteen diapers. And a warm bottle of water, and a container of formula. Wipes. A change mat. Infant Tylenol. The list went on and on and on.

I watched an online tutorial on how to get the baby carrier on. Then I started to worry I'd drop the baby accidentally, and decided to just put him in the car seat thing that went into the car and also into the stroller.

Long story short, I was now running ten minutes late, my hair was in a messy bun on top of my head, I was wearing jeans and an old band tee that I loved, and I probably looked so sleep-deprived that I actually appeared insane.

I hadn't slept well since my parent's accident, so I was used to living on minimal sleep. Janette had said that it would take time for Huey to adjust. I just had to stick it out.

The cafe was busy, but it wasn't hard to find where Huey's uncles were sitting, since everybody in the cafe was angled in their direction. Mostly so they could get a better look without being obvious, but some people—mostly women—were openly staring.

I mean, when I spotted them, I understood completely. They were handsome as hell in suits. But casually reclining in jeans and tight t-shirts?

Hooboy.

When I stepped further into the cafe, it was the tall, dark and handsome one who spotted me first. Devan, that was the name they'd used yesterday at the hearing. He was Alana's foster brother too, apparently.

His dark eyes burned into me, his face tense, and I felt stripped bare. I wanted to fidget on the spot, but I held my gaze steady as I stared back at him. I navigated the stroller around all the chairs and people, and when I made it to the table, Devan's eyes dropped to Huey.

And his face softened completely.

He lifted an eyebrow and gestured to the car seat Huey was still strapped into. I nodded. I looked over at the other two men at the table, but their eyes were focused on the baby too.

Devan held Huey in his huge hands, supporting the baby like he'd held him a million times. "You're getting so big, little man. I've missed you." He turned his eyes to me. "I stayed with Alana for the first month after he was born. I was only gone two weeks when…" He trailed off. He'd been gone for two weeks when she died. I could imagine the guilt he must feel.

Huey cooed and reached for the dark-eyed man, like he knew him already. Like he loved him. Like this man was familiar in a world where he'd been passed around strangers for two weeks, missing his mother.

River and Rigby were watching him too, and when Devan put the baby over his shoulder, patting him softly until he drifted off to sleep, I couldn't help it. I burst into tears.

River slid away from me like I was contagious, and Rigby just gaped. I didn't look at Devan as I tried to push down my sobs, but they just kept pushing past my lips like a wrecking ball. "I'm… sorry," I choked out, scrubbing my cheeks with my hands. "It's… just… tiredness. I'm okay."

I firmly believed it, too. I was okay. Of course I was okay. Hell, if I kept repeating it, maybe I would actually *be* okay.

Rigby stood up and came around the table, pulling me to my feet and wrapping me in his arms. He was a perfect fucking stranger, and he was hugging me, and it made me *feel better*. His hand stroked up and down my back softly, as he murmured things that I couldn't really hear because I was short as hell and only came up to his pecs. But the steady rumble of his voice was reassuring.

"It's okay. This is a lot. Come on, now. It's all right."

A tissue appeared in my peripheral vision, and I

realized River had grabbed one from my diaper bag. I gave him a tight smile of thanks and pulled back, embarrassment settling in over my body as I realized I'd just cried into the chest of a stranger, in public.

Everyone was staring at me now, and my face flushed hot with shame. I'd had the baby less than a day and I was already a mess. Everyone could clearly see that I had no fucking idea what I was doing.

River seemed to give the surrounding crowd the stink eye. "Swap places with me."

I swallowed hard as he gave me his seat, with its back to the rest of the cafe. Chewing my lip, I nodded appreciatively. "Thank you. I promise I'm not normally like this."

Rigby made a soothing noise as he led me to River's vacated seat. "Naw, it's okay. It's been a crazy couple of weeks for all of us. I'd be worried if you didn't want to cry." Somehow, this big blond giant validating my feelings did kind of make me feel better.

A waitress came over as soon as my ass hit the seat, and took my coffee order. Or at least I thought she did; she didn't actually drag her eyes away from River and Rigby.

Finally, I thought I might actually have myself under control. Then Huey started to fuss. I panicked. This shit didn't come naturally just because I had boobs and ovaries. It was mostly just winging it and Googling and second-guessing shit.

I held my hands out for him, but Devan just stared

me down. "If you have a bottle ready, I can feed him." Rigby cleared his throat, and Devan glared at him. "*Please.* If it's okay with you."

I looked between the three men. The fact they'd obviously been talking about me before I arrived—hell, probably had hour-long discussions about me at some point—made me feel a little self-conscious.

Well, even more so, considering there were still wet patches on Rigby's shirt from my tears.

I gave Devan a tight smile. "Sure. There's one in the little insulated bottle holder thing." I rummaged around in the chaos of the diaper bag. Eventually, I'd be better at this; I had to keep telling myself that. I passed the still warm bottle to Devan. "He's been a bit fussy taking it, though."

Devan nodded, hitching the baby into the crook of his arm and testing the milk on his own wrist. Happy I wasn't scalding his nephew from the inside out, he put the bottle to the baby's lips. Huey took it so easily, I wanted to cry all over again.

Maybe it was just me. Maybe Huey hated me.

The waitress returned with my coffee, and she seemed a little awestruck by the sight of a huge man holding a tiny baby. My animalistic hindbrain had perked up, like *look at this specimen with his young. He would make an excellent mate for the season.*

No. Just no.

The waitress managed to drag herself away, and I took a fortifying sip of coffee. I made a happy humming moan as the caffeine hit my veins like liquid gold. A throat cleared, and I whipped my gaze away from the man and the baby.

River was looking at me intensely. "Miss Stone—"

"Nova. Please call me Nova."

His dark, straight eyebrows pulled in tight. "Nova. I just wanted to get one thing straight. I am going to see my nephew. He mightn't be my flesh and blood, but some things are bigger than that."

I frowned at his tone. "I said I wouldn't stop you. That's why I'm here, remember?"

Sleep deprivation made me snippy. I sucked in more coffee to counteract the bitchiness seeping into my tone.

River shook his head, leaning forward. "I don't mean once every now and then. I want him to know me, know *us*. I want him to be able to lean on us. We can't do that if we live half a country away in Michigan. I don't want to be just a name that comes and visits him once every five years."

"We want custody of Huey. We are willing to reimburse you for the privilege," Devan said, his dark blue eyes staring at me.

My jaw unhinged. "He's not a fucking puppy you can buy!" I hissed, trying not to draw attention. "The court appointed me as his parent for a reason. You mightn't like that, but it's the truth. I don't care how much fucking money you want to throw at me."

How dare they? What kind of person do they think I am?

I tried to stand, but Rigby put his hand on my arm.

"Nova, wait, please." He gave the other two men a stern look, like they were idiots. "That's not what they meant—"

"Don't lie to me. Yes, it was."

Rigby sighed, screwing his face up into a wince. "Okay, yes, it was. But…" He looked at River beseechingly. "You have to understand the guys. The promises they made to Alana. They're many things… Idiots, sometimes," he muttered. "But their word is their bond. And the bond they had with Alana and Huey is something they take very seriously."

I shook my arm out from underneath Rigby's distractingly warm, large hand. "You don't understand. Huey is all I have left. Without him, I'm alone." My voice was shakier than I would've liked, but the truth of that fact hit hard.

River placed both large hands on the table. "I will pay you twenty-five million dollars to relocate to our home in Ann Arbor with Huey."

That's when white spots danced across my vision.

CHAPTER
Five

DEVAN

"ARE you out of your freaking ever-loving mind?" Nova hissed, and I shifted the now sleeping Huey back into his stroller. It hurt me to think that this might be the last time I held him, especially if this went badly.

I cleared my throat. "I was there the moment he was born. I was the second person to ever hold him in their arms. I looked down at this scrunched, potato-looking alien thing and told him I'd love him forever, and do anything for him. I don't intend to take that back now when he needs me the most," I said in a soft voice.

Rigby's eyes were hot on my face, because he knew me. Soft didn't mean gentle with me. Soft meant shit was about to go down. Not that I'd ever hurt her, this weirdly defiant woman in front of us. I'd never raised a hand to a woman, and given my past, I'd chop off my hands before I ever would.

"You can't buy a *baby*, and you can't buy *me*. The fact

you think I would move to an entirely different state, into a house with three strange men, tells me you're arrogant, stupid, or serial killers. Honestly, have you never listened to a true crime podcast?" she muttered under her breath, making Rigby grin.

But her eyes were still on me, those weird hazel orbs that looked like Huey's. There was no doubt they were related; that color was too unique. Hers had a little more green than Huey's, and maybe a touch of gold. They must have inherited it from their father.

Just the thought of that man made me irrationally angry. I breathed quietly through my nose as we all sat in silence.

Rigby, that fucking golden retriever of a human being, nodded. "I can understand that it would be a daunting idea. We're happy to do anything to help ease your mind. Criminal history checks. References from the coaches. I'll even give you my mom's number, if you want?"

Since I'd been an adult, my criminal record was clear as filtered water, so I wasn't worried about Rigby's declaration. If my minor record was released, she might have a problem, though.

Nova was still frowning, and honestly, I was kind of glad she hadn't jumped on the money straight away. "None of those things tell me what you're like as people. What if you kill kittens for fun? What if you gaslight and manipulate me? That shit happens. I don't *know* you." She shook her head. "This is crazy. My home is here. My life is here."

River continued to stare at her, like he could use his mind to bend her to his will. "I'll give you the numbers of all of my ex-girlfriends if you want. They probably won't say nice things about me, but they'll tell you I'm not violent." They'd say he was an emotionally unavailable asshole, though, which wasn't wrong. River raised a single brow. "You just said you had no one. I know from the court case that your job is virtual, which is why you could stay home all the time with Huey. You can do it from anywhere."

She was still shaking her head. "This is *insane*. You must know that, right?" She sucked in a fortifying breath. "I mightn't have family here, but I have friends. A life."

I met her eyes and held them. "Anyone who'll stick around now that you have a tiny baby to care for instead of going out and partying every Friday night? Anyone who won't think listening to you talk about diaper rash and sleep schedules is tedious and boring?" She frowned at me, her jaw tense. "Look, I understand this is an unorthodox proposition, but think of it from Huey's point of view. Instead of one parent, he'll have four. You won't have to do it all yourself. You won't have to do every single night feeding. When he's sick— and he *will* get sick—there'll be other people to lean on instead of having to do it all yourself. Being a single parent is hard. It's twenty-four hours a day, every day of the year."

I gave her what I hoped was a reassuring smile. "You're a good person. I can tell because you took Huey in, even when it had to be painful for you. I know that you'll want what's best for him—we have the money, and the time, to give him that. You'll still be able to live your own life as well, instead of paying for the mistakes of your father for the rest of your life." She winced at that, and Rigby shot me a look that said *gentle*. "We'll put in safeguards for your protection. Get the lawyers to draw up agreements to hold us to our word. Move out to Michigan temporarily, for three months, and see how you feel. If it's too much, we'll figure something else out. But think about giving us, and Huey, this opportunity," I said softly.

After a moment, she nodded, and I lifted my chin at the guys.

River slipped her a piece of paper with his number on it. "Rigby and I have to go back to Ann Arbor for preseason training, but Devan is here for a couple more days to pack up Alana's place. He can answer any questions for you, and we'll honor any of his promises. If you could maybe message me updates on Huey when you can? I'd like that. Alana used to..." He trailed off, and it was only because I knew him that I could hear the raw pain in his voice.

We'd loved Alana. She was a year younger than us, and when we'd met in a co-ed group home, all uncontrollable teens, we'd bonded. I think, perhaps back then, Alana had a crush on River, but he'd never seen her as more than a little sister to protect. Just as I had.

And we'd failed her.

Nova took the number and punched it into her phone. She snapped a picture of Huey and sent it across immediately.

River smiled. "I'll add you to a group chat, so you can send it to us all in one go."

She finished her coffee in one huge gulp and stood. Rigby disappeared to pay the bill, and River and I stood as well. "We'll help you to your car."

We navigated out of the cafe under the scrutiny of the whole crowd, and I hoped to hell no one had been listening in on our conversation. Otherwise, we were all going to be prime time news later.

We made it to her car, and I noticed she had a baby spit stain down her back. I forced myself not to grin. I helped her unclip the car seat from the stroller, then carefully clicked it into the attachment in the car. I knew this brand from when we were setting up Alana. It was top of the line and had the highest safety rating on the market. Nova didn't skimp on safety, and I could respect that.

Didn't help that the rest of her car was a death trap on wheels, though.

I stroked a finger over Huey's soft, downy hair and stepped away. Rigby came up to join us, and I briefly wondered if maybe we were too intimidating, standing here all together. River stroked Huey's cheek, and even Rigby gave the baby a soft kiss. He was an easy baby to love.

Nova walked around to the driver's seat. "I want you to know I'll think about it, okay?"

"That's all we ask. I leave on Friday, so call me if you have any more questions, or need help or anything."

She nodded and hopped in her car. The car took two tries to turn over, and then she was driving away. I shook my head, the edge of grief still sitting there in my chest, where it had been ever since we heard Alana had died and Huey was in care.

Alana had never wanted her child to be in foster care like we had. I'd promised her that after Huey was born. But still, he was driving away with a stranger, and I hated it.

"Even if she says no, we should get her a new car. That shitbox isn't safe," Rigby grumbled, and I agreed.

"She's going to say yes," River grunted, heading back to the Range Rover. "She doesn't have a choice."

We would do what we had to, but I kind of hoped that Nova did the right thing. I didn't want to break her, but I would if it meant keeping my word.

I hadn't expected her to call me. She seemed like the kind of person who'd do it all herself, even to her own detriment. I could relate to that. So three days later, when the phone rang in the middle of the night, I was awake and on my feet before I'd even answered the phone. I nearly dropped it when I saw her name on the screen.

"Nova, are you okay? Is Huey okay?" I could hear him crying in the background, and her crying at the other end of the phone.

"I'm sorry to call so late." She sniffed. "But I can't get him to sleep. He just keeps crying. He only sleeps during the day, and I—" Her voice wobbled, from either tears or from her bouncing an obviously distressed Huey. "I don't know what I'm doing wrong and I'm so tired and I'm worried that I'll fall asleep and drop him or hurt him and I can't—" She let out a sob, and my heart broke. "I didn't want to call my neighbor because then she'll know I'm a failure and that's stupid and I'm so sorry…"

"I'll be there in fifteen minutes, Nova. Unlock your front door and go lie down with Huey on the bed. If you fall asleep, he'll be safe there until I arrive. Can you do that, sweetheart?"

Her sobbing, "Yes," came down the line, and I was already jogging down the stairs of Alana's apartment building.

Packing up Alana's life was painful for many reasons. One, it was evidence that she'd been hiding how hard she was doing it from us. There was barely anything in her apartment that wasn't baby stuff. It was a by-product of being a foster kid, and something both River and I had worked really hard to shake—the inability to accumulate more than two trash bags worth of stuff.

I listened at the other end of the line as Huey screamed his little lungs out, Nova sniffling as she moved around to do what I asked. "You still okay over there?"

"Yeah." She hiccuped. "It's okay, Huey. Shhh," she whispered, her voice rough. "Devan's coming, then you won't be stuck with just me."

God, I didn't know who I wanted to hug more in that moment. "Are you in bed now?"

"Just building a blanket wall so he doesn't fall out," she almost slurred. Jesus Christ, how fucking tired was she? "I've laid him down, but he's so sad. I've fed him and rocked him, and his diaper is dry. I'd normally take him for a drive in the car, but I'm worried I'll—"

I knew what she was worried about. "It's okay, Nova. You're doing the right thing. You made Huey safe, and that's what all moms should do. There's no rule that says you have to do it alone."

The phone call switched over to the speakers of the car. She didn't say anything else, but I listened to the sound of Huey's cries—and her soothing noises that were more sobs than anything else—the whole way to her house.

She'd left the door unlocked like I asked, and when I walked into the room, she was still awake, though her whole face looked strained with the effort, her eyes opening and closing slowly. I walked over and picked up Huey, putting him over my shoulder and rocking him softly. Nova curled up in a ball, her sobs muffled by her pillow.

Reaching down, I put a hand on her shoulder, squeezing. "It's okay. Sleep. You'll feel better in the morning."

She nodded, and I moved toward the living room until her soft voice stopped me. "Devan?"

"Yeah?"

"You were right. I can't do this on my own. I'll come with you to Ann Arbor."

My heart leapt in my chest, and I knew it was a shit thing to do, holding her to something she said when she was obviously distressed, but I couldn't help it.

"You'll never have to do it on your own again. I promise."

And I always kept my word. Always.

CHAPTER

Six

NOVA

I WOKE UP IN A PANIC, my hand moving to the cool side of the bed where Huey should be. As my brain came back online, I remembered calling Devan in the middle of the night. Of him picking up Huey and soothing him. Of falling into a restless, distressed dream state for hours until I passed out from absolute exhaustion.

I remembered telling Devan that I'd go to Michigan with him. I wasn't having second thoughts.

After the first night of sleep deprivation, I'd thought, *No. I can definitely do this.*

The second night was hard.

The third night of trying to do it alone was absolute torture. I needed help. The only person who'd suffer if I clung to my pride was Huey.

The very thought that I could have dropped him

from sheer exhaustion terrified me. I climbed out of bed, and the brightness of the day told me it was late. I looked down at my pajamas, which were covered in food and sweat and baby spit, and grimaced. I needed a shower, but first, I needed to make sure that Huey was all right. That Devan hadn't run off with him in the middle of the night.

My heart pounded at the thought, and I raced from my room and into the living room. The kitchen was empty but when I turned the corner, I saw Devan, sitting on the floor beside Huey's play mat.

Huey was clean and dressed in a new onesie. He was kicking his legs and gurgling happily, and my panic subsided. It was replaced by some dark sort of jealousy that he was obviously so content with Devan. And that jealousy was directly because I feared I was inadequate. That I wasn't enough.

Devan looked up from the baby and gave me a soft expression. "Feeling better?"

I smiled tightly. "Yeah. Is Huey okay?" I swallowed hard. "Should I have called an ambulance? What if it was his heart?" Fuck. What if I'd caused him damage by not taking him to the hospital?

Devan stood, walking over to me, but keeping one eye on the baby. "I don't think it's his heart. They gave us a list of things to look for when they discovered the heart defect, and he doesn't have any."

I knew that, logically. I'd Googled the shit out of it

when I found out that Huey had a congenital heart defect. No blue fingernails or lips. His breathing was okay, as was his color. He was drinking fine. But how was I supposed to know what the baseline for a baby even was?

Devan squeezed my forearm. "He's fine. Happy. Look at him," he insisted softly, and I did. He was so small and fragile, the sweetest baby I'd ever seen most of the time, except when he was crying in the middle of the night like he'd been possessed by a demon. "It's probably just colic, but we can go and get him checked out if you'd like."

I nodded, because I did want that. I wanted to be sure he was okay. He was on my co-pay, though they said it would be another few weeks before the paperwork was finalized. Didn't matter, though; I'd pay out of pocket if I had to.

Devan's eyes darted up and down my body, and I cringed. I looked like shit. "Why don't you have a shower, and I'll make some lunch?" he suggested, completely reasonably.

I turned away before I did something dumb and cried again. I couldn't even blame hormones. I was just a mess.

I went into the small bathroom and stood under the showerhead for twenty minutes. I hadn't had a shower longer than two minutes in almost a week. I scrubbed and shaved everything I possibly could, just in case it was another five days before I got this opportunity again.

Dressed in soft sweats and a tank top, I emerged back into the main part of the house. The smell of hot carbs told me that Devan had found my frozen pizza stash. I hadn't had time to go grocery shopping for me in ages.

The man in question was standing in the kitchen, making a box of Rice-A-Roni. He looked odd cooking in the kitchen, standing in the place my mother had made almost every meal I'd ever had growing up. It was an almost painful reminder that everything was different now.

Feeling my eyes, he looked up from studying the directions on the back. "I didn't realize anyone ate this shi—stuff." I shrugged, not about to tell him that I hadn't really had the will to cook anything for myself in months. Probably not what he wanted to hear from the woman who had custody of his nephew.

"It's been a long couple of weeks. I need to get to the store." I sighed. "Devan, about what I said last night..."

His body froze, his spine going rigid. I could almost see him forcing himself to relax. "I'm not going to hold you to something you said when you were almost delirious with exhaustion, Nova."

I almost smiled at his disgruntled voice, and shook my head. "I meant it. I'll go back with you, and we'll make this work. But there'll be rules..." I trailed off, because the smile he gave me was heartstopping. Literally, I felt like I'd swallowed my tongue. The dark-eyed moodiness completely transformed, making him look way younger.

He sucked in a deep breath, bouncing slightly on the spot. "I promise you won't regret it, Nova. It'll be better for both of you." He looked at me like I'd given him a gift, and I wasn't sure how I felt about that. Happy, I guess. Apprehensive, maybe?

"There'll be rules. And I want to see all that contract stuff that Rigby promised me. And only for three months, just to see. If it doesn't work, I'm coming back here, so I want it in writing that you guys will let me and Huey return if it doesn't work for us all."

Devan nodded. "Whatever you need to feel safe, we'll give it to you."

I chewed my lip. "And I don't want the money. Put it in a trust for Huey or something, but I don't want it. I don't want you guys to think you can buy me," I said firmly. I was turning down twenty-five million dollars, and the opportunist in the back of my brain was screaming that I was an idiot. I should take the money. Set myself up for life.

I wouldn't, though. I worked for what I had. I'd take what they offered for Huey, so he'd have the best possible chance in life, but he wasn't my meal ticket and I wouldn't exploit him like that.

The man across from me narrowed his eyes, tilting

his head as he stared at me, like he was trying to figure out my angle. I just held my chin higher. Finally, he nodded. "Okay. We'll figure out the logistics. I'll call our lawyers now, get them to contact yours. We'll make an agreement so airtight in your favor, you won't have any opportunity to doubt our intentions." He stepped around the kitchen counter, moving toward me. He didn't walk like a normal male; he swaggered like a man who was entirely in control of himself. It was a little intoxicating. He held out his hand. "You're making the right choice."

I wrapped my palm around his and shook. God, I could only hope he was right.

Mr. Lief called me that afternoon to say he'd received word from the personal lawyers of River Cooper. Together, they'd drafted up an agreement that definitely leaned in my favor, including financial and punitive repercussions for any wrong-doing on their part. If I felt uncomfortable or harassed in any way, I could sue the shit out of them for breach of contract or something. I didn't understand the jargon, but Mr. Lief said they were contractually shackling themselves to my whims. He said it with a bit of disapproval, like he couldn't even fathom someone signing a contract where the terms were so one-sided.

Whatever, as long as they sided in my favor, I was okay with it.

I'd given Devan my email address, and within hours, proof started pouring into my inbox. First, there were the criminal checks from all three men. Rigby had a speeding fine from three years ago, but that was it.

Then came the testimonials. I wasn't sure what they'd done, but I soon had emails from all their teammates, business associates and most of the coaching staff of the Ann Arbor IceCaps, as well as three of River and Rigby's ex-girlfriends. River's all said the same thing. He was a good guy, loyal to a fault, but when it came time to get serious, he ran away like his tail was on fire. Rigby's were a little kinder, but most of them said they couldn't stand being second to ice hockey. I could understand that. I didn't want to date them, though; I just didn't want them to murder me in my sleep.

There were no ex-girlfriend testimonials for Devan. When I asked about it that night, because he brought me Vietnamese food for dinner, he just shrugged. "I don't have any ex-girlfriends. I've been busy growing the business." There was probably more to it than that, but I wasn't here to psychoanalyze the man.

All the references said basically the same thing. They were good guys. Men of their word. They were a close-knit bunch, but they would give you the shirt off their backs if you asked for it.

I stopped short of asking Rigby's mother for a reference. For some reason, the idea of talking to his mother terrified me. No, in all honesty, I would date a man for years with less background information than these guys had willingly handed over in twenty-four hours.

I just had to take a leap of faith now.

Well, that, and tell Chloe and her parents. I'd actually be closer to Chloe, kind of, because she worked at Virginia Tech. It didn't stop her from telling me I was absolutely fucking insane. And then calling her mom, who marched over and demanded to meet Devan in person.

That's what I was doing right now. Holding Huey while Rita gave Devan the third degree. She asked him where he grew up (in foster care in Minnesota, along with River), what he did for a job (he was an investor, and when he told me how much his company was worth, I might have swallowed my pho the wrong way), and did he drink or take drugs?

His parents were both alcoholics, then later drug addicts, and his mother had died when he was ten, overdosing on sleeping pills. I tried to keep the pity from my face; I'd only known him a couple of days, but I had a feeling that he'd hate it if I felt sorry for him.

Finally, after Rita had grilled him better than the CIA ever could, she tilted her head for me to walk her out. Handing Huey to Devan, I followed her outside. Even that had been a relief—being able to just hand the baby to someone. I'd never underappreciate the joy of having two free hands again.

Rita looked out over the lawn, and my mom's flower garden. "Do you know what you're doing?"

I chewed my lip. "I think so."

She nodded. "And what does your gut say about them?"

I'd thought this over, and despite the fact they were all big enough to snap me like a twig, I didn't get any bad vibes from them. My parents had been all about trusting your gut. "It says this is the right decision."

She sighed, resting her forearms on the porch railing. "I'm not going to lie and say I'm not worried, Nova. You barely know them, and you're moving so far away from anyone you can reach out to for help. But on the other hand, I can understand why you feel you need to do it. I'm struggling with this whole situation, and they were only my friends." She didn't need to elaborate on the fact she meant my dad's illegitimate love child now being mine. That one was pretty obvious. "Just know, this isn't your only choice. I can help you more if you need it—you just have to ask."

I gave Rita a smile, this woman who'd somehow stepped into a maternal role without hesitation, right when I'd needed it the most. "I know."

She straightened. "I'll miss you. I'm going to text you the number for my brother Greg in Detroit. He's ex-Army, so if you need help, you call him and he'll come and get you, okay? His wife is scary too, so don't fret. They'll have your back. I want you to memorize that number until you can mutter it in your sleep, got it?" I nodded, tears pooling in my eyes. "And you better message me every two days or I'm sending him to your house whether you need it or not." She reached out and pulled me into a hug. "You're so damn brave and strong. I wish I'd been half the woman you are when I was your age, Nova Stone. You'll be the best damn mother to that baby anyone could ask for. Don't let anyone tell you differently."

CHAPTER

Seven

RIGBY

I PACED AROUND, making sure everything was perfect. I'd even called someone in to redecorate two rooms, one into a nursery and the attached room into something a little more feminine than the general rooms in our house.

I was in sweats, freshly showered from practice. The regular season would start soon, and I wanted to make sure that Nova and Huey were settled and happy. I tried to do what my mom used to tell me to do and think through *why* I was feeling what I was feeling.

Why did I feel this anxious about something that really shouldn't matter to me? I mean, I loved the guys —they were my best friends, and I'd do anything for them. I'd liked Alana too; she'd been damaged and broken, but she was sweet enough. She'd tried to come on to me a couple of times, but there was a code, you know? Don't fuck your best friend's sister.

I'd been with them when she died, felt their devastation at her loss, so maybe that was it. I was anxious to secure this last little piece of their family for them. It might be the thing they needed to start healing and shake off the heavy cloak of their grief.

However, as much as I tried to pretend that was it, I knew it had more to do with the girl herself. Nova. She tugged on something deep in my chest, and whatever it was, I couldn't shake it. When she'd cried at the cafe, I'd wanted to pick her up, set her on my lap and promise I would make everything better.

Which I guess I kinda did. Minus the lap sitting.

There was something about the brokenness she tried so hard to hide that spoke to me, and it definitely didn't hurt that she had a body that was perfect. Soft curves and a juicy little peach butt. Those big hazel eyes that were so damn captivating, it was hard to drag your eyes away.

Logic told me that lusting after her was a bad fucking idea. Like, really bad. We wanted her to be comfortable here, and sex made shit messy. So she'd stay in the spank bank, and outwardly I'd try and be her friend, patch up her broken bits.

My mother always said I was empathetic, even when I was a little kid. Always bringing home the kids who everyone else picked on, or abandoned kittens, or broken things I'd found on the side of the road so I could fix them and make them work again.

I was self-aware enough to know that it was this

pattern that had drawn me to River in the first place, way back when we were both rookies for the Atlanta Lightning. He hid it well, but some wounds never healed, and even if they weren't visible, they were still there, festering below the surface. It was in the way he eyed every other man around him as a possible threat. The way he struggled against direct orders on the ice, even though he knew he couldn't make it far without following the coach's demands.

He'd isolated himself from the other players. But I was persistent as fuck, and I made him love me. It was basically my superpower. He eventually introduced me to both Devan and Alana, his family, and it was the beginning of a great friendship, until I was traded away to Minnesota.

Somehow, five years later, we were both back on the same team after a bunch of years being traded around, and we made a great fucking team out there. The friendship grew, and when I bought this big-ass damn house, I'd asked if he and Dev wanted to move in with me. I hated being alone.

We'd turned this place into a bachelor pad of epic proportions, and it had seen its fair share of crazy parties. But not anymore. Now we'd have a girl and a baby in the house. The whole dynamic was about to change.

"Will you quit the fucking pacing? You're making me seasick," River grumbled, but I'd known him long enough now to know that he was just as nervous as I was.

Dev had messaged about forty minutes ago to say they'd landed, and we'd sent a private car to collect them from the airport. As much as we wanted to collect them, apparently there was a lot of stuff and they'd need the space two hockey players took up.

"Sorry. Don't know why I'm nervous."

River narrowed his eyes. "I feel like this goes without saying, Rig, but she's off limits. You know that, right? This is too important to fuck up because you can't keep it in your damn pants."

I glared at him. "I'm not the one that's going to fuck this up, you grumpy bastard. No one wants to live in a home where they have to avoid the troll under the bridge every day to get a coffee." I stood in front of where he was perched stiffly on a recliner. I stared down at my best friend, the man I loved like a brother. "If you hold her at arm's length, she's never going to feel comfortable and she's never going to stay. I know it's hard opening yourself up to the possibility of being hurt, but you gotta take the risk, man. It'll be worth it." He punched me in the thigh muscle, corking it, and I grunted out a pained breath. "Asshole!"

"Don't psychoanalyze me, dickhead."

I gave him the finger. "Truth hurts."

"Not as much as your thigh."

It did fucking hurt. I leaned into him, giving him

several short sharp shots to the ribs with a laugh, trapping him against the back of the recliner.

But we were hockey players, and we knew how to brawl. He tipped us out of the recliner and landed on top of me, pulling my shirt up over my head to trap my arms, then gave me a fucking mean-ass nipple cripple.

I managed to get one arm and head out of my shirt and cracked him in the kidneys. "Fuck off, you giant hairy bastard. Leave my nipples alone!"

Someone cleared their throat. "And on that delightful note, welcome home."

River and I both froze. As one, we looked toward the front door, at Dev standing there with two rucksacks and a diaper bag over his shoulder, and Nova with a baby in her arms.

Well. This was awkward.

I pushed River off, scrambling to my feet beside him. "We were just playing."

Nova's eyes bounced between us, her eyes sparkling. "That was obvious from the intense nipple twisty. No one tweaks nipples in a real fight."

Her gaze dipped down to my nipples, and I realized I was still shirtless. Deciding it was probably best to desensitize her to it now—because who wanted to wear a shirt all the time?—I just shrugged. "Been in many fights?"

"Not lately," she quipped back. Her eyes were laughing at me, even if she was clearly trying to keep a straight face. My nipple throbbed like a bitch, and I resisted the urge to rub it. "Have you?"

I winked at her. "Only on the ice."

Dev made a grumpy noise. "How about you clowns go out and get the bags? And put a shirt on."

I gave him the finger. "In a minute. I want to show Nova her room."

River rolled his eyes at me. "He's basically been watching the Lifestyle channel for a week to get it right. We could've just hired an interior designer but…"

I waved him away, moving around the recliner to Nova. I gave her a hug, wrapping her gently in my arms, the baby between us. "I'm glad you're here. Come on, let me show you your room and the nursery."

Dev grunted something not very nice, before telling her, "Don't mind Rigby—he's a hugger."

Normally, I'd snark something back and then force him to hug me, but I didn't have time. Both of the guys pretended not to like it, but when I hugged them, I felt their bodies relax. They just weren't used to it—another byproduct of their upbringing.

"Touch is one of the cornerstones of human development and happiness, Dev. Hugging makes you happy. You should try it." I gave him a haughty look and held my hands out for Huey. "May I? There's a whole bunch of stairs between here and there." Not that I thought she'd drop him.

Nova handed me Huey with only a little hesitation, and I held him in my hands and pulled a goofy face at him, making him smile. Or maybe he was pooping. I didn't know enough about babies to decipher.

She eyed me up again, her eyes lingering on my abs, and I swallowed down my grin. Looking over at the guys, I saw they were both glaring at me. I rolled my eyes at them and moved toward the stairs.

"Let's go. If you hate it, you can always change it. Just didn't think you wanted to sleep inside beige. The other room was gray, and honestly, that's even worse. I kept it pretty neutral, so you can redesign it to your taste." I looked over my shoulder to make sure she was keeping up. She was looking around the place, her head whipping from side to side. "We'll give you the full tour in a minute, but I think it's nice to know where your own space will be, right?"

She nodded but didn't say anything.

"Okay, so all the bedrooms are on this floor," I explained. "When Huey gets bigger, we'll put a baby gate up here, stop him from making a run for it down the stairs." I pointed to my bedroom on the left-hand side closest to the stairs. "This is my room. Just knock if you need anything, anytime." I tried not to make it sound sleazy. "Down that hall is Devan's room. And off to that side is the games room and home cinema." I moved off to the right, down another short hall. "Down here were the guest rooms, but we've turned the middle one into a nursery and I got them to put a doorway between your two rooms. The nursery has two doors; the other one opens out into the hallway just outside

Devan's sitting room, so just let him know if you ever need a hand with Huey. I promise you, he'll be all too happy to help."

I shuffled the baby on my chest a little higher. "We'll all be happy to help. You just need to ask. Isn't that right, champ?" I cooed at the baby. I was kind of nervous for this part. "The doors all lock from the inside, though, just in case you're worried. I want you to feel safe here until you know you can trust us completely."

There was a short, plain hall, then it opened up into the bedroom. There was a soft pink abstract painting on the wall, and I'd tied it with the blush comforter set on the brand new bed. Hints of gold and deep forest green were dotted around the room, including the occasional chair in the corner and a pale wood bookcase, with just a couple of books to make it look less like a hotel.

"Like I said, change it however you like. The ensuite is through there." I pointed off to the left. I scratched the back of my neck self-consciously when she said nothing, so instead I led her into Huey's room. It was like hockey met the zoo, and I heard her soft laugh as she came inside. "With two uncles as professional hockey players, there weren't a whole lot of ways this could go, I'm afraid."

I'd had a hell of a lot of fun decorating this room. There were polar bears and penguins on skates, as well as our logo, and everything was done in the blues and yellows of the IceCaps colors. Lying across the rail of the crib was a tiny little IceCaps jersey, and she picked it up.

"River got him that. I'm pretty sure he investigated how small ice skates actually came. He can't wait to teach him."

Nova huffed out a chuckle and turned around in a circle, gazing around the room. "It's beautiful, Rigby. Thank you. Both rooms... I mean, you didn't have to go to all that effort."

Stepping closer, I handed her back the baby. "I know this seems like a lot, but I swear it to the hockey gods, you're going to be happy here. The guys... they don't know how to express themselves sometimes, but they're happy you're here too. Huey needed a mama, and it's going to take a little while to come to terms with the fact that this all turned out for the best, even if they have no legal rights to Huey. A house full of bachelors and a nanny is no way to raise a kid, but they've never had the influence of a mother in any way that wasn't painful."

She frowned, and I bit my tongue. Ah shit, I'd said too much.

Pasting a grin on my face, I guided them back out into the hallway. "Dev's room is through there if you need him," I said, pointing to the closed door. "Now, let me show you the rest of the house. Did I tell you we have a pool?"

CHAPTER

Eight

NOVA

I WAS OVERWHELMED. This wasn't a house—it was a freaking mansion. It had a pool, cinema, gym... and Devan's sitting room? A full-blown library. The ensuite to the nursery had been converted to a butler's pantry, and had everything I'd need to make bottles in the middle of the night, or bath him, or anything.

Rigby bounced around me like an excited puppy, wanting to show me everything all at once. A half-naked puppy. A sexy, half-naked puppy. He showed me every square inch of the house, Huey cradled easily in his arms as if he weighed absolutely nothing at all.

When we got to the kitchen, I gasped. "Oh. My. God."

He grinned, and it was a heartstopping expression on his handsome face. "Right? None of us can really cook—we usually get shit sent in—but even I know this kitchen is impressive. Do you like to cook?"

I *loved* to cook. More specifically, I liked to make chocolate. It had been nearly impossible in my tiny apartment, and not much easier in my parent's house. But with these marble countertops, and a six-burner stovetop?

Holy shit.

I tried to push down my excitement. "Uh, not really. Not meals, anyway. I quite like making desserts."

"Just so happens that I like eating desserts. Cakes or something?"

"Chocolate," I said noncommittally, taking a fussing Huey back from him.

Rigby's eyes went wide. "From, like, scratch?"

I shrugged. "Kinda. When I have time."

I could almost see the chocolate bars in his eyes. My cheeks flushed, and I turned away from the kitchen. Could you be sexually aroused by a double oven? Because I think I was.

It definitely wasn't because of the way that Rigby's back flexed as he strode toward the family room. Dev and River had finished hauling all of Huey's and my stuff up to our rooms, and were now sitting on the couch, watching sports on the huge flatscreen mounted to the wall.

"You finished being a guide dog?" River asked Rigby, who just gave him the finger.

"Better than a beast of burden, asshole," Rigby replied, flopping down on the other side of the sectional.

Dev looked at me, shaking his head. "The answer to your question is yes, they are always like this." Huey took that moment to give another disgruntled cry. "He's hungry?"

I nodded. "I was just wondering where you put the diaper bag, or even the suitcase with all the formula?"

River unfolded from the couch with an ease of a much smaller man. "I packed it all away in the kitchen. Let me show you." He strode past me and into the kitchen area, then through to a butler's pantry that ran along the back. He opened up a floor-to-ceiling cupboard. "I don't know if Rigby showed you in here, but this is where we keep all the food. It goes without saying you eat whatever you want. This place is your home too now." He looked down at me, his piercing golden eyes riveting me to the spot. He didn't look away until I nodded my agreement.

"This is the Huey cupboard. I thought it would be easier for you, and us, if everything was in the one place. Filtered water is over there." He pointed to a spout on the huge sinks. I'd seen bathtubs less deep.

It was thoughtful, I'd give him that. Normally, this wouldn't be a problem. But River's kitchen was the size of my whole apartment. Huey's "cupboard" was the size of my closet. Honestly, what are we going to fill this with?

But when I looked inside, I realized someone must have bought out the baby store, because there was everything I could even think to need and then some.

Tins of formula, rows of bottles, a sterilizer, sippy cups, weird little grippy plates so Huey couldn't throw a plate at my head once he started solids. Pacifiers. Teething rings. Everything. Things I couldn't even name, let alone have on my shopping list.

I swallowed the hard lump in my throat. "Thanks. If you could hold him, I'll make him a bottle, then put him to bed. We're both tired."

River stared down at me for a long time, his hands reaching out to take the baby. He was assessing me, that much was obvious. I just didn't know if he found me wanting or not.

So instead, I went through the process that had become such an ingrained routine that I could do it half-asleep. Literally.

By the time the bottle was ready, River was nowhere to be seen. I walked into the living room, and Rigby lifted his chin. "He went to get him ready for bed." The giant stood, ambling over to me and wrapping me in a hug. "I'm happy you're here."

He still had no shirt on.

I tried to think of any other person in the last three months who'd hugged me just because they wanted to, and not because I needed it. Chloe wasn't a hugger, though she did hold me when I cried. Rita wasn't a hugger either, but they both expressed their affections in other ways.

Rigby was one hundred percent touchy-feely. If I was sane—which, considering I'd moved myself and my infant in with a bunch of strangers, was up for debate—I'd be uncomfortable being this close to a guy I barely knew. But instead, I let myself lean into his warmth, into his strength, and allowed my whole body to relax for the first time in months. I let someone else shoulder my weight, just for a moment, and closed my eyes.

Rigby didn't speak, didn't loosen his grip. His thumb rubbed small circles on my shoulder blade, but that was it. He didn't ask me to hug him back; he just encompassed me in his huge arms and let me rest.

Finally, I let out a shuddering, cathartic breath and stepped back. Rigby let me go just as easily. I could feel Devan's eyes on my spine, but I didn't turn around. I just looked up into the pretty blue eyes of Rigby. "Thanks. I needed that."

He gave me that soft smile, his eyes filled with empathy. "I know. Anytime."

I knew in my soul he meant it too. Hell, a part of me wanted to step back into his arms again already. To ask him to carry me to bed, to tuck me in, to take away all the responsibility I held for just one night.

Instead, I gave him a tight smile. "Goodnight." I chanced a look over my shoulder at Devan, who was watching me with an intense expression. I cleared my throat, feeling my cheeks flush. It probably looked like I was trying to hit on his housemate. "Goodnight, Devan."

"Night," he said gruffly.

Over the last couple of days, as I'd packed up my life for an extended, and unknown, period of time, Devan had been a quiet force in the background. He'd spoken less words to me in three days than Rigby had said to me in one tour of the house. But he'd been there whenever Huey needed anything, and had allowed me to focus on getting my life organized.

He'd also done small, thoughtful things that I still didn't know how to interpret. Like hiring a company to come and secure my house and put in alarms that would go to a local security firm.

I would never have had the money to do that. But was he doing it to be kind, or did he do it to make me feel indebted to him, to them?

I made it up the stairs, and then got briefly turned around. Left was the cinema? Or was that Devan's room? I knew if I moved to the right, I'd get to my room eventually, or the library, and then I could slip across the nursery to my room. I totally took a wrong turn and ended up in the library, but that was okay. I'd make it out eventually.

The library was extensive, and had everything from business texts to hardback classics, even some paper-back crime novels. What interested me the most was the small case of romance novels.

Who read those? A girlfriend?

Shit, why hadn't I asked them about girlfriends? Jesus, I was a dumbass. They were pro athletes. When I'd been doing a little research, I'd found Devan in a

Forbes "30 under 30" article, which was basically a wish-list for debutantes. Of course they had girlfriends.

It didn't matter to me, of course, because that wasn't why I was here. It'd be fine. Yep, fine.

The door to the nursery was already open a fraction. River must have brought Huey in through this door instead of going through my room. I was touched by his thoughtfulness.

"...so your mama was in the middle of the river in a shopping cart, and neither your Uncle Dev or I could swim—that's one of the first things I'll teach you, especially since we have a pool—so we ended up buying three gallon bottles of milk and chugging as much as we could, because we didn't want to waste it. By the time we finished drinking what we could and pouring out the rest, I had this huge pain in my stomach, but we still had to rescue your mama. We tied those bottles together with rope and threw them out on the water, and your mama had to leap from the shopping cart and do this weird dog paddle back to shore while we pulled her in. As soon as she reached the bank, your Uncle Dev turned into the bushes and must have puked up half a gallon of milk." He chuckled, and I continued to stand outside the door, holding my breath and not making a noise. "I promise I won't let you forget your mom, but Nova seems like a pretty good stand-in. You're gonna be a lucky boy to have two mamas who love you so much. Some of us didn't even get one."

Argh. My heart.

I tiptoed back down the hall and opened the door to my bedroom a little louder than I normally would have. When I ducked around the corner into the nursery, River was holding Huey, all clean and zipped into his sleep sack thing. Huey was grumbly, and instead of taking him, I handed River the bottle and pointed to the rocking chair in the corner.

Bless Rigby. He'd thought of everything.

"Do you want to feed him and put him down? I can get started on putting our stuff away."

His eyes darted between me and the grizzly baby. "I'd like that."

He was almost too big for the chair, but somehow he managed to shift himself around until he was comfortable, tucking Huey in the crook of his ample arm. The baby took the bottle like a ravenous piranha.

"Just give me a shout if you need anything," I told River softly, moving out of the room and back into the space that would be mine.

It was a beautiful room. You could sleep a family of nine in here, though; it was huge. Windows on two walls, a walk-in closet and an ensuite. The thread count on the sheets must have been a million because they felt like silk.

Slipping into the closet, I unpacked my clothes onto the hangers. My parents had never been rich. We'd been firmly middle class—enough to buy a decent pair of sneakers once a year, but not well off enough to shop anywhere but Target for clothes. Once I grew up and got a job, I'd been even poorer, because no one ever tells you that adulting is so freaking expensive.

So I thrifted and hit the end-of-season sales, and had created a wardrobe I was happy with. But stuffed into one-eighth of this closet, it kind of seemed miserable. Shaking my head, I pulled out the remainder of my worldly possessions, placing them on shelves around the room. I held a photo of my parents in my hand, and for the first time in my life, I didn't know what to do.

The smiling man in the photo, the one who'd loved me, taught me to ride a bike, come to all my volleyball games, sang happy birthday to me out of tune every birthday for my whole life... he was also the same man who'd abandoned Huey. Who'd inadvertently caused the death of his mother. If she hadn't been alone, maybe she would have made it.

"You can put it up, if you like. We're angry at him, but he's Huey's dad, and yours too. We wouldn't deny either of you that."

I spun quickly, clutching the picture to my chest. I hadn't even heard River come into the room. With a sigh, I placed the photo on the dresser. "I'm mad at him too." I didn't look at River as I said it. "I miss him so fucking much, but I'm so angry at him."

River hovered at the door. "Rigby tells me that feelings are complicated. If they weren't, we'd all float around the world like Teletubbies. His words, not mine." I snorted, because I could imagine Rigby saying that. "We have a therapist here in Ann Arbor. Both Dev and I go and see him, because… we are pretty fucked up." He let out a humorless laugh. "He must be good, because there's no way I would have admitted that ten years ago. Anyway, I know you were seeing one in Tucson, but I wasn't sure if you were going to just video call in your sessions or if you need a new one. I'll leave his number on the counter, just in case." He wiped his palms on his sweats. "So, goodnight."

Turning away, he headed back through the nursery and out the other door. "Night, River," I whispered to his back. Then I got into my pajamas and climbed into a bed so soft, it was like a dream.

I didn't lock the doors.

CHAPTER
Nine

RIVER

"PICK UP THE PACE, Cooper! This is training, not your casual Saturday spin around the lake!" Coach shouted at me from the stands.

I was sweating hard as I skated up and down the ice, running drills until my back was soaked. You couldn't beat the feeling of being on the ice, your muscles burning, the bite of the cold that you feel in your lungs. That smell that only an ice rink can create. Chemicals. Sweat. Ice.

"Wake the fuck up!" Coach called, and we pushed harder, faster. "We aren't getting the Cup if you fuckers are asleep out there."

He said this every training, no matter if we were sweating blood or not. Coach Tooniski, better known as Coach Toons, swore like a sailor whose mother was a prostitute. He was also the best coach the IceCaps had in a decade, so I'd take the abuse and only mentally flip him the finger. We all knew deep down that he was making us better. He might swear and yell a lot out on the ice, but he also took care of the players, not just the team.

When I'd asked for a reference for Nova, he'd sat down straight after training and written me out a glowing recommendation. He'd looked me dead in the eye and told me that if I needed any fucking help, then just let him know, day or even in the middle of the goddamn night. Direct quote. He meant it too. And he'd say the same thing to every one of the guys on the team.

The goaltending coach was Dana Soukal, a forty-five-year-old Czech woman who said very little outside of coaching, but had a look that could shrivel your balls from twenty-five feet away. The rookies were petrified of her, the few players who tried hitting on her never looked her in the eye again, and I was fairly sure she wore PVC and cracked a whip on the weekends. The goalies grew balls of steel, but had some of the best stats in the NHL, so you couldn't argue with that kind of record.

However, underneath all that tough exterior was a deceptively soft heart, and the hunger to succeed. She made us better, even if she was tough. You had to be in this sport, man or woman. But especially if you wanted to be a female coach. Fuck that shit. She'd also written us a reference, and while it didn't have as many curse words, it was genuinely positive.

Probably didn't hurt that Rigby was terrified of her,

and therefore super polite. Thank goodness he wasn't the goalie.

I probably deserved Coach Toon's ire, because my head wasn't in it today. It was back at the house, with a woman who barely came up to my chest and a baby that made me both happy and sad at the same time. He was where he should be, but also, he was a blinding reminder that Alana was gone.

And that I had an aching attraction to his new guardian.

I huffed, checking Ludo as we did our two-on-one drills. Bouncing off me, Ludo laughed as he got out in front and drove me into the boards.

"Asshole," I grunted with the impact.

"Not my fault you're skating like my grandma out here." Ludo was young, twenty-two, and had been playing with us for twelve months. I liked the smug little fuck.

"Not unless your grandma is Soukal."

"She mightn't be my grandma, but I'd still let her spank me and call me a bad boy," he whispered, his eyes darting to the woman in question in case she heard. See? Smug.

"Only if you don't mind her using her skates to slice off those brass ones you call balls, kid."

Ludo laughed, and we ran the drill again.

Vanmussen, our captain and a veteran in the team, skated up to me. The guy made it look easy, but I knew that had more to do with rigorous conditioning than it actually being effortless. "How'd the thing go, Cooper? Julieta's been asking me to ask you for days." Julieta was Vanmussen's wife. Tiny and fiery, she had her six-foot-two husband wrapped around her little finger.

He'd given me a personal recommendation that had made my eyes sting, writing things that no one had ever said about me, at least to my face. That I was a good man. That I was honorable and would give my last breath to the team, to his family. He wrote about the time I went around and did all his yardwork when he'd injured his knee, because Julieta was having her little sister's quinceañera at their house the next day. How me and Rigby were the two men he could rely on in the team, that he knew would share the burden of leadership with him.

His words affected me far more than I'd ever say. I didn't think anyone had ever praised me for anything but my hockey skills. Hockey was what I had. But Muss thought I was a worthy man, and that meant something to me. He hadn't even asked what the reference was for; he just wrote it from the heart. I'd eventually told him, because I needed advice and he was the only good dad I knew.

"Good. They arrived yesterday."

Muss slapped me on the back. "Man, I'm so fucking glad to hear it." He dropped his voice low. "You're gonna be an amazing dad, River. I know it in my heart. Julieta always says it when she sees you with the kids at parties." Muss and Julieta had four kids between the ages of one and seven. We joked that he wanted to have a baby for every Stanley Cup win he'd had in his career.

I shrugged. "Never had much of an example, man. But they have DIY videos on the internet for everything now, including how to be a parent."

Muss just nodded. I didn't talk much about my past, and he never pressed. But I think, on some level, he knew that my childhood had been a giant fuck-up.

He gripped my shoulder again. "I'm here if you need me. Julieta said you guys should come over for dinner soon. I'm sure… what's her name again?"

"Nova."

"I'm sure Nova would like to know another mom in town. Some things you can only ask another woman, you know?"

I nodded. It was a good idea. "I'll let you know."

Muss punched me lightly in the chest. "You do that. Now get out there and run some two vs. twos. Ludo's grandma could beat you right now."

I rode home with Rigby, freshly showered but still aching from the workout. We'd be ready for this weekend's season opener, but it was against our bitter rivals, so I knew it was going to be a tough one. They were mouthy and mean, and I always wanted to punch their right winger in the face.

It was still mid-afternoon, and I couldn't help but

wonder what Nova and Huey had gotten up to today. Dev had taken the day off to get them settled, but tomorrow he'd have to go back to work. He'd been away too long, and I knew his little control freak heart would be losing it.

Would she be okay, home by herself all day with a baby? She'd looked so lost last night, staring at the photo of her parents, and it was easy to forget that we weren't the only ones grieving. I'd wanted nothing more than to hold her in my arms last night, and the sensation scared the fucking shit out of me.

"We should talk about Nova." For a moment, the silence in the car was weighty.

"Didn't we already talk about this?" Rigby said lightly, his hands resting lightly on the steering wheel. It had taken six years of friendship for me to relinquish enough control to let him drive. I hated being out of control of my life, even with something as simple as driving.

I gave the side of his face a hard look. "No, we didn't. I know you, Rigby. You avoided answering, which means we did *not* talk about it."

Rigby sighed, his jaw bunching. "I'm not going to put the moves on her, River. I wouldn't fuck this up for you guys for a convenient lay. I barely know the girl." That should've been reassuring, but I wasn't lying; I knew him. He wasn't done. "But if she comes onto me for anything serious, I'm gonna see where it goes. I feel this draw to her, man. I can't explain it." He took his eyes briefly off the road to stare at me. "You know, though, don't you?"

I dragged my eyes from his face and back out the window. Was I attracted to her? Fuck yeah, I was. She was beautiful. All dangerous curves and those lips that were just this side of too pouty, so all you could do as she spoke was imagine what they'd feel like. And she smelled like something soft and feminine, something I could never identify.

"What the hell are you even talking about?" I grumbled, not looking at his face where his eyes could read all my secrets. I wasn't sure why I was even friends with this bastard, but he'd weaseled his way into my life and I loved him as much as Dev now.

"True or false, River 'I-have-no-feelings' Cooper. You've pictured Nova naked at some point."

"False."

"Liar. You aren't fucking dead. I bet you've jerked off to her in the shower too." I flipped him the bird, and he huffed out a laugh.

"Doesn't even matter, because what are we going to do? Draw straws for her? It's better for everyone if none of us touch her."

Rigby snorted. "Okay, sure. So, say she stays. That's what we want, right?"

"Of course."

"She's a beautiful twenty-four-year-old woman. So fucking beautiful. She's not an old maid. Eventually, she's going to want to get laid. Find a nice boyfriend or something. Are you cool with her bringing men home, and then fucking them down the hall from you? Because the very idea makes my balls shrivel up."

It made me irrationally mad. Possessive. Exactly what Rigby was trying to get at.

We pulled into the driveway of the house. "You have two options here, Coop. One, you can let yourself feel something. It's rough, and could lead to heartache, or it could lead to something wonderful."

"You'd stand aside for me?" I couldn't believe him.

He gave me a crooked smile, but it didn't quite reach his eyes. "I would do just about anything for you to be happy. Dev, too. If you haven't realized that about me yet, I'm going to have to hug you more."

Sometimes, I didn't deserve this guy. I shook my head. "You'd be better for her. For them. At least you're in touch with your emotions. I haven't seen mine in twenty years."

Somehow, the idea of her being with Rigby didn't make me quite as angry.

"Don't rule out Dev, either. He watches her like he's hungry. I don't know what it is about her, man…"

I didn't, either. "What's the second option?"

He chewed his lip. "You buy her a place of her own. Give us all a degree of separation. Because I can't smell her shampoo, or watch that tight ass go up and down the stairs, or meet her sad hazel eyes without wanting things. To make shit better for her, either with my words or my dick."

I shook my head. "We'll see where it goes, man. I want her here where we can help. If she falls for one of you assholes, I'm okay with that." But not a stranger. Not some other fuck that Huey would call Daddy.

Rigby gave me a long look, and then sighed heavily, getting out of the car without another word.

CHAPTER
Ten

NOVA

THE GUYS HAD LEFT straight after breakfast for training, but not Devan. Apparently, he didn't need to be back in the office until tomorrow, so he'd spent the day entertaining Huey while I unpacked stuff. Babies had a lot of stuff, even though the guys seemed to have bought out an entire baby store before we got here.

Once I was fully unpacked, I came downstairs to find Huey in his car seat on the porch. His uncle was out in the drive, securing the base into a luxury SUV and swearing softly under his breath.

I watched him for a moment, unseen. He was really kind of beautiful for a man, and I wondered if he had some kind of Latin American ancestry, because those lips were made for kissing and his soft, golden skin was made for touching. He didn't smile much, and he wasn't overly chatty, but there was a quiet intensity about him that made him almost magnetic.

Which was bad. Bad, bad, bad.

I squatted down next to Huey's car seat. "I'm in so much trouble, little man," I murmured, but it didn't matter—he was already asleep.

Devan must have felt my eyes on his ass, because he looked over his shoulder. He frowned a little and waved me closer. Casting one more look at Huey to make sure he was fine, I walked over to the black Range Rover.

Devan handed me the keys. "This is yours."

I blinked. "What?"

"The car. It's yours."

"No."

"Yes."

"No, Devan. I can't... This is a hundred-thousand-dollar car. I can't have it. What if I go home in three months?"

He put his hands on his hips, and I realized he was mirroring my own stance. "Then you go home in a car that has the highest safety rating of its kind, and my nephew will be safe from suffering the fate of his father." I staggered back, like he'd punched me in the chest. He reached out, his face apologetic. "Nova, I'm sorry, I didn't mean that."

I wanted to run away, to hide in my room, but that was a child's thing to do. I was an adult now, responsible for another human being, another life. And as much as it hurt, he wasn't wrong. If my parents had been in this car when they'd crashed, instead of my mom's fifteen-year-old Honda, they might still be alive.

But they hadn't, and they weren't. I wouldn't begrudge Huey that safety because of my pride. I wouldn't give Devan the satisfaction of telling him he was right, though.

Reaching out, I took the keys from his hand. "Thank you."

I spun and walked back to the house, scooping the car seat up on the way past. I felt Devan's eyes on me until I made it into the foyer, where I let out a shuddering breath. I took the stairs slowly and carefully, moving Huey into the crib, then grabbing the baby monitor.

Moving into the bathroom, I turned on the shower and stripped off my clothes. I stood under the water and cried, until Huey's tiny waking whimpers filtered in over my own. Wrapping myself in a towel, I dried my face and got on with my life, like a man I was just beginning to know hadn't just reached inside my chest and ripped open my heart again.

I was sitting on the floor, watching Huey have tummy time—because that's what the books said he should be doing—when Rigby found me.

"Hey, Nova. Hey, little dude." He smiled down at Huey, who was doing his best impression of a worm that had just accidentally been unearthed. "Can I come in?"

I lifted a hand, inviting him into the nursery. There was a big colorful rug on the floor, and Rigby casually flopped down onto it beside Huey.

"So, I think we might have a barbecue tonight, before fall really settles in and it's no fun to use the pool anymore. It's still really warm outside," he said softly, and I shrugged. I still felt a bit raw from Devan this afternoon, but I was trying not to pout about it. Holding grudges wasn't going to help me get through the next few months.

"Sounds nice."

Rigby rolled onto his back and looked up at me. His body was long and strong, and it almost felt illegal for anyone to look that good. My eyes drifted to the small sliver of skin peeking out from just above his sweats, making me swallow harder than normal.

Not to mention the way his sweats bulged in a certain area. Nope. Was definitely not looking at that.

Why couldn't Huey's rich uncles be ugly as hell? Sweet, average-looking guys who didn't make me question everything all the time. Not temptation on a stick. Or on a rug, as it would seem.

I looked down at my nails, like they were suddenly so interesting. I also ignored the low chuckle that echoed around the nursery.

"Nova?"

I sucked in a deep breath. "Mmm?"

"Devan told me what he said today. That was wrong of him."

I shook my head. "No, it wasn't. It hurt so much because he was right."

Rigby growled softly, sitting up. "I'm going to hug you now." That was all the warning I got before he dragged me across the rug and between his thighs, his arms wrapping around me until my head was tucked under his chin.

I breathed deeply, because I needed this. I shouldn't, and it was probably giving him all sorts of wrong impressions. Well, right impressions, but not ones I could act upon.

His hand stroked up and down my spine. "Poking at someone's pain to make a point is wrong, Nova. Whether the underlying message is right or not doesn't matter." He rested his cheek on the top of my head. "Do you want to talk about them? Or the accident?"

I shook my head. It was too soon. I was still running from the pain.

"I'm here if you do. Or if you just need a hug. Devan says that touch is my love language, and those two surly fuckers needed it more than anyone I'd ever met. When we first met, they used to flinch whenever I even patted them on the back. They were so unused to anyone showing any kind of affection, let alone physical affection. Alana helped, but she was just as damaged as they were, maybe even worse. Her childhood was... traumatizing. There was a reason the guys were so protective of her their entire lives." He snuggled into my hair, inhaling deeply.

I *knew* this should feel weird. Deep down, I knew I should break the contact and move away. But I couldn't force myself to do it. He was right; I needed this. My body craved it. It was so fucking nice, just to be in the shelter of the arms of someone bigger and stronger than me.

He sighed against my hair. "This is nice. I think maybe I needed this, too."

We sat like that a little longer, both of us watching Huey as he waved his arms around on the playmat, trying to reach the brightly colored bugs next to him.

Eventually, I sighed. "Devan was right today. It's hard to overcome my pride and accept things from you guys. It's like you're trying to trap me with *things*, when I'll never be able to pay you back. I haven't done any work in two weeks, my savings are dwindling, and it's just so easy to let you guys take care of everything."

His hand stroked up and down my back. "What's wrong with that?"

"I feel like I'm being bought, and I hate it." I huffed, thinking I should definitely move away to make my point, but honestly, his warmth felt like it was filling up an empty well inside me.

"Nova, you have to understand. These guys have nothing else to give yet. They don't know how to be parents, because they have no good examples. They don't see themselves how I see them, but they will.

They're the kind of friends who are there for you whenever you need it. They *care*, and no one has told them that's all there is to being a parent. You need to care so damn much, just show up and show love. That's it. The rest we can all learn on the fly, though I'm fairly sure Dev's read every baby manual on the planet and has each one memorized."

He huffed a laugh. "What I'm trying to say is that they don't know how to show Huey, and show you, that they care outside of grand financial gestures. But they'll get there—just give them time. Emotionally stunted fuckers," he grumbled, and the vibration in his chest tickled my cheek. "But don't be scared to call them on their bullshit. They need Huey, and I know it's a lot, but I think they need you too."

He squeezed me one more time and then moved away. "I better go and put the grill on. We bought Huey swim trunks—they're in the third drawer, along with some swim diapers. Put on your swimwear too, because what's the point of having a damn pool if you don't use it?" He stood with a groan. "It was leg day, and I feel like I'm paralyzed from the quads down." He gave a little stretch, showing me the V of his obliques, making my mouth water.

I climbed to my feet too. "Rigby, can I ask you a serious question?"

He tilted his head, giving me true golden retriever energy. "Sure."

"Do you have a girlfriend?"

His grin was wide and instant. "Nah, sweetheart. No one has been able to handle all this, but one day. I hold out hope." He gave me a burning look, or maybe that was wishful thinking. He held my eyes a little longer, then swaggered out of the nursery, leaving me breathless and bewildered in equal measures.

CHAPTER
Eleven

DEVAN

I WAS GOING to pass out from lack of blood to the brain, because when Nova emerged from the house in a robe, her shapely legs on display, half the blood in my body went straight to my dick. The rest followed after as she slipped out of her robe and stood there in nothing but a bikini. It wasn't skimpy or anything—more of a 1950's style, with the waistband sitting just below her navel—but Jesus, it hugged every single curve. The pale gold of her skin made me want to strip her down and lick every inch of her body.

I stood in front of the grill, hiding my dick from everyone and pretending to watch the steaks. Rigby had bounded up to her, holding his arms out for Huey, and she'd given him over easily with a laugh.

River came to stand beside me, his face shut down. "They look like a family, almost. The kind you see in holiday commercials."

I snorted a mirthless laugh. "They do."

"He likes her, you know."

I didn't take my eyes off them. "I know."

"We should let him go for it. He'd make a good father for Huey. A good partner for Nova."

This time, I turned to look at my oldest friend. He'd held me together for as long as I could remember; hell, we held each other together. I loved him more than anyone on the planet, even Alana. "They aren't possessions for us to give away."

He gave me a pissy look. "You know what I mean. Not stand in their way." Yeah, I did know what he meant, but I also knew River better than any other person he'd ever known. He wanted Huey more than anything. Wanted to be the parent we never had. Wanted to give him everything that little River had never gotten, and not just material things. Love. Security.

"You'll make a good father too, Riv. Don't count yourself out just yet." I cleared my throat. "As for the partner bit, that's not really up to us. She might seem small and delicate, but I don't think Nova's going to care about anyone's opinion but her own."

She did seem more comfortable with him, but that was the Rigby effect. He was just one of those people who lit up a room and made everyone feel like they mattered. How he'd ended up friends with us was still a mystery.

"Rigby said if it isn't one of us, it's going to be some random guy raising Huey."

And fucking Nova. Yeah, he didn't say that bit out loud, but it was there, written all over his face.

"So what, Rigby is the sacrificial lamb? Or is that going to be you?" I didn't even suggest myself, because no matter how badly my body wanted Nova, I was not good husband material. I wasn't good *anything* material. I'd come from a bad batch, and there was nothing I could do about it. It was genetic.

"It's that, or we set her up in her own place, 'where we can have a degree of separation.' His words, not mine."

I shook my head instantly. "Rigby didn't see her back in Tucson, man. When I walked in, she was in the middle of a sleep-deprived breakdown. She needs help. Needs us. She shouldn't have to do it by herself."

River was nodding, and I had a feeling the sly bastard had just talked me into a corner. "So we agree then. We let her explore where she wants to go with us. If she's happy, and wants to, I don't know, pursue her other needs with one of us, you're on board. Or are you happy with her going on dates and finding some other fucker who'll have their hands all over her body? Someone Huey will call Daddy?"

I scoffed. "Aw, do you want Nova to call you Daddy too?"

He gave me a shove. "I wouldn't say no." He let out

a breath that whistled between his teeth. "She is beautiful."

Fuck yeah, she was. A kind of effortless beauty. Even in the middle of the night, her hair crazy and unwashed, eyes puffy from crying and lack of sleep, she'd been beautiful. Not in the traditional sense, but I was still a little awestruck by her. She was one of those people whose beauty on the outside was reflected on the inside. Like Rigby.

Not like me or River, though. Our exteriors hid a defective core.

"I'm not going to try and gaslight her into liking one of us, River. You know how I feel about that shit." PTSD for the win. "If she wants to date, we should let her. We don't own her. She's young and up until three weeks ago, carefree. If she finds a guy who's a fucking douche, we'll figure it out then. I'm not going to force her into anything."

River scowled at me, and I knew the expression sometimes scared the shit out of his hockey opponents, but I'd been on the receiving end of the scowl for a lot of years now. It had lost its effect. "I'm not suggesting that, asshole. Look. Just *look* at them."

I did. Nova was laughing at Rigby as he gently moved Huey through the water on one of those little infant rings. Huey was loving it, his hands splashing in the water. And every now and then, when Rigby wasn't watching, she looked at him with hunger in her eyes.

Okay, so we probably wouldn't be forcing her.

Problem was, I'd seen River look at her with that exact same hunger earlier. "Okay. And when shit goes wrong? What, we kick her and Huey out? Or do we kick out Rigby?"

He shook his head. "We'll cross that bridge when we come to it. You know Rigby. He's not going to do anything to hurt her."

"But will she hurt him?" I loved that fucking kid. I wasn't going to set him up for heartache.

"It was his idea, dickhead. He's not doing anything he doesn't want to do."

I sighed. This had so much potential to blow the fuck up in our faces. "What if she wants you too?" He scoffed, and I punched him in the arm. "I mean it, man. You don't see the way she checks out your ass when you walk away. It's like your hockey ass is a magnet and her eyeballs are pure metal."

"You're a dick," he grumbled, walking away, but I saw how he watched her. He peeled off his shirt, and Nova's eyes immediately made their way to him. Fucking athletes. Going out with Rigby and River to a club had always been a lesson in humility.

Rigby commanded a room, but River... He could walk in and everyone would turn to look. He didn't like being the center of attention, but always was anyway. He just had that brooding presence, on top of the looks, that made women swoon.

For a long time, I'd been happy getting their cast-offs, because I never wanted anything serious. Still didn't. But if I did, I'd want someone who looked at me the way Nova was looking at River right now.

My eyes slipped to Rigby, who was watching Nova gape with a smug, amused expression, not a hint of jealousy. I didn't understand it. People were fucking hard.

I just needed to get laid.

As if he felt my eyes on him, Rigby turned in my direction. "Why don't you get in the pool too, Dev?"

"Can't," I yelled back. I pointed the tongs at the nearly done steaks.

"Can't or won't?" he called back, and I had a feeling he wasn't talking about the pool.

I met his eyes. "What's the difference? The result is the same."

Rigby just raised his eyebrows and shook his head. He swam over to where River was standing at the deep end of the pool, leapt up and grabbed him by the back of the calves, pulling him into the water. Nova laughed from the shallow end, where she was sitting on the steps with a still-splashing Huey.

Idyllic. But why did it make my chest hurt so bad?

CHAPTER
Twelve

I WAS ONLY HUMAN, okay? I wasn't particularly special, didn't have any hard luck stories that made me edgier or more badass than any other woman in the world. Well, at least until now.

Believe me when I say *nothing* in my life had prepared me for sitting around the table with three half-naked men as we ate steaks that each cost more than my weekly grocery budget, and drank fancy craft beer in the freaking candlelight.

Swimming had tired out Huey quickly, and when I gave him his bottle, he'd nodded off into that deep, floppy baby sleep almost immediately. He'd hardly stirred when I'd changed him into his onesie and put him in his sleep sack.

The baby monitor was now in the middle of the table, and Rigby was regaling everyone with a story about the time he'd tried to rescue a baby moose from the frozen lake behind his house. I could imagine a thir-teen-year-old Rigby saving a moose but losing his dad's tractor in the lake. How could you even be mad about that?

His dad had grounded him for a month, because both moose and tractors were dangerous when coupled with a frozen lake, and he'd forgone his allowance forever after that. When he'd been drafted, he'd bought his dad a state-of-the-art new tractor, and they all still laughed about it.

But it wasn't the grounding that gave me an insight into how Rigby had ended up the guy he was—it was the part where he dropped his voice conspiratorially. "After I'd been yelled at for a solid two hours about how dangerous everything was, my mom came in with a huge cake, covered in chocolate mousse"—I laughed at that part, because the *irony*—"and said that what I'd done had been dangerous, but courageous acts deserved recognition, especially when it was to save something weaker. I ate the whole damn thing. I was so sick afterwards, but it was the best hero cake I've ever had."

I looked at River, remembering the story he'd told Huey last night when he got him ready for bed. Would he have turned out like Rigby, open and willing, if someone had baked him a cake after he'd saved Alana from the river? We'd never know, but I stored away the Hero Cake idea for when Huey was older.

We talked a little about the team, and the opening

game that was on Friday night. River looked over at me, his beer raised to his lips. "You'll come, right? Bring Huey?"

I must've been feeling soft with the beer, because I nodded. "Sure. I'll pick him up some of those tiny earmuff things in case it gets too loud." I felt Devan's eyes on me, saw his brows pulled together in a thoughtful expression. His intense expression did things to me.

"Woo! Baby's first hockey game. Gah, I'm already so proud," Rigby hooted.

I laughed and sucked down more of my beer to cool my overheated cheeks. Being the center of their focus was... a lot.

They went back to talking about the upcoming game, and I settled back in my chair and just watched them. River was passionate as he talked, his eyes alight, and fuck, he was even more handsome than usual. Devan joked about buying the opposing team and firing Rigby's archnemesis, and everyone just laughed.

"You could do that?"

He turned his intense expression in my direction. "Several times over."

I was wildly out of my depth with these men. "Fuck me," I breathed. Whoops, the booze was making my tongue a little loose. "That came out wrong. I mean, that's a lot of money. I knew you guys were well off but that much must be terrifying."

That sexy-ass frown again. "Why do you say that?"

I shrugged, wishing I hadn't said anything now. "Money makes people crazy. My mom always said so. She said that there was always the pursuit to make more, be more, that you could never appreciate what you had. When you were living from paycheck to paycheck, you had to learn to appreciate the things and people around you. But you can't do that, right? I did my research, saw an article in *Forbes*. You must always wonder if someone wants you or wants your money, and that would be terrifying." I looked at the other two men at the table. "It must be the same for you as well. Do they want the man or the pro athlete?" I gulped down the rest of my beer to make my tongue stop working.

"So you think you have to be mediocre to be happy?" Devan asked, and I shook my head.

"No! I mean, people still take advantage of each other, even when you have nothing to give. But I think it would be the exception rather than the rule. I can't help anyone get any further in life. They can join me in my just-above-the-poverty-line glory, or they can move on." I put a smile on my face. "Don't mind me. I haven't had a drink in… way too long. And beer always makes me a little too chatty."

They all appraised me silently, and I felt about two inches tall. Fuck, now they were going to think that all I wanted them for was their money. Damn beer.

"Not that it makes any difference to me. I don't want anything from you guys, except for an extra set of hands to look after Huey." I looked at Devan, today's disagreement in the forefront of my mind. "Obviously."

"Mmm, obviously," he agreed. "I hope you can maintain that slightly cynical optimism."

"That's an oxymoron," Rigby chimed in.

River slapped him on the back of the head. "You're an oxymoron."

Just like that, the intense conversation was done. And damn, the rest of the night was just nice. It wasn't awkward, and when Rigby got up to light the fire pit, we moved down there. I could still see Huey on the baby monitor that sat between me and Devan, and I felt normal for the first time in so long.

Well, as normal as I could be surrounded by three hot guys I now cohabitated with.

"So you're a virtual bookkeeper? What does that even mean?" Rigby asked me.

I shrugged, stretching out my legs on the outdoor sofa. I gave a little shiver as the cool night air competed with the warmth of the fire, and River pulled a blanket from somewhere, throwing it over my legs. I couldn't help my little gasp of surprise, but when I looked at him, he was eyeing the firepit flames, not turned toward me at all.

I cleared my throat. "Basically, I run the numbers for small, independent businesses. Most of my clients are artists who sell their paintings on the internet."

"Do you like it?" Rigby asked, and I huffed out a laugh. That was such a pro athlete thing to ask. Not everyone could make millions doing the thing they loved most in the world. Most people didn't even *like* their jobs. But you had to eat, and that meant trudging your way through a job you didn't like, day after day.

So I hedged. "I like that I don't have to go into the office every day. I like most of my clients."

Devan tapped his beer bottle against his bottom lip. "But do you like your job?"

I gave him an exasperated sigh. "I mean, it's a job. It isn't my passion. It's not like I wake up every day and say 'I can't wait to balance chequebooks today,' you know? But it's a steady income and I'm my own boss, so I can't complain."

Rigby laughed. "Could be worse. You could be pounded into the boards by a solid wall of muscle everyday."

"Sounds pretty good to me." The words were out of my mouth before I could drag them back. Every single set of eyes turned to me, their focus like lasers as they stared at me. "I mean the hockey part, not the pounding. I mean... Woo, is that the time? I better go to bed."

I shifted to my feet and stood up, the world swaying a little in my peripheral vision. Drinking while sitting in front of the fire was a trap; you never knew how hard it was hitting you until you needed to move.

Rigby stood quickly. "I'm going too. I'll walk you up so we can all rest easier knowing you aren't going to fall down the stairs."

I expected River and Devan to protest, but they

didn't. They just watched me with expressions that I couldn't decipher. Maybe they thought I was an alcoholic? Though the fact I was tipsy off three bottles of beer probably didn't lend much credence to the idea.

I muttered a goodnight under my breath and hightailed it inside. I could hear Rigby's chuckles from behind me, and I turned to look over my shoulder at him.

"You're a bit of a lightweight there, sweetheart." I flipped him the finger, and he just laughed.

"We aren't all pickled. I'm out of practice. In college, I could have drank that beer upside down at a kegger and still passed a sobriety test."

"Really?"

I sighed at the bottom of the stairs. Why were there so many? "No. I was a lightweight then too. But I wasn't this bad. Did you add an extra ten stairs while we were out? How the hell do you climb that after a big game?"

"Normally, we go out for drinks after a game, and I don't come home until the following day if I'm lucky."

I faux-gasped. "Rigby Engman, are you a manwhore?"

He laughed as he took two big steps toward me and lifted me in his arms like a bride. "Reformed manwhore. There's only so much meaningless sex you can have before it becomes a chore. Still feels nice, but so does fucking my fist in the shower, and my fist won't poke holes in the condom or talk to the media about me."

I looked up at him with wide eyes. "People haven't?" I breathed, horrified at the very idea of selling private details to the press, let alone trying to baby-trap someone. Who does that shit?

"Not to me, but to others." He curled his arms, pulling me closer to his chest. "Enough to be a warning to us all. I know that River is picky as hell, and had a booty call that he made sign an NDA contract. Though he hasn't seen her in a while," he said thoughtfully. "And I make it *real* clear about what I expect early on. You get better at picking the girls who just want to ride you so they know they can, and the ones looking to trap you as a meal ticket."

I frowned. That was so fucking sad. "I'm sorry."

He laughed, cuddling me to his chest. "I know, right? Poor little manwhore."

Still, I wrapped my arms around his neck tighter, hugging him closer. "Abusing your trust isn't a joke, Rigby. Next time someone does that shit, point me at them and I'll beat their ass."

Rigby snorted as he climbed the stairs easily, even with my body weight. "Are you going to get into a catfight for me?"

I frowned up at him as we reached the landing. "Not *for* you. I'm protecting your honor. It's chivalrous."

"Can women be chivalrous?"

"They told me I can be anything I want to be," I

announced like a PBS special, making him laugh. He stopped outside my door, lowering me to my feet.

"That you can, baby girl. You can be anything or anyone you want to be." He stared down at me with intense eyes, his hand cupping the back of my neck like he was going to kiss me.

I realized I wanted him to. Really, really bad.

Instead, he stroked my jaw with that huge mitt he called a hand. "Goodnight, Nova," he murmured softly.

"Goodnight, Rigby," I breathed back. He stared down at me for what felt like an infinite amount of time, before turning and walking back down the short hall toward his own bedroom.

I stayed in the hallway until his door closed softly, breathing deeply. Moments later, the water of Rigby's ensuite shower turned on. My brain jumped to what he might be doing there, and I shook my head vigorously.

No. Bad Nova.

But it didn't stop me from dreaming of lips sliding across my body and Rigby's sexy smirking face staring down at me.

CHAPTER
Thirteen
RIGBY

I SKATED onto the ice as they called my name, the crowd going wild, and I couldn't help my grin. Out there in the sea of faces was Nova, and I was determined to find her. Devan hated the family box, so they'd be out in the crowd, but still in good seats.

I lifted my hand and waved at the crowd, until I found her. Right on the glass, dressed in my jersey. I'd gotten it for her this morning, as well as two tiny onesies that looked like little jerseys for Huey, one with my number and one with River's. They were cute as hell. I hadn't been clucky before, but holding those tiny little jerseys did something to me.

Beside her, Devan had one of those baby carriers strapped to his chest, which looked kind of ridiculous but judging by the eyes of all the women around him, was just one step above being naked when it came to seduction.

I skated to the space in front of them and put my gloved hand on the glass. Nova looked at me with wide eyes until she leaned forward and covered her hand with mine. I winked and skated away, leaving her staring after me. I probably shouldn't have called attention to her like that, but I was excited she was here.

Ludo skated up to me, nudging me with his shoulder. "New girlfriend, Engman?"

I gave him an intense look, but didn't answer as I continued warming up.

"Just saying, at least it'll be easier for everyone else to get laid if you're off the market. There's a lot of disappointed faces on the females out there tonight. They put you on the jumbotron."

Ah hell, she was definitely going to kill me.

"We're just friends," I grunted, and he raised his eyebrows at me but didn't say anything more.

Coach yelled across the ice at us, and we made our way back to the bench for one more spiel before showtime. I dragged my mind away from Nova, compartmentalized how she'd felt in my arms the other night, how hard it had been not to kiss her. Instead, I focused on the ugly mug of Coach Toons. I had a game to win, because there was no fucking way I was going to lose in front of Nova.

Considering we shared a state, we should've gotten along with Detroit. But we didn't. We had a bitter rivalry, like if we trounced each other enough times, one of us would reign supreme in Michigan. There were always fights and blood, and the crowd went bananas for it. Maybe I should've gotten Nova to come to a more gentle game.

I rammed a guy into the boards as we fought for the puck, but I didn't see his teammate until he rammed me with his shoulder, jumping into it and wiping me out. I grunted as my body hit the ice hard, and then River was there, his gloves landing near my head as he punched the guy who'd illegally hit me.

Winded, I gasped for air as the trainer came over, and I shooed him back off the ice because I just knew this shit was about to get insane. "I'm fine. Get off the ice."

The refs blew their whistles, but they knew the score. That was dirty, and it had to be settled.

Muss skated over and pulled me to my feet. "You good? Get your head?"

"I'm good," I yelled. My shoulder hurt like a bitch, but I didn't have a concussion.

River was pounding into the fucker that hit me, and when one of Detroit's guys came up behind him, I didn't think, just launched myself into the fray, grabbing him up in my arms. If you couldn't hear the heavy thud of fists meeting flesh, it would almost look like we were hugging.

"You dirty fuckers," I grunted.

"Break it the fuck up!" the ref yelled, ramming his hands down between us.

I grinned down at the Detroit player I was hitting,

his jersey gripped tight in my hands. Laurens. Not a bad guy, considering the whole team were fucking dickwads.

"I'm done," Laurens huffed.

"Yeah, me too. I still have all my fucking teeth, and I'd like to keep it that way." I looked at the ref. "We're good."

Bless his heart, he took my words at face value, but I didn't get up off Laurens for a bit. "Sorry for the dirty hit," Laurens told me, though he wasn't the one who'd hit me. "Just how he plays."

Yeah, Rusket was one of the best defensemen in the league, but he played fucking old school. Dirty.

"You guys should work on that."

Laurens just grunted and threw me off, as River and Rusket got sent to the box.

The game was close, but we scraped through 3-2. After River and Rusket got into it, tensions had remained high, which was tough on the body but made the crowd go crazy with bloodlust.

Yeah, I definitely should've had Nova come to one of the more gentle games. But this was the first one of the season, and we'd wanted her here.

As the sports medicine team went through and iced everything that needed to be iced, I steamed my muscles in the shower, then put on my suit to go talk to the press. Everyone wanted to know how we'd fare this season, like we were ever going to say anything other than we were going to go all the way to the playoffs.

I sat through the inane questions. Yes, we were aiming for a Cup win. No, I didn't have any injuries from Rusket's hit. Yes, I thought the team was in the best shape it had ever been in.

None of that was a lie, but damn, these press engagements were taxing as fuck.

When I finally made it to the family room, I didn't miss all the eyes on Devan and Nova. The expressions were speculative.

Nova was holding Huey, rocking him gently, and I couldn't keep the goofy, lopsided smile from my face. I bounded up to them and hugged Nova and Huey gently. "Did you like the game?"

"It was so violent," she whispered, her eyes wide.

Ah crap.

"I fucking loved it. It was brutal. Is it always like that?"

Both my eyebrows rose, and my eyes must be as wide as hers right now. Not what I thought she'd say.

Devan snorted. "Turns out sweet little Nova has a bit of a violent streak."

She waved a hand. "Please. So it's fine for the beer-bellied old guy behind us to hoot and holler when River did that thing with his gloves, but if I enjoy men fighting, it isn't feminine?"

Devan held up his hands. "I didn't say it wasn't feminine. I just said you were bloodthirsty."

She lifted a hand to rub the bruise on my cheekbone from Rusket's shoulder. "I don't like that you got hurt, though." Her mouth fell open as she looked behind me, and I had a feeling I knew why.

River looked like shit. His eye was black and swollen, and he had some butterfly bandages on his eyebrow.

"I take it back. I don't like it at all," she whispered to me, before turning to River. "You look like you went ten rounds with a gorilla."

He snorted and held his hands out for Huey. "You aren't wrong."

When she handed over the baby, I heard the collective "*Awww*," from all the women still loitering in the room. The baby did kind of look cute in the giant arms of my bestie.

"Slept through the whole thing," Devan told us. "Didn't even wake up when you scored that goal in overtime and the crowd went fucking nuts."

I stepped closer to Nova, tucking her under my arm. She just fit so nice; I liked hugging her. I didn't want to look into it more than that. Nova was tense beside me, but eventually relaxed into my side. "He's going to be the best little hockey fan the NHL has ever seen," I told her proudly. "Let's get out of here. I need to go home and eat enough food to supply a high school cafeteria."

Not that there was anything cafeteria-like in our fridge. That shit was all nutritionist-approved, superior macro-fuelled diet. There wasn't a single Twinkie, let alone pizza and chicken nuggets.

Still holding the baby, and grabbing his game bag, River led the way out of the room like we weren't the center of attention.

"The game was great, but next time, we'll wait for you in the parking lot," Nova whispered as she walked beside me. "That was intense."

"Whatever you want, as long as you keep coming," I murmured in her ear, keeping her tucked tightly under my arm as we walked out. There was space between our bodies, so it was more friendly than anything, but I wondered if that's how everyone else saw it too. As we walked through the back entrance of the arena to the parking lot, I pulled her closer. "You look real good in my jersey," I whispered in her ear and was rewarded with a deep flush of pink to those gorgeous cheekbones.

I didn't say she'd look even better out of it, but picturing peeling her out of my number made my dick achingly hard. One thing was for certain, though—I wanted Nova Stone, and I was pretty sure she wanted me too.

CHAPTER
Fourteen

NOVA

I'D NEVER BEEN one to obsess over pro athletes. Honestly, before like a month ago, I would've been hard-pressed to name one professional sportsperson who wasn't Wayne Brady. Or was it Tom Brady? Whatever.

But now, watching those guys slide around on the ice like wrecking balls with knife feet? I finally understood. They weren't just fit and hot. They were commanding. They were the most primitive kind of attractive, the type based on raw masculinity and not much else.

Well, not Rigby. My attraction to Rigby had a little to do with his physique and a whole lot to do with the fact he was a beautiful damn human, from what I could see.

However, the family room where we met them afterward had been intense. Not to mention, all the wives and girlfriends were dauntingly beautiful. Like, supermodel beautiful. There was actually a Victoria's Secret model there; I'd recognized her from social media. Their collective gaze had weighed and measured me, and I'd been found wanting. I could feel it in my bones.

So after we got home, put Huey to bed and ate some kind of meal kit food that you reheated in the oven, I was more than ready to be in my own bed. Not to sleep, though.

No. Both Rigby and River had stripped out of their suit jackets and rolled up the sleeves of their dress shirts as soon as they stepped in the door, and holy forearm porn, Batman. I couldn't stop looking at the way River's fingers flexed around his bottle of beer, or the subtle veins in Rigby's thick forearms.

Damn.

I made my escape upstairs as quickly as humanly possible. Ensuring that I grabbed the baby monitor and shut the door to the nursery, I threw on the oversized Disneyland shirt I used as sleepwear. Then I reached under the bed and unzipped a side pocket of my duffle bag, pulling out the Pink Rocket. It had been a gift from Chloe last Christmas. She'd put that shit right under the tree too; my dad had almost choked on his eggnog when I opened it and didn't hide the contents fast enough.

But it was a thoughtful gift in a very Chloe kind of way. She was all about spreading empowerment by taking control of your own orgasms. She had a whole fifteen-minute TED Talk on how the invention of rechargeable batteries had revolutionised the sexual landscape of this country. Whether that was true or not, I was going to have to take the edge off this hunger I had or I was going to do something dumb, such as climb Rigby like a damn tree.

I dived deep into my spank bank, pulling out all the hot actors with rippling abs, and that one billboard in Times Square that had caused a social media uproar and given a woman a heart attack. I thought about a scene I'd read in my latest book where the male lead bent her over in an alleyway and took her where anyone could see them. I tried to think of *anything* but the three hot men I was living with.

I failed.

I tried not to think of Rigby's strong arms as he carried me up the stairs. Would he hold me against a wall and pound into me, like I was the only thing he needed to survive? Would River watch us from the end of the hallway, then come over and join us, pressing me tightly between their muscular chests as they licked and kissed across my skin? In my fantasies, they shared me between them, tasting me and taking me like I was a dessert so sweet they had to share.

And Devan... He would wrap his hand around my throat as he pushed inside me, those eyes staring down at me, commanding me to come when he said...

I was so fucking close to coming. So close.

"Hey, buddy. Did you wake up?" A whispered voice

came from the nursery, and I bit my lip to keep from crying out.

Fuck. I was *so goddamn close*.

I bit my lip as I increased the speed on the Pink Rocket, needing to get this finished fast. I accidentally hit the g-spot vibration setting and rocketed up in bed on a moan.

Shit, fuck. I looked at the baby monitor and Devan was there, his eyes on the door between the bedroom and the nursery. Watching his face in shades of gray, I slapped one hand over my mouth and went harder, crying out as my body shook with orgasms. Devan's eyes intently watched the door, almost like he could see me coming as I thought about him.

It just made me come harder. I imagined he was watching me as I came, and I whispered his name in a gasp. His whole body was held taut, like he could hear me, but I knew he couldn't. I hoped.

I let my loose limbs flop to the side. Then I raced to the bathroom, had a shower and pretended I didn't just come to the thought of Devan choking me while he watched me orgasm.

The following morning, everyone left early. Rigby and River had a player meeting and physiotherapy, and Devan had an early morning meeting. I was home alone for the first time with Huey, and it was a weird feeling. It was a university town, so there were a lot of young people with backpacks running around, generally being carefree.

I reminded myself I was still young, and while I mightn't be carefree, I wasn't someone's grandmother. I just had a built-in bestie for a while. Like, eighteen years. Huey was a gift. I knew that.

But when I saw the college students, some my age, it was easy for the bitterness to creep into the edges of my happiness. This wasn't how I'd seen my life going. I was meant to get my degree, go on a bunch of depressing online dating app dates until I found one that broke the mold of horrible. We'd date for a couple of years until we got engaged. Then I'd have a decent, proper career, we'd settle down, and I'd have a family when I was about thirty.

Who would date a woman who was saddled down with a baby already? A baby who came with three oversized and intimidating protectors?

I sighed, deciding I needed to get out of the house. I had yet to use my new car, though Devan had driven us to the stadium in it the other night. It was the most comfortable car my ass had ever sat in.

I packed up some stuff, including a couple of bottles for Huey and a sandwich for me, and loaded it all into the SUV. It was lucky this place had such a huge driveway so I could get a feel for this giant tank of a vehicle.

Finally, when I rolled out onto the road, I was confident that I could drive this beast into battle and win. It was a beautiful day, and I'd read about a sweet park south of the river that was a nice place to take kids. We'd go and have a picnic, because that seemed like the parental thing to do, and if I had to be trapped inside one more day, I'd go insane.

Eventually, I'd need to come off hiatus for my clients, but not yet. I wasn't ready to go back to working, staring at a computer screen for hours on end. I hadn't even tried to juggle it yet with Huey.

Next week, I'd start getting back into the daily grind. This week, I'd just enjoy getting to know my baby brother a little better.

I drove five miles under the speed limit—probably annoying all the people behind me—until the navigation system told me to turn off. I could see why people raved about this park. It was sweet, filled with children, rolling green lawns and flowers.

I loaded everything into Huey's stroller and walked around the paths for an hour. When he grizzled hungrily, I circled back toward the car until I found a place to lay down a picnic blanket I'd pilfered from the house, and sat down to feed Huey.

"Your son is beautiful," an older lady commented as she strolled past. "You should put more clothes on him, though. You don't want him to get a chill."

I looked up at her, wide-eyed. "Thank you for your advice," I replied politely. I didn't correct her about Huey being my brother.

She looked down at my left hand, then back at my

face with a slight frown. "It must be tough being a teenage single mother," she said, shaking her head. "Babies having babies. Who is there to teach you all the lessons you need to keep your baby alive?"

I stared at the woman. "Excuse me?"

"Look at the sunburn on his arms already. Did you even put SPF on his arms before bringing him out?" Hadn't she just told me that he'd get a chill? "Having a baby isn't like getting one of those designer dogs people pay a fortune for. If you're going to have a baby, you have a responsibility to care for it properly, or give it up to a family that will." The old lady's lip curled in disgust. "This is what the lack of Christian values has given this generation. Whores and bastards. You should be ashamed of yourself. Poor little thing is going to have to drag itself up and will probably end up in prison like all the other fatherless miscreants."

I was stunned. Last night, if anyone had asked me how I'd respond to someone saying these things, I would have said with immediate ferocity. But in reality, I sat there and just gaped at her, my eyes filling with tears.

A mother with a toddler on her hip marched up. "Listen, you old hag. No one wants your opinion, or your disgusting vitriol, so why don't you do us all a favor and drop dead already," the mama bear growled, and the old woman sniffed, giving us both a disdainful glare and striding away.

But the damage had been done. I was already standing, pulling the bottle from a grumbling Huey's mouth and putting him back in the stroller. I threw everything else in the cargo area underneath.

All the while, the mother with the squirming toddler watched me with sad eyes. "Don't listen to her. You're doing a great job, and she's obviously nuts."

Fuck, I was going to cry. I'd thought I was over this crying shit. "Thank you. I'm sorry, I have to go."

The woman nodded, watching as I all but sprinted back to the car. I unlocked it quickly and slid Huey into his seat. I hopped into the driver's side, then promptly burst into tears.

It was just my luck that at the moment my phone rang. Instead of answering it, I cried more. Then it rang again. And again.

Finally, I answered. "Hello?"

"Are you okay?" River's voice was breathless down the phone. "What's wrong?"

I sniffed, sitting up straight and scrubbing my forearm across my eyes. "Nothing. I'm fine."

"Don't move. I'm coming."

"River—" But I was talking to dead air.

CHAPTER

Fifteen

RIVER

WHEN NOVA DIDN'T ANSWER her phone, something in my chest constricted and didn't let go until I heard her voice. When I realized she was crying, a new sensation filled my chest and it was something I could immediately recognize: protectiveness.

"Don't move. I'm coming."

I hung up before she could protest. I lifted my chin at Rigby, and he excused himself from the sponsors he'd been schmoozing to walk over to me.

"What's wrong?"

"Something's up with Nova. I'm going to get her. Can you cover for me with the GM?"

Rigby frowned. "Fuck that. I'm coming with you."

I slapped him on the shoulder. "Stay—I've got this. And one of us being missing is way less conspicuous to Coach than us both being gone."

He stroked a hand down his face. "Fine. But

message me straight away and let me know she's okay."

I nodded, and as Rigby made his way back across the room, smiling and drawing the eyes of every person in the vicinity, I snuck out the door. I strode through the team offices so fast, no one even thought to stop and talk to me. Once I was in the car, I called Devan.

"What's up?"

"Can you track Nova's phone for me?" I wasn't an idiot. Devan had his issues, and one of those was this insane protectiveness that almost bordered on suffocating. Trauma did that; he needed to be in control the whole time, and he hated unknowns. Which meant I knew he had a tracking device in Nova's car, and probably on her phone too.

He didn't ask why. He just went silent for a moment, then came back on the line with a harsh breath. "She's at the County Farm Park. I'll be there soon."

I didn't try to stop Dev. There *was* no stopping him. But he had to come from the other side of the city, so I'd make it there first. I broke several traffic laws, but within fifteen minutes of getting the address from Dev, I was pulling up beside Nova's new car.

There was no one in the driver's seat, and I began to panic. Maybe she'd stepped out to walk through the gardens? I climbed out and rushed to the car, dragging open the door and then stopping.

Sitting in the passenger seat, feeding Huey, was a

tear-stained Nova. "I'm sorry. I'm fine, I promise. You can go back to work."

She didn't look fine. Her face was puffy and too pink, and her voice was scratchy like she'd been crying hard.

"What's wrong? Are you hurt? Is Huey okay?"

She shook her head, muttering, "I'm fine." Then she looked down at Huey and cried harder. Was the baby okay? He looked all right. He was eating and kicking his legs. Definitely didn't seem hurt in any way.

"Is there something wrong with the baby, Nova?"

She shook her head. "Only that he's saddled with an incompetent teenage mother and is going to end up in prison with melanoma because I don't know how to put sunscreen on him," she sobbed out.

I blinked several times. I would have laughed if she hadn't been crying so hard. "What? Nova, quit crying; you aren't making any sense."

She just cried harder, and I didn't know what to do. I rubbed her arm, while Huey seemed oblivious to his caregiver's emotional trauma, happily sucking down his bottle like he didn't have a care in the world.

When Dev turned up, I'd never been happier to see his face. Considering he'd once rescued me after I was handcuffed to a puck bunny's bed for three hours, that was really saying something.

He pulled open the door, took one look at Nova, another at Huey, and raised an eyebrow. I shrugged, because I still had no fucking idea what was going on. He stuck his head in the passenger door.

"Did someone hurt you?" he growled.

"Only emotionally."

Dev frowned. He untangled Huey from her arms and gave me a loaded look. "I'll burp the baby. Tell River what's wrong." With that, he closed the door again, and Nova looked at me with those big hazel eyes that broke my heart.

Why was she still crying? *Ugh, fuck it.* Sliding the seat back as far as it would go, I picked Nova up and pulled her into my arms. She let out a little squeak, sitting stiffly on my lap until I wrapped my arms around her, pulling her tightly to my chest. She tucked her head beneath my chin, her sniffles loud through the car.

I stroked her back until her tears dried up a little. "Tell me what happened."

As she recounted the absolute bullshit some old lady was spewing at her, I did my best not to feel incredulous. This was what she was crying about? We were sitting in a car that cost more than most people's houses. Obviously that woman's views didn't apply to Nova, so why did it upset her so much?

"And why are you crying in the car?" I murmured softly against her hair. God, she felt nice in my arms. She just fit so perfectly, and it made my chest feel way too full. Rigby was onto something with this hugging thing.

"She was right. Well, not about the teenage pregnancy thing, obviously. I'm twenty-four, so it's been a hot minute since my teenage years. But I don't have any idea what I'm doing, and who do I ask? I'm motherless. And fatherless. I have no one to ask about these things. I don't have anyone to ask if I'm fucking this up." She sniffed, and her tears started again. "I miss my mom."

Ah. I had nothing to help that kind of hurt. It was a wound only time would ease. So I stroked her back and let her cry, giving her all the reassurance I could without saying a word. I also formulated a plan. Because I wanted Nova to be happy—not just because she had custody of Huey, and keeping her happy meant keeping him.

I liked Nova. She was sweet and fierce. She was stronger than she gave herself credit for. She was a good mother, even though she didn't believe it, and didn't know every nuance to motherhood like someone who'd had six or nine months to prepare. But she was giving 110% to the job.

"Listen, Huey is a happy baby, and he loves you already. He lights up when you're around. In a couple of short weeks, you've become his safe space. The rest we'll figure out on the way. We'll make mistakes, but in the end, Huey *will* grow up to be a happy, emotionally healthy kid who definitely won't be in jail or have skin cancer, I promise."

She let out a weird snort-sob. She was overwhelmed, that was obvious. And her meltdown had less to do with some old bitch and more to do with her grief. Still, I pulled her shoulders back, and pushed her hair back from her sticky cheeks.

She looked down at the wet patch on my chest from her tears, and her already pink cheeks darkened. I saw when embarrassment overcame her distress. I watched as she got mad at herself, saw the frustration in her eyes.

"He'll end up a basket case because I'm a basket case. I'm sorry." She scrambled off my lap, and I swallowed hard to stop myself from grabbing at her hips to make her stay where she was, tucked against my chest.

I shook my head. "He'll be fine. Spoiled rotten, probably, but he'll know so much love. I swear it." And I did. Huey would have the childhood Dev and I never got. I swore it on Alana's memory.

"I guess—" She froze, her eyes looking out the windshield. I turned and saw an elderly woman walking into the parking lot.

Anger welled in my chest. "Is that the lady?"

"River—" she started.

"Is. That. Her?"

She nodded, and that was all I needed. I climbed out of the car, ignoring Nova's pleas. I strode over to the old bitch who'd needlessly caused Nova so much heartache. When the old woman's eyes met mine, they lit up, first in obvious appreciation, and then—when she reached my face after ogling my body—in recognition.

"Oh my gosh, River Cooper! I am such a fan. My ex-husband was a massive IceCaps supporter—only good thing that bastard left behind. I took his box seats in the divorce. I come to all your games!"

I told myself to breathe through my nose, pasting a friendly smile on my face that didn't reach my eyes. Good. This had just gotten better. "Is that right? It's nice to meet you too, Ms…?"

"Sullivan. Margaret Sullivan."

I gave her a shark grin. "Excellent. Consider your membership revoked. I'll talk to Corporate when I get back to the arena."

The woman gaped. "Excuse me?"

I got up in her space. I didn't use my size to intimidate often, but now was the time. "You don't get to approach people in a public space and force your disgusting views on them. You don't get to emotionally hurt people who belong to me with false representations about them being a single mother. You don't get to air your prejudices in public like the heinous bitch you are. You aren't worthy to wear an IceCaps jersey, and if I ever see you near my girlfriend again, I will personally destroy your fucking life.

"Keep your bullshit opinions to yourself, because you have no fucking right to assume shit about anyone. It's shitty people who are the real fucking problem with the world—not single mothers. Judgemental old hags like you, who believe you're somehow superior because you got married, then turn a blind eye when your husband fucks his secretary over his desk every lunchtime rather than touch your shrivelled old ass with a ten-foot pole. Speak to her again, and I'll sue you for every penny you got in your shitty divorce."

"Your girlfriend?" she breathed.

Ah fuck. That had just slipped out. Instead of clarifying, I turned and strode away. I wasn't kidding. I'd talk to Corporate. There was a conduct clause in the membership application, and I'd personally ensure that she was banned from the IceCaps arena. I'd have to explain to membership services, but I'd given Gavin in that department a lift to and from work every day for a week when his car was in the shop. He owed me one.

I strode back over to the car, the woman's eyes still on my back. Nova was watching me, her pillowy lips slightly parted. Devan was putting Huey back in his car seat.

"Are you okay to drive?" I asked Nova.

She nodded, but her eyes were shiny again. She cleared her throat. "Thanks. For defending me, I mean."

Against my better judgment, I reached in and cupped her cheek. "Always." I sucked in a breath. "Head home. We'll meet you there. I just have to swing back and pick up Rigby."

She nodded again, and slowly reversed back out of the parking lot. Then she crawled away.

"You think she drove that slow all the way here?" Dev snorted, and I grinned.

"Probably."

"Is she okay?" The mirth left Dev's face. He was worried about her too.

"She will be, I think. We're going to dinner with Muss and Julieta tonight; she needs mom friends. She needs a support network."

Dev frowned. "We're her support network."

I rolled my eyes at my control freak friend. "She needs a support network of *moms*. She needs someone to tell her she's doing it right, not three bachelors who also have no idea what they're doing."

Dev grumbled, but nodded. "Fine. I have to head back to the office, but I'll be home before dinner."

He climbed into his Porsche, waving as he left. Every set of eyes in the parking lot watched him go, including Margaret Sullivan's. I gave her the coldest look I could muster and then turned my back on her forever.

I climbed back into my own car, and as soon as my phone connected to the car's speakers, I made some calls. First to Julieta, and then to Corporate. I was going to throw my weight around and make sure that woman never got close to Nova again.

CHAPTER
Sixteen

NOVA

I WAS STILL mad at myself as I pulled into the driveway of the house. My cheeks flushed hot if I even so much as thought about my mini-meltdown in River's arms. I was stronger than this, goddammit. I wasn't someone who had a breakdown about the words of some bitter old bitch. I stood up for myself. I'd stand up for Huey too.

But not today. Today, that woman had pressed her fingers right into new wounds. She'd made me bleed as easily as if she was wielding a knife. And then I'd cried all over River. So fucking embarrassing. I wanted to crawl into a dark hole and not come out for a week. Long enough to forget all about today.

I looked down at Huey, who was happily sucking on his fist as I unclicked his car seat from the base. He didn't look sunburned. He was fine. I knew he was.

We'd only been in the sun for about ten minutes. He was clean and happy, and I was doing a good job.

I repeated that mantra in my head over and over. *I just had a minor crisis of confidence, I can do this.* I'd look up a list of things to do before you took your baby out, and then I'd follow that list every time.

I needed a shower. I needed to wash all this damn angst down the drain and start again. I carried Huey up the stairs, moving his baby rocker into my room. It swayed gently from side to side and had tiny zoo animals along the top of it.

Putting it outside the bathroom door, I set it to a gentle sway and gave him his pacifier. Leaving the door to my ensuite open a bit just in case, I climbed into a cool shower and just breathed. I centered myself on the feel of the water on my skin, on the things I was thankful for. Resting my head on the cold tiles, I just let my body relax.

I definitely tried not to think about the hardness of River's body under mine earlier. The man was basically zero percent body fat, and his thighs were like fucking rocks. He was strong and broad, and being in his arms had felt like the most natural thing in the world. Climbing out of his lap had been so damn hard, but embarrassment was a powerful motivator.

The next three months were going to kill me. I had no idea what I was going to do after that, though. The guys had been great—attentive, sweet, and so damn helpful with Huey. They'd been nothing short of amazing. The reason I couldn't live here after three months had nothing to do with them, and everything to do with me and the fact I was stupidly attracted to them.

I was going to ruin everything, and the one who'd suffer was Huey. He didn't know it yet, but he'd suffered enough. Maybe I'd find a place here in Ann Arbor. What did I actually have back in Tucson? Just a few friends, Chloe and her family.

I needed to call Chlo. She'd know what to do. But even as I thought it, I knew I wouldn't be able to afford an apartment in Ann Arbor, let alone a house. Even if I sold my family home.

With a sigh, I turned off the shower and stepped out. Wrapping a fluffy towel bigger than a blanket around my body, I opened the ensuite door to check on Huey.

Unsurprisingly, he was sound asleep. But it was the man sitting on my bed that made me freeze.

Rigby was in dress pants that were stretched to their maximum capacity, and a blue button-down shirt. And he was looking at me with concern etched across his face. "I just wanted to check on you," he said, his voice rough, but his eyes never dropping below my chin. "River was freaked out when he left the players' meeting."

Swallowing hard, I tightened the towel around my chest. That made his eyes flicker to my chest for a second. "I'm fine. Another day, another emotional crisis." I gave him a self-deprecating grin and moved to my walk-in closet. It was huge, and I walked to the back, grabbing my underwear and pulling them on under my towel.

Then I dropped it and grabbed my bra. My nipples decided it was time for high beam, knowing I was mostly naked and Rigby was right out there, on the bed.

"Do you want me to go?" he called, and I bit my lip. Had we reached this stage of our friendship? No. But part of me didn't care.

"No, it's okay," I called back. I reached behind me and tried to fasten my bra, but my hands felt shaky.

"Need help?"

I froze. I saw the reflection of Rigby in the large mirror at the end of the closet, leaning against the door jamb. I met his eyes, and there was no doubting the lust I saw there. He wanted me as much as I wanted him; I knew it in my soul. Well, somewhere distinctly lower knew it too.

So instead of saying anything, I just nodded. He ate up the distance between us in two long strides. I held the cups to my breasts as his long fingers deftly worked the hooks and loops of my basic bitch bra. Dammit, I should have put on my fancy underwear. Something lace. Not this old lady bra. Too late now, though.

I watched him in the mirror as he finished his task, then brushed his fingers down my spine reverently. My skin felt ten times more sensitive to his touch as he traced them down to the small of my back before lifting them away.

He looked up and met my eyes in the mirror, and his expression stole my breath. "You're so fucking beautiful, Nova." He lifted his hand again, and I watched in the mirror as it landed on my hip. He paused, as if waiting for me to move away, not realizing that I couldn't move my legs because my knees were weak.

He traced his hand up the curve of my hip slowly, like he was memorizing the sensation. Those huge hands wrapped around my ribs. His thumb brushed the underside of my boob but missed my aching nipple.

"Baby, I'd really like to kiss you," he said softly, his body now so close to mine that I could feel his warmth. "Can I kiss you?"

Obviously, the answer was yes. I wanted him to do more than kiss me. I wanted him to lie me on the floor of this huge closet and fuck me into oblivion. But it was a bad idea. I knew that.

My head nodded of its own accord. Rigby spun me quickly in his arms, and I gasped at the sudden movement. He took full advantage of my parted lips, swooping down to capture them in a kiss that I'd remember until the end of time.

I clutched his shirt as his mouth dominated mine, the press of his lips against mine firm and powerful, like he was consuming both my kiss and me. It was heady. It was erotic. All I could do was hold on for dear life. He continued to devour my mouth, his tongue tangling with mine, tasting me.

Finally, when I was gasping for air, he pulled back. His hooded eyes bounced from my swollen lips to my eyes that felt like they were open far too wide. "I've wanted to do that since the first time I saw you in that courtroom. That mouth begs to be kissed." His hands slid from where they were clutching my lower back, up until they reached my shoulder blades. His face moved into a frown. "Are you okay?"

I just blinked up at his concerned face. "I... Damn."

He grinned, and any coherent thought I'd been mustering disappeared. "I'm taking that as a compliment." His head dipped down, and he brushed another soft kiss across my lips. "I came up here to tell you we're going to Muss and Julieta's house for dinner."

"Oh. Okay." Yep, apparently I was malfunctioning. Jesus, I needed to get laid. If a kiss could render me mostly mute, I was obviously out of practice.

I had a brief flash of Rigby above me, looking into my eyes as he filled me with... *Argh. Stop, brain, stop.* My cheeks flushed, and Rigby gave me another one of those crooked grins.

"I'll let you get dressed." He let me go, but his fingers trailed across my skin as he dropped them. He winked as he turned, striding to the door with a cocky swagger. He stopped in the doorway. "Hey, Nova?"

"Yes?" I breathed.

"I can't wait to kiss you again." Then he was gone.

Holy fuck, my body was on fire. *I* was on fire. I was not going to survive Rigby Engman. I really needed another cold shower, but instead, I pulled out a dress from my wardrobe. I had to get my shit under control. But every time I thought about Rigby's kiss, my body flushed again.

I was so screwed.

CHAPTER
Seventeen

DEVAN

"SEE YOU TOMORROW, MR. MAYSON," Elise from Accounts cooed, and I gave her a tight grin while internally groaning. I was going to have to get her transferred, or talk to Carol in HR. Psychological studies show that bonding during high-stress workplace situations is akin to that of sexual relationships. It's why so many people marry—or fuck—their work colleagues. Throw in the fact that most office workers see each other more than their family or friends, and it's no wonder that one in every three employees would sleep with a coworker.

Add in a boss who kept getting added to those dumb fucking eligible bachelor lists, and it was a fucking minefield. A stress I didn't want or need. I would never in a million years date a damn employee. Not Elise. Not my secretary. Not Carol in HR, who was actually fifty-three with three grandchildren and a CPA as a husband.

I grunted goodbye to Elise and moved back into my office, shutting the door. I was done for the day, even though I often worked late. I didn't examine why I suddenly wanted to rush home at 5 p.m. every day. Probably to see Huey, because he seemed to grow bigger and bigger every time I looked at him.

It definitely didn't have anything to do with his pretty guardian. Or the fact she'd been so damn sad today in that park. I'd wanted to destroy that old bitch who'd made Nova cry. It had been an urge so visceral; it had poured through my veins like acid. That in itself scared me. I knew Rigby thought I was aloof—he always teased me about being the tin man—but it was only because if I didn't keep a firm control of my emotions, I knew where they could lead me.

I still had nightmares about the things that had happened when my father lost control of his emotions. When he was strung out and in his psychosis if he couldn't get a fix. I couldn't blame the drugs, though; my earliest memories were of him screaming at me.

I wouldn't walk in my father's footsteps. I'd keep it under control. Which meant it was best if I felt nothing at all.

I nodded to my personal assistant, a financial aid kid who'd done an MBA and who would've been paying off his debts for the next thirty years if it weren't for this job. I wasn't giving him a free ride; he worked fucking hard for the six-figure salary I gave him. But I also knew he had a mom and three younger sisters that he helped support and put through college. I liked him.

Taking the elevator down to the parking garage, I breathed a sigh of relief that no one hopped in with me. If I had to pretend to write emails to avoid small talk, I would, and my reputation as a hard-hearted ice monster really didn't need much more evidence.

Pulling my Porsche keys from my pocket, I folded my body into the seat. Most CEOs at my level had a driver, but honestly, I couldn't stand the idea of giving up control to another person. I drove my sports cars so everyone just thought I was vain, and no one ever questioned me. Not that I didn't like my classic Carrera 911, but I wasn't the Car Guy everyone seemed to think I was.

Pulling out of the parking garage, I navigated through the peak hour traffic with growing annoyance. It gave me too much time to think. Normally, I would've thought about work, or it used to be about Alana and Huey, or River's pesky knee injury, or a hard hit one of the guys had taken that week.

Now, the only thing that snuck into my thoughts was *her*. The girl I couldn't have. Somehow, that just made me want her more.

Growling out a frustrated noise, I smacked my hand on the steering wheel and turned up the radio. It was ridiculous talkback radio, but it did its job of distracting me.

When I pulled into the garage at home, I took a moment to center myself. Grabbing my briefcase with a couple of business case studies I wanted to go over this week, I climbed from my car. I didn't bother putting on my suit jacket again, instead just strolling into the house through the garage door.

And stopping dead.

Holy. Shit.

Nova had dressed up to go to dinner at Muss's house. She looked… breathtaking. Her dark brown hair was curled lightly, hanging down her back in shiny, soft waves. She was wearing a sundress in a burnt orange color, making her golden skin look radiant. It had tiny buttons all the way down the front, hitting her mid-thigh, and I wanted to undo every single one of those buttons with my teeth.

I clenched my jaw as she turned in my direction and smiled so widely, I could barely breathe. "You're home! Look how cute Huey is in his outfit," she said excitedly, lifting Huey up. I couldn't help but smile. He did look fucking cute in a little pair of dark shorts with attached suspenders, and a tiny bow tie that clipped onto his blue button-up.

Studiously not looking in Nova's direction, I held my hands out. "Looking dapper, little guy," I cooed, and he grinned at me, melting my heart again. He did it every single time. Kid was going to give me cavities, he was so damn sweet.

Nova grinned, her eyes trained on the baby too.

Then she let out a little gasp. "Wait, wait!" She disappeared for a moment, returning with a tiny pair of socks shaped like black high-top Converse sneakers.

"Did you turn our son into a hipster?"

She froze. I froze. It had slipped out, but I refused to take it back. He *was* our kid. My son. Her son. River's son. Maybe not by blood, but in every other way that counted. He would be raised with so many parental figures, he'd know nothing but love. I wanted him to know that this wasn't some kind of game, that we truly *wanted* him. Her too—I wanted her to know that we wanted him. I didn't want her to walk away in three months.

And not just because of Huey.

Nova cleared her throat. "Well, this is his first dinner party, I think. We went all out."

I nodded, forcing myself to look up into her pretty hazel eyes. "He looks great. You both do." She flushed pink, and I decided that was my cue to get the hell out of here before I made this even more awkward. I handed Huey back to her. "I'll just run upstairs and get ready. I'll be down in twenty."

Racing upstairs, I was already unbuttoning my shirt before I made it to my ensuite. I'd been on edge all day when it came to the woman downstairs, and I had to do something about it before I exploded and did something stupid. I really needed to get laid. ASAP.

As I climbed into the shower, I wrapped my hand around my cock almost immediately. Seeing her, all beautiful and happy, brought back what I thought I'd heard last night. I'd tried to convince myself I'd been hallucinating. That she'd just been sleeping, or talking on the phone, or doing anything but what I thought she'd been doing.

Touching herself.

I'd gone in to check on Huey before I turned in for the night, and heard a low hum. It was almost too low to hear, but I had great hearing from a decade in foster care. At first, I'd convinced myself that it was just her brushing her teeth with an electric toothbrush. People did that.

But then I heard the unmistakable sound of a swallowed moan, slightly muffled, like she was trying to be quiet. And I'd stilled, like a statue. It had suddenly made sense why Huey's nursery door had been shut.

I hadn't been able to move. Even just thinking about that sweet, soft noise made my dick ache, and I stroked it harder and faster, imagining it was Nova's tight cunt wrapped around my dick.

What made it better—or worse—was that I could've sworn she said my name as she came. As those muffled cries turned into one long moan of release, I would've bet my fortune on the fact that it was my name she'd breathed. Had she been thinking about me as she fucked herself? God, even the thought made me pump harder and faster until I was shooting my load all over my bathroom tiles.

I was so, so fucked.

Drying myself off, and still cursing my lack of control, I threw on some jeans and a light blue button-down. Running some product through my hair, I decided that was enough to go visit Muss. Of everyone in the team, Rigby and River were closest to their team captain. He was a nice guy, who'd been in the league for a long time. Sometimes that made people arrogant, but Muss was a genuine person who cared about the team, and also about the players in it. He loved hockey, but he loved his wife and kids even more.

I respected him, and there were very few people I could say that about.

I made it back downstairs in seventeen minutes, and everyone was waiting for me in the kitchen. Rigby and River were having a beer, and Huey was already strapped into his car seat. Nova was laughing at something Rigby was saying, her body leaning in close to his as she joked back. Their arms touched, his fingers brushed across her hip.

And jealousy was like a punch in the balls.

River was watching them from the other side of the island countertop, his eyes lingering on Rigby's hand too. Feeling my eyes, he turned, and I saw the reflection of my own feelings in his expression. Envy. Jealousy, even.

Something had happened between Rigby and Nova, and it was fucking bad, bad news for us all. Even though it was what we'd wanted.

"Let's go. We're late."

Nova stopped laughing at my tone, which was probably a little colder than I'd intended, but Rigby, that little fuck, just turned and smiled wider at me. "No worries, Dev. We're just waiting on you. On both of you."

River frowned. "I've been here the whole time."

Rigby just shook his head, shooting me a crooked smile. I didn't think he meant for the dinner party. I was pretty sure he meant something a little more serious. I didn't want to think about what I couldn't have, so I just scowled at him and strode toward the garage.

This day needed to be over already.

CHAPTER

Eighteen

NOVA

CLINT AND JULIETA VANMUSSEN lived on a huge estate, but it wasn't flashy. A single-storey place, it had sprawling grounds, with everything from trampolines and swing sets to what I thought might be a half-pipe. The gardens were beautiful, and judging by the dirty, grass-covered boots by the front door, they actually did their own gardening.

There was the general commotion of children inside the house. Rigby was grinning as he rang the doorbell, and a huge man with a shock of white-blond hair answered it quickly. His smile was wide and straight as he took in our small group.

"Cooper, Engman! Hey, Dev. Good to see you, man," he said, thrusting out his hand for a shake before his eyes settled on me. Then they softened. "You must be Nova. The boys speak highly of you. I'm Clint." He put out a hand, and I shook it.

Clint must have been in his late thirties, and he was still a handsome man. Not as hot as the men I lived with, and maybe his attractiveness had nothing to do with his square jaw and everything to do with the warmth that came off him in waves.

"Thank you for inviting us to your home. The guys say great things about you too, when they aren't cursing you out for being a taskmaster."

Rigby gave me a mock disapproving look. "Hey, what happens in Vegas, stays in Vegas, babe." He hefted the car seat in his arms. "This is Huey, the most perfect baby in the universe."

Julieta appeared behind her husband. She had wavy dark hair and eyes that seemed almost too big for her face, but they sparkled like she was up to mischief, in a good way. "Did someone say baby?"

Clint rolled his eyes. "Julieta has baby fever, like we haven't been changing diapers consistently for the last seven years. At this rate, I should just buy shares in a company. I blame you guys; she's been talking about it since the game Nova and Huey came to last week."

Julieta elbowed her husband. "You don't seem to mind the baby-making practice," she said with an arched brow. She reached over and hugged me. "So good to see you, Nova. And you, handsome little man, look how cute you are," she murmured at Huey before looking around at the guys. "Are you and Dev doing matching outfits already?"

Dev flushed as he looked down at his outfit. He did

kind of match Huey, with his blue button-down and dark jeans. "Accident," he grunted, and Julieta laughed.

"Sure it was, big guy. I'm not judging. I think it's just adorable. Come on inside, I'm stealing your girl for wine time. I stopped breastfeeding this week and Mama needs to get wine drunk ASAP. Your girl is going to help me out. You guys are on kid duty." She patted her husband on the butt before pulling me into the kitchen. She turned to me, one eyebrow raised. "I have serious questions for you, girl."

Oh shit.

"Red or white?"

"Uh… white?"

"Bubbles or no bubbles? Just kidding—the answer is always bubbles. Let's hit up the wine cellar. Man, tonight is going to be fun. Clint got food from my favorite sushi restaurant, because he might complain about my baby fever, but as soon as I suggest getting pregnant, that man is on me like a basic bitch on a pumpkin spice latte. I have a short window to drink and eat raw fish, and I intend to revel in it."

I followed her down the stairs, slightly glad she didn't want much by way of conversation out of me, because that wine cellar was the kind of thing dreams were made of. It had racks of wine behind sealed doors on one side, and on the other, an entire wall of books surrounded a huge abstract artwork. Right in the middle were two overstuffed couches in a soft cream suede and fluffy as hell throw rugs. It was paradise.

"This is Mommy's room—a kid-free zone. I keep the soft cheese down here with the wine. It's a one-stop shop. If you need cheese, wine, and smut-filled romance novels, girl, I got you."

As if to prove her point, she pulled out a wheel of cheese, an entire packet of artisanal crackers, and two fancy cut-crystal wine glasses. After pouring us a drink, she pointed to the couches. I had a feeling that Julieta was a force unto herself.

"Sit down and put your feet up. You deserve it, Mama. Cheers!" She lifted her wine glass. "Now, tell me what happened today."

I sucked in a deep breath and unloaded the whole story. As Julieta got fired up on my behalf—including a few threats about slashing the woman's tires—I decided then and there, I wanted this woman as a friend.

"Spill! Which one of those fine men whets your whistle? Because I don't know a whole lot about your situation, but I do know that hockey players have some sexy-ass bodies and you're stuck in a house with two of them. Unless you're a cyborg, a lesbian, or blind, I know you must *at least* be ogling one of them. Not to mention Dev with that smolder, holy shit."

I giggled, falling to the side because staying upright seemed to be more difficult now that I was filled with a bottle of wine and the best sushi I'd ever eaten. "No, you don't understand. I couldn't."

Julieta waved me away, chastising me in Spanish before switching back to English. "Girl, of *course* you can. You just put some pretty lingerie on that sexy body you're rocking," she said with a sigh. "I had a body like that once. Baby number three was a giant and just ruined all this. Clint likes it, though. Horny bastard." She shook her head. "What was I saying? Oh yeah, you just put on lingerie and say 'Hey, I have a need that only you can fix.' Walk away with a lil butt wiggle and they'll come panting behind you like hounds."

My face was flushed, and I covered my cheeks with my cool hands. "I can't, Julieta," I whined. "They are so pretty, and I couldn't choose... and what if I fucked it up? I can't do that to Huey. No, I need to get laid somewhere outside the house."

Julieta muttered something under her breath about it being a waste, though I wasn't sure of what, exactly. Then she lifted her hands in the air, leaning across to slap them on my thighs. "I got a brother! He's a bit of a hound dog, but he's almost thirty and it's time he settled down. I can set you up." She stood, tipping a little to the side, and then sat back down again. "Yes! That's what I'll do. I'll give you his number. I mean, he's my brother, and I really don't want to think about him having sex"—she screwed up her nose—"but once, a girl turned up on my parents' doorstep begging for Zayn to take her back because he'd ruined her for other men. I feel like that's a damn fine review."

I lifted my bottle of champagne at her. "Set me up. I

haven't seen any action that wasn't self-inflicted in months. My vagina is about to retire and move to Florida!"

"To taking your vagina out of retirement!" she toasted loudly, until someone cleared their throat at the bottom of the stairs.

Clint was standing there, an amused smile on his face. "Sorry to interrupt. Just checking Julieta hadn't reached the part of her night where she drunkenly gets naked."

"I do not!"

He snorted. "One word. Barcelona."

Julieta flushed bright red, but narrowed her eyes. She pointed a bottle of champagne in his direction. "You were going to get laid tonight, but I've changed my mind."

I tipped back my own bottle of champagne as Clint and Julieta bantered. They were a cute couple.

"Julieta, we both know three-hundred-dollar bottles of wine always make you horny. Your threats are empty."

I spat my mouthful of champagne back in the bottle. "How much?" I gasped.

Clint laughed, and Julieta whacked him with the back of her hand. Then she winced, clutching the hand to her chest. "*Dios,* when do you get a dad bod already? You're built harder than a rock."

Clint leaned closer to whisper something in her ear, and it didn't take a genius to know what. He stood back to his full height and grinned at me. "Don't stress it, Nova. We're part owners of a vineyard in California. We get most of the bottles for free."

I stood up and dutifully drank the rest down, even though I must've been chugging the equivalent of a glass and a half. "Thank you for tonight—you have no idea how much I needed this."

At least, that's what I thought I said. I took three steps, swerved wildly to the right, and then there were hands gripping my upper body, holding me still while the room whirled around me. I looked up into the pretty face of River motherfucking Cooper. Why was he so fucking hot?

He raised an eyebrow. "Because I work out six hours a day?" he replied, and I realized I'd said that last bit out loud. Fuck.

"You said that bit out loud too," Clint said with a laugh.

I flung my head back so hard, it was a wonder I didn't get whiplash, then stared at the ceiling. I was so screwed. I needed to get laid. "Julieta! Give your brother my number."

Suddenly, I was being hefted into River's arms, while Julieta laughed hysterically. "I will!" she promised, cackling as River snarled something at her.

He climbed the stairs with me over his shoulder easily. I should've been embarrassed, but I was too drunk to be shy. Plus, I had a great view of River's tight ass from here.

The ass in question slapped my butt. "You need to sober up."

"What? Why? And don't spank me. I like it." He groaned, and then Rigby was bending down in my vision. "Rigby! You're so fucking handsome. If things were different, we'd *definitely* have sex. Actually, if things were different, I'd be a total ho and just have sex with all of you, because this is the twenty-first century and body counts are a stupid social construct that suit men and not women. What if I want to have sex with all three of you, huh? Why couldn't I?"

"I don't know, Fireball. Why couldn't you?" Rigby teased.

"Don't encourage her," River grunted. "Let's go."

"But I can't because that would ruin *everything* and Huey needs this more than I need your dicks… so I'm going out with Julieta's brother, Zayn, and I'm going to make my vagina come back from Florida."

Rigby frowned. "Over my dead body, Nova Stone," he told me, gripping my face tightly as we made it to the car. "No one touches you but us."

I shook my head. "No can do, Eleanor Rigby. Huey needs you more than I need sex, and I won't ruin it for him. Shit! I forgot Huey! River, put me down. Have to get my baby."

River set me on my feet beside the car. "Devan has *our* baby right there, see? He's strapping him into the seat." I looked through the open car door at Dev, who was indeed clicking a sleeping Huey into the frame of the car seat.

"You're so pretty when you hold a baby. It's really unfair." I huffed and climbed into the back seat, getting a better look at Devan and Huey. "He's so perfect. I didn't know I could love another person the way I love that baby."

Dev looked up at me, his eyes the color of midnight, making me feel kinda light-headed. God, I wanted to kiss him so fucking bad.

His eyes widened. "You know you're still saying every thought out loud, right?"

I scrambled backward and ended up on Rigby's lap. He just laughed and sat me in the middle seat, buckling me in tightly and throwing an arm around my shoulders until I was pressed against his side.

My phone dinged, and I looked down to see Julieta giving me Zayn's number with a bunch of winky and laughing face emojis. Rigby plucked the phone out of my hand and deleted the message.

"Hey! I needed that." *Like, real bad.*

Rigby kissed my temple. "The only person who gets to help you take your vagina out of retirement is in this car."

"Are you flirting with me? Are we going to go home and have sex tonight?" I asked, my body feeling flushed. Oh man, I really liked that idea; the consequences could go to Hell.

"No, because you're drunk."

"If I wasn't drunk?"

"We'll talk about it later. Why don't you sleep it off?"

I snuggled my face into his chest. "Can't."

"Why's that?"

"Because I'm going to throw up. Dev!"

The car swerved to the side, and Rigby had my belt undone and the door open before I could even get my brain to catch up.

"This is so not sexy," I moaned, and lost more seafood than Seaworld all over the side of M-14.

CHAPTER

Nineteen

RIGBY

WHEN NOVA APPEARED the following morning, she looked a little like death. After she'd puked on the highway last night, she'd passed out and we'd had to put both her and Huey to bed, which had been kind of hilarious.

Now, with her hair piled on top of her head and her pallor distinctly gray, I couldn't help but grin. "Aw, Fireball, you look like hell."

"Shh, Rigby. You're being too bright," she whimpered. "I need water."

I grabbed a glass and filled it to the brim, handing it to her when she finally staggered to the breakfast bar. She downed the whole glass in one go, then gave it back to me. I dutifully topped it up, sitting it down in front of her.

Leaning on my elbows, I grinned at her. She was

cute, even if she did look like a zombie. "So, you had a good time last night?"

She winced. "I think so. It's a bit blurry there toward the end." She glared at me. "Did I do anything, you know, embarrassing?"

I dragged my bottom lip between my teeth to stop myself from grinning. "Embarrassing? Nah."

She narrowed her eyes at me. "Rigby…"

"It was fine, Nova. I'm glad you enjoyed yourself. You deserve some downtime."

She huffed something under her breath, then laid her head down on the cool marble benchtops. "Where's Huey?"

"Dev took him to work. The joy of being the boss, plus we figured you wouldn't want to nurse a hangover and a baby."

"Ugh, I'm a failure already."

I walked over to where she was sitting and picked her up in my arms. She squeaked, but wrapped her thighs around my hips. I gave my dick a stern word about appropriateness, and I wasn't sure if he was flipping me off, but he stirred anyway.

"You are *not* a failure. You're a human being. Moms get days off too. You aren't a slave who has to be on the job twenty-four seven when there are other capable adults in the house. Now, close your eyes, Fireball. I got you a surprise."

"Fireball? Are you calling me cheap and sweet?"

I hefted her up onto the countertop. I definitely wanted to eat her out up here, just lay her back and then dive between those soft thighs. Clearing my throat, I stepped away, glad her eyes were closed so I could adjust my cock in my shorts. "No, because of, like, a supernova, you know? A burning ball of fire? Plus, it suits your personality, especially after last night. You're sassy when you're wine drunk."

"So you're calling me a burning ball of gas? Much better."

I rolled my eyes, but she couldn't see that either. "Don't move."

Rushing toward the butler's pantry, I grabbed the big basket of stuff I'd ordered on her first day here. I had no chill. I just wanted her to feel so at home that she'd never leave. Racing back into the kitchen, I sat it on the space next to her and stepped back.

"Okay, you can open them now."

She looked at the gift basket, a confused frown on her face for a moment, until she started to unwrap it. Then she pulled out a knife. A palette knife. And then a large bag of chocolate nibs. Molds. Piping bags. Thermometers.

"What's this?" she whispered, her eyes wide.

I grinned, stepping back into her space. "You said you wanted to make chocolate in this kitchen. It's a welcome home present. Sorry it's taken so long to get here."

She looked down at the basket, her fingers running over all the instruments inside. "Rigby…" She swallowed hard. "This is very thoughtful of you."

I hugged her, because I could. Because I craved it. "You deserve nice things. I mean, it's just a gift basket and not a car, so you don't have to be all weird about it."

Nova slapped my shoulder. "Too soon."

I laughed and just held her to my chest. I wanted to grill her about the things she'd said yesterday. Wanted to profess just how badly I wanted her too, but I didn't. Not yet. She wasn't ready for what I wanted to suggest.

None of them were.

"You're such a good man, Rigby Engman." She sighed against my chest. "And you have an ass sculpted by the gods."

Her words spread pleasure through my body, centering somewhere significantly lower than my heart. We'd have to talk about that eventually too, but not right now. Right now, I wanted to enjoy this moment.

"It's completely selfish, Fireball. I love chocolate." I'd love to lick melted chocolate from every inch of her body right here on this countertop. "If you ever need anyone to try samples, I'm your man."

I wanted to tell her that if she ever needed a man for *anything*, I was here. Right. Here. But the time wasn't right, and I could be patient. She needed more time too.

She surprised the hell out of me by gripping my face between her palms and kissing me hard. Her tongue slipped into my mouth, and I let her take control of the pace, the depth, everything. I just enjoyed the taste of her, the feel of her beneath my hands.

Eventually, she pulled back with a gasp. "You're something else," she whispered between long inhales, and I grinned.

I kissed the corner of her mouth, a light touch, barely there. "You deserve all the good things life has to offer. But it's incredibly hard for me to not push you back and fuck you with my tongue right now," I said with a laugh, though I wasn't really joking.

She looked at me for a long moment, and I began to panic. I'd gone too far.

But she surprised me. She always surprised me.

"Why don't you then?"

That was a yes. *Oh my god.* I wanted to be cool and calm. I wanted to take my time and woo her until I was between her thighs. But I was too fucking excited.

"Baby..." I breathed, and kissed her hard again. Ripping my mouth away, I grabbed her hips and pulled her closer to the edge of the countertop. I tugged at her tiny little satin shorts, and she gasped as her ass hit the cold tiles.

I didn't stop kissing her. Not yet. I reached under her camisole and rolled her right nipple between my fingers, making her gasp into my mouth. I pulled back a little, my smirk completely smug because she already looked a little dazed. I hadn't even started yet.

"I'm going to make you come so hard, you'll see stars. Would you like that?"

"Please, Rigby," she gasped as I pinched her nipple lightly.

"Mmm, that's right. But I want something from you, baby." I was more nervous about this confession than I wanted to let on, but I needed this too. "I need you to use that sexy as hell voice to tell me if I'm doing something you like. Tell me if I'm doing good. Can you do that for me?"

She blinked at me a little, and I desperately wanted to know what was going on in her head. "You've got a praise kink?" I nodded, and after what felt like an eternity, her smile widened. "I see you, Rigby Engman. Be my good boy and make me come all over your face."

My whole body shuddered with pleasure. *Holy. Shit. Hoooooolllllyyy shiiiiit.* I went hard as a brick in an instant. But you bet your ass I was between her thighs before she'd even finished her sentence.

I'd realized I had a praise kink pretty early in life. When I was in the tenth grade, my history teacher who was hot as fuck, Miss Bolinski, had told me I did such a good job getting an A on my quiz, and I'd popped a boner. It was years later when I'd realized it wasn't *just* because Miss Bolinski was hot.

Some of my exes had hated it. There was this social expectation that men should be dominant and take what they wanted. That the dynamic should only be one way. That was fine; I'd been just as happy to pin them down and be all alpha. But it had tainted this for me, so many rejections.

So for Nova to just readily accept it? I was going to reward us both by making her come so many times, she was going to be chanting my name.

I wasn't submissive—I was pretty sure about that. I didn't *need* for her to tell me what to do. I also didn't need to be dominant the way Devan had to be in control. I liked to play with the dynamic and keep shit interesting.

I licked and sucked my way up her thighs, before I blew a breath on her overheated folds. She moaned, and her hands scraped through my hair, taking some strands in her fists. Running the flat of my tongue up her slit, I flicked the tip of my tongue over her clit and lifted my eyes in time to see her head fall back. So I sucked it gently between my lips, and she gave a little shriek.

She needed a little reminder. I looked up expectantly, and she didn't disappoint. "You look so good between my thighs, eating me out," she gasped, her cheeks flushed, and I grinned and went back to work. I licked, sucked, and swirled my tongue over her clit, then alternated pushing it deep inside her, tasting her on my tongue, smearing her across my cheeks.

And the whole time, she softly told me things around her wild moans.

That I ate her so good.

That I knew exactly what she wanted.

She was so close, and I plunged two fingers inside her, my tongue swiping at her clit and my left hand squeezing my dick so I didn't come. I just let her ride my face, listening to her words of affirmation.

When her thighs clamped hard around my ears, I gave up holding off my own orgasm. I came hard with her, blowing my load in my boxers and licking up every ounce of her release from her thighs.

She slumped back against the marble and panted, and I was breathing heavily right along with her. Standing back up, I curled over her, my hands slipping beneath her shoulders until I could kiss her with the taste of her own release on my lips.

She pulled back. "I think you've destroyed me, Rigby Engman. I didn't even know it could be like that." She turned my head to the side, licking a stripe up my jaw until her lips rested beside my ear. "You're such a good boy, Rigby. I don't think I've ever come that hard." I shivered beneath her hands, and she chuckled low. "This is going to be so much fun."

I grinned down at her. Who knew she'd be into this as much as I was? "You're fucking perfect, Fireball."

She buried her face in my neck. A movement across the room caught my eye, and when I looked over, River was there, his dick tented in his pants. How long had he been standing there? Had he seen the whole thing? Had he seen her coming beneath my mouth? Had he heard her words?

I wasn't embarrassed. Well, maybe a little, but if

Nova liked it, I was going to own it. So I gave him a smirk and a wink, and he just stared fiercely, before spinning on his heel and walking away.

He'd had a taste of what he was missing now, and I had a plan. I just needed to put it into action.

CHAPTER

Twenty

RIVER

TOONS WAS GOING to bench me, and I wouldn't blame him. I was so fucking distracted out there, because every time I tried to get my head in the game, all I could see was Rigby fucking Engman tongue-fucking Nova on my kitchen benchtop. The place where I made my meals, he'd eaten her like a feast.

Skating with a fucking hard-on was torture.

Muss came up behind me, bumping me with his shoulder. "Get your head in the goddamn game, Cooper."

Shaking off the lust that was settling around me, I skated harder. Unfortunately for the other team, I harnessed all that sexual frustration into aggression. I hit so hard that the rookie from Washington went flying across the ice and their defense got all up in my face.

Good. I could use a fucking fight.

But Rigby was skating between me and the big

defenseman. I couldn't hear what the guy was saying over the hollering of the crowd, but whatever it was, he glared at me and slid away.

"You're gonna get yourself thrown out of the game and penalized if you keep hitting dirty," my former best friend grunted.

"Fuck off," I growled, and he frowned at me but skated away. I wasn't actually mad at him. I loved Rigby. I was man enough to admit that I was a jealous bastard, though. I'd wanted it to be me.

Nova was in the crowd somewhere with Julieta, who looked equally as hungover. I'd seen Nova after Rigby had debauched her on the Italian marble, and she'd looked better, but I'd still told her she didn't need to come to the game if she didn't want to. She'd just shaken her head, looking so fucking happy, and said she was rarely baby-free so she wanted to. I wanted her to as well. We had a week of away games coming up, and I wanted to get in as much Nova and Huey time as possible.

Dev had messaged to say that he was taking Huey straight home, after sending me several photos of Huey in his car seat at the head of the boardroom table for the weekly departmental meeting. It was probably unprofessional, but everyone was shit scared of Dev so no one would say anything.

She was out there wearing Rigby's number on her back, and that made the jealousy rear its head again. I bodychecked one of the Washington forwards into the boards, skating away before he could start something.

I played hard and dirty, but in the end, we won 7-3, so when Coach Toons gave me the stink eye in the locker rooms, I knew he wouldn't say anything. It was a messy defense strategy but it was still effective.

I showered for six hundred years in the locker room, hoping that I'd be able to skip the bullshit press box, though I doubted it. I was an old face in the IceCaps now, and the press always wanted to talk to me, no matter how badly I just wanted to flip them all off.

I scowled as I got redressed in my suit. Coach Toons waved a finger at me before I could storm into the conference room. "Not you tonight, Cooper. Engman, take his place. Cooper's scowling mug will break the damn cameras."

Rigby lifted his chin in agreement. "No worries, Coach." He walked up to me and slapped me on the back. I resisted the urge to punch him in the face. "What's wrong, Coop? You seem all pent up."

I growled in the direction of my best friend, his shit-eating grin really getting on my nerves. First he got the girl, and now he got the fucking glory?

"Your bad mood doesn't have anything to do with a pretty girl who may or may not live down the hall from you, and may or may not have been half-naked in your kitchen this morning, right?"

"You're gonna want to get out of my face *right now*."

Rigby reached over with one arm and gave me a

side hug, the disarming bastard. "We'll talk about this at home, Riv. No need to be so grumpy about shit that you don't need to be grumpy about." With that, he strode out of the locker room and down the hall toward the conference room with Perrier, the goalie.

Ludo came up to me, his tie still undone around his neck. "Lover's tiff?"

"Fuck off, Ludo." I picked up my bag and strode down the tunnels beneath the stadium. I needed to find a bar. I needed to find a pretty little puck bunny who'd be happy to take the edge off this fucking horniness.

That's what I'd do. Rigby or Julieta would get Nova home. I'd go down to Biscuits Bar and get fucking slammed until I could find a girl and *not* imagine she was Nova as I fucked her.

"River!"

Shit. I'd thought about Nova too hard and she'd appeared. I seriously considered ignoring her. I thought about pretending I hadn't heard her shout for me down this near-empty hallway. But I couldn't. Because I wanted her so bad, my body was turning before I'd even made a conscious effort.

She bounded up to me with a grin. "Good game!"

It was deceptively easy in that moment to see her as just any other beautiful woman, in her jersey and her sneakers, a grin on her face from watching sixty minutes of a brutal sport. She wasn't Huey's mom. She wasn't the woman raising my best friend's baby. She was a woman barely out of college, fresh-faced and happy.

And irresistible.

I grabbed her by the hips and spun her against the wall, my mouth landing on hers hard. She froze in shock, her lips still beneath mine, but only for a heart-beat. Then she was kissing me back. Her hands went up to my shoulders, gripping me tightly, like she was holding on so she wasn't swept away.

I groaned into her mouth. She felt electric in my arms, my fingers flexing against the soft curves of her hips, wedging her tightly to my body even as I had to stoop down to kiss her. I wanted to go deep, taste more of her.

I picked her up and pressed her against the concrete wall, and she hissed at the cold sensation. I didn't care. I'd warm her back up again. She wrapped her legs around my hips, clinging to me as our tongues fucked.

I almost didn't hear the distinct clicking sound of a shutter, or the cleared throat that echoed down the hall. I was too consumed by her.

But when I turned around, several cameras were pointed in our direction, and the ASPN reporter was giving me a look with one perfectly raised eyebrow. Andrea Esperanza. I'd slept with her once on the road, and it had been a mistake.

"New girlfriend, Cooper?" she asked, but her voice was frosty. Yeah. I'd hit and quit it once, totally drunk after a particularly hard loss out in Seattle. Andrea

looked harder at Nova, who was looking at the sophisti-
cated reporter like she wanted to run away. "Isn't that
the girl Rigby Engman was flirting with at the last
game?" Andrea gave me a disappointed and yet
somehow gleeful expression. "Your best friend's girl is a
bit cliché, even for you, River."

There was no way I was ever going to get Andrea to
change the narrative. So I did the only thing I could
think of in that moment. "You're right. This is my new
girlfriend. Now fuck off, Andrea." With that, I turned
on my heel and strode away, Nova's hand in mine.

Fuck, fuck, fuck.

I didn't stop swearing until we reached my car. We
had to wait for fucking Rigby to be done. My best
friend, who'd told me *repeatedly* he was interested in
Nova. And I'd just claimed her in front of the nation.

I climbed into the driver's seat and slammed my
hand on the steering wheel. "Fuck!"

"I'm sorry," Nova said softly, hunched in the corner
of the car like she was scared of me.

I sucked in some deep breaths. I never wanted her to
fear me. Never.

"You have nothing to be sorry for. I kissed you. I
said those stupid things. That's all on me."

"I kissed you back…" She trailed off, and my mind
was drawn back to the memory of her lips on mine. She
shook her head, like she was trying to escape those
memories too. "I shouldn't have. Rigby and I… I mean,
this afternoon we—"

"I know what you did this afternoon, Nova. I was in the house," I snapped.

Watching from the hall like a fucking peeping Tom.

Her face flushed red, and she turned back toward the window. I messaged Rigby, telling him I was heading home. Telling him I was sorry, because now he'd have to go in there and deal with fucking Andrea trying to blindside him.

Me: Reporters caught me kissing Nova. Think I stole your girl. I'm sorry. Taking Nova home.

God, I felt like such a bastard. He didn't message me back, and maybe I was too late. Maybe he was already in there, being grilled about Nova and I, instead of talking about the fucking sport we were all here for. He was going to punch me in the face, and I definitely deserved it.

I started the car and pulled out into the heavy traffic leaving the arena. We were silent the whole way home, and I felt like a complete and utter asshole.

Because I didn't regret kissing Nova. I just regretted getting caught. I was an asshole because I wanted to do it again. Over and over, until I was branded on her lips forever.

CHAPTER

Twenty-One

NOVA

MY THOUGHTS WERE WHIRLING so fast that it was hard to latch on to any of them. Except the one that thumped around in my brain like a shoe in a clothes dryer.

I'd kissed River. And really, really liked it.

We drove home silently, and as soon as River stopped the car, I had the door flung open and was all but running up to the nursery to check on Huey. Not that I thought he was anything but happy and healthy —and probably sound asleep—but I needed an excuse to get away and center my thoughts.

Didn't help, though. Once I'd laid eyes on Huey, who was sound asleep in his crib, I went and flopped down on my bed and chased my thoughts for what felt like hours.

I'd let Rigby tongue-fuck me in the kitchen this afternoon, and hours later, I was enjoying his best friend's lips on mine. Did that make me a whore? Did I care if it did?

I didn't regret either action, which was what made it worse. What I regretted was the possible consequence of me not being able to keep my libido in check.

Huey needed the guys; that was becoming more and more clear. They loved him, and he adored them. The relief of having others to lean on during this parenthood thing was so all-consuming, I would almost become a nun to keep it. I wasn't sure I could go back to doing it alone. I would if I had to, but I was strong enough to admit it would be hard to be a solo parent.

I also didn't want to come between River and Rigby. I'd only had to peek at River's face to see the regret painted all over it. He regretted that he'd kissed me, and that hurt. I hadn't expected it; I hadn't even initiated it. But I'd hoped for it, somewhere deep down, and that's why it felt so bad.

Hell, while I was examining all my damn feelings, I wanted Devan too. Just as much as the other two, maybe more, because he was so out of reach. He was aloof, but somehow it just made me want him more. I felt his eyes on me like a physical brand sometimes, and that shit was heady.

There was a knock at the door, and I buried my head under my pillow. "I'm sleeping," I shouted into the mattress, and I heard the door squeak open.

Someone crept in and sat on the bed. I didn't need to

turn my head to know it was Rigby. I could smell his cologne. "You yell in your sleep then."

I sighed, rolling to the side. I wasn't a coward. "I kissed River."

Rigby raised an eyebrow. "I know."

Ugh. Why couldn't he storm out of here in jealousy so I didn't have to explain this next part? I tugged at my lip with my teeth. "This afternoon, we did something that could be construed as the start of something..." I sounded dumb. Maybe he gave oral sex to women willy-nilly, and I was about to come off as clingy. "I shouldn't have kissed someone else before we'd talked about what that meant." I winced.

He reached over and patted my arm comfortingly. "I don't mind. I don't own you."

"Oh. Okay. I didn't mean that I wanted things to be more exclusive or anything. You can, uh, do whatever you like with whoever too. I don't own you either." My cheeks flushed, and the very idea of Rigby kissing another woman made acid burn in my gut. "Glad we cleared this up. I am tired, though." I turned my face back into the pillow so he couldn't see me.

Rigby chuckled softly. "Come on, Fireball. That's not what I meant. The guys are downstairs and I think it's time we all talked, don't you?"

"No. I'm happy burying my head in the sand, thank you very much." Arms wrapped around my torso, and he hefted me up and over his shoulder. "Rigby!"

"Come on, my little ostrich. Nothing was ever resolved by pretending it didn't happen."

I snorted, snatching up the baby monitor on the way past, despite hanging upside down. Rigby carried me easily, and honestly, there was a hindbrain part of me that just enjoyed that shit. The fact he could throw me around so easily was just… mmph.

We bounced down the stairs, and it wasn't particularly comfortable, though his large hand was around my upper thigh, nice and close to some other parts that were feeling suddenly neglected.

Too quickly, he dropped me on the floor in the living room. River was pacing around, and Devan was sitting on the edge of the couch, his shoulders curled as his elbows rested on his knees. He raised his eyebrows at Rigby carting me around like a bag of wheat, but didn't say anything. River looked at me, then at Rigby, then kept pacing.

"Does anyone want to fill me in about what's going on?" Devan asked lightly, his eyes bouncing between us.

"It doesn't matter—" Rigby started, but River interrupted.

"Like hell it doesn't."

Devan leaned back into the couch like he was watching a daytime soap opera. Okay, I guessed this was kinda on me.

"River kissed me." I looked at the man in question. "I kissed him back. Some reporter took a photo."

Devan looked surprised, but still kind of confused. "Well, that's interesting, but I don't know why we're having a house meeting about it. You're both consenting adults—what's the problem?"

My cheeks heated. Actually, my whole body felt like it was one huge blush. "The problem was that earlier, uh, Rigby and I, we, uh…"

"I ate her out in the kitchen," Rigby finished, his mouth curled into a cocky smirk. I gave him the stink eye, but then looked down at the floor, unable to meet Devan or River's gaze.

"Did you enjoy it?"

My eyes shot to Devan's face. Surely he wasn't talking to me? But he was staring right at me, his eyes molten.

I swallowed. "Uh, yes?"

He cocked his head to the side. "Would you do it again?"

I wanted to have some kind of fucking principles, but I couldn't lie to Devan. So I hedged. "Look, I don't want to create any drama here—"

Devan was in front of me in the blink of an eye. "Do you want to do it again, Nova? Would you let Rigby eat your pussy again, if he asked?"

I wanted to look at the other men in the room, but Devan's eyes were like magnets. I couldn't look away. "Yes," I breathed.

He stepped closer, and I backed up a step. And then another, but Devan followed. "And River? Did you like his mouth on yours? If he pressed you up against this wall, his lips inches from yours, would you kiss him back? Let him tongue-fuck your mouth?"

My back hit the wall. "Yes," I said on a shaky breath.

His arm came out and pressed against the wall beside my head. "What about me, Nova Stone? If I stroked my hand down that soft body, buried my fingers inside your panties, would I find you wet? Would you want what I had to offer?"

"Yes," I whispered, partially because I was embarrassed at the admission, partially because it felt like he was stealing the air from my lungs with his intensity. My knees felt like jello. His hand came up to cup my cheek, his eyes running all over my face. I wish I could see what he was thinking.

Then he stepped away, and my palms hit the wall behind me like it could hold me up. He went back to the couch. "Tell us your plan, Rigby. I know you have one."

Rigby raised an eyebrow at him as he walked over to me, herding me toward an armchair. He looked over at River. "Sit down, man. You're making me nauseous just looking at you."

I sat down like a good girl, and River sat beside Devan. Rigby stood in the middle of the room, his eyes bouncing between us all.

"So, the reporter from ASPN grilled me about my girlfriend during question time." He looked at me. "It took me a while to realize they were talking about you, because unless they had a camera in the house, or were pulling old images off the 'Gram, to the world I was single as fuck." I winced, because I had a feeling I knew where this was going. "When I worked out she meant you and the fact I called attention to you last week, I just said you were a new friend."

River rolled his eyes. "Yeah, but did you say it like that, with that I-just-got-fucked smirk on your face?"

Rigby shrugged. "I didn't know that Andrea was trying to get a gotcha moment. I didn't see your message until after the press shit was over. So maybe." I groaned and swiped a hand down my face.

"Do you think she's going to spin a story?" Devan asked, his brows pulled down into a worried line.

"Given that River fucked and forgot her last season, I'd say she's *definitely* going to run a story that makes him look like an asshole, Nova like a harlot, and me like a cuck."

I flopped back into the cushions of the couch and covered my face with my hands. This was a disaster. I hadn't even been here two weeks, and it had become a shitshow. "What do we do?"

The last thing I wanted to do was draw attention to myself and Huey. I wanted to stay as far from the limelight as possible.

"That depends on you, Nova. It depends on what you want—from me, from River, from Dev. It's all in your hands."

Well, no pressure then.

CHAPTER
Twenty~Two

DEVAN

I WAS HARDER than I'd been in a long time. Women had always been a peripheral thing; first was my family, then the business, and somewhere like fifteenth or sixteenth on the list, was sex.

It wasn't that I didn't enjoy it. I mean, what's not to like? But the emotional complications that came with taking a woman home, fucking her and then trying to get her to leave again made it undesirable unless I really needed to blow my load inside someone.

Fuck me, I wanted that someone to be Nova right now. She looked mortified as Rigby asked his question. What did she want from us?

Up until today, I would've said she wanted nothing from me. But after that little scene we'd just had against the wall? The way I'd affected her almost as much as she affected me said otherwise.

"What do you mean?" she squeaked out.

I gave her a loaded look. "I think you know what he means, Nova." God, I wanted to lay her over my lap and do depraved things to her. I had no right at all, but I wanted it so fucking bad it made my balls ache. "What I want to know is if he's out of his fucking mind?"

Rigby rolled his eyes at me. "This is going to surprise you, but I love you surly bastards. Love you enough that I want you to be happy. But you forget I also know you. You're so fucked up, with more baggage between you than all the international airports in the world, it would almost be unfair to ask a woman to heal that trauma for you."

It was like a punch in the chest, but I didn't deny it. It was true. I would never inflict my issues on a woman. Therapy helped, but some shit had been imprinted in my DNA.

"What's your point?"

"It means you guys would never be enough for a woman. You could give her what she needs physically, but you'd be emotional sandpaper."

"Rigby..." Nova said softly, already trying to protect our feelings. She was too good.

River was shaking his head. "He's not wrong. Let him finish."

"You both need time to heal from your past. Hell, you should have already begun healing, but you're both stubborn bastards. It's almost too late. Too late for you to feel real happiness. Love."

I felt like I was in an episode of Dr. Phil, but I didn't

interrupt again. He was getting to a point, but I wished he'd hurry up and try to do it without emotionally flaying us in the process.

"I propose polyamory."

I blinked at him, waiting for him to get to the punch-line of the joke, as I tried to formulate a response.

River beat me to it. "What the actual *fuck?*"

"You've lost your mind, Rigby. We need to get your head checked, because I think you've taken one too many sticks to the temple," I added.

Rigby waved his hands. "No, no, hear me out. These are our options right now. Number one, we stop all this. We get Nova her own place, because she's too fucking tempting to resist." He threw Nova a heat-laden smirk. "Number two, we take this to a physical level and Nova can just bed hop until she wants to choose one, or none, of us. Satisfying, but not actually a long-term solution. I don't think Nova is going to be happy to be a bed warmer forever."

I looked at Nova, and she was chewing her bottom lip like she was going to gnaw it right off. I wanted to lean over and replace her teeth with my own.

The idea of tasting her, being with her, and then her choosing someone else, hurt more than I wanted to admit. I wanted all of her or none of her; they were my two choices. Anything else made fire burn in my chest.

"What's the third option?" I asked impatiently, though he'd already told us. I just wanted him to lay it out for me like I was a layman.

The coffee table groaned as Rigby sat down on it. "We go into this with an idea of commitment. Of permanence and exclusivity. River and me, we're on the road six months of the year, longer if we make the play-offs. That's no way to have a committed relationship with anyone. But you'd be here. A steady presence, taking care of Nova and Huey when we are away. I'd smooth over the rough emotional edges you guys have, so you don't cut her with all your damage. She wouldn't be shouldering the entire emotional load of your relationship until she quits."

I wanted to argue that wasn't how it happened, but the few committed affairs I'd had—because they were never relationships—would support his theory. I looked over at River, trying to judge what he thought, but his face was unreadable. Nova just looked shell-shocked.

"I bring nothing to the table," River said softly, his face still a blank mask.

Rigby tried—and failed—not to roll his eyes. "It's not a business transaction, Coop. It's a relationship. You get out what you put in."

Surprisingly, it was Nova who moved across the couch to sit beside him, her fingers twining with his. "You bring something."

River surprised me when he didn't move away. Shit, maybe Rigby was right. "What do you think of this?" he asked Nova, the first person to ask, like she wasn't literally the center of this whole little charade.

"I should move out."

I froze, my whole body going cold, then hot. I really didn't want her to leave.

"But I don't want to," she added softly. I stifled a relieved breath. "I'm not sure I could just have sex without getting feelings, either. I want to pretend I can, and maybe for a while I could. But emotions are messy, and you guys are, well, you."

What did that even mean? But Rigby clearly knew, and he was leaning forward eagerly. "So you want to try this?"

"I'm not saying that, either. I've never even been on a date with any of you. I'm not about to jump headlong into some alternative relationship with you all." Rigby looked crestfallen. "But I'm open to seeing where it goes, if you guys are open to it too."

He nodded eagerly. "Of course. We'll go on dates, all the normal stuff."

"What about the press?" River asked, dropping a lead balloon right on all the progress we'd made.

Rigby shrugged. "We'll cross that bridge if it becomes a problem. Until we become official, we toe the party line. We're good friends. Nova is special. When we're all in, we'll talk to the executive team about making some kind of official announcement."

I looked between them. I hadn't fucking thought about the team. "It won't affect your careers?"

Nova looked anxious at the thought. It was River who waved a dismissive hand. "If Ludo can get caught fucking a puck bunny in public at least once every season, they can deal with this."

Silence was loud in the room. I didn't know about anyone else, but it was because my mind was whirling.

Just like in business, I thought shit through, weighing up the risks and the benefits. There was a chance that Nova would come between us. We were rock solid, especially River and I, but love made men crazy. There was a chance she wouldn't want me at the end. The thought literally made my stomach curdle. There was a chance we would take a financial hit if the announcement of our relationship went badly. I was less worried about that.

The guys could lose their positions in the IceCaps, but they were too good not to be picked up somewhere else. Though not necessarily together. Alternately, they could be transferred during the draft, and how would the relationship they were suggesting work if we were in different states?

Worst of all, if we fucked it all up, Nova would take Huey and leave for good. We'd lose them both.

What were the benefits? Nova naked beneath me was an obvious one. We'd be a family, a proper one, and that held more sway with me than I'd thought it would. As much as it burned to think, Rigby was right too; the chances of me having a successful relationship as is were slim to none. I was too cold. Too abrasive. Too scared. I could probably fake my way through it for a while, but what examples did I have for a healthy, successful relationship?

None.

On paper, the risks outweighed the benefits. But when River looked at Nova, I found myself holding my breath for her answer. "I want to try, but I'm not committing to anything. If it happens naturally, I'll leave myself open to the idea. But I won't cause issues between you guys, and I won't risk Huey's happiness, now or in the future."

Rigby grinned at her, that shiny, happy smile that made girls throw their panties at him. "That's all I ask, Fireball." He looked over at River, and I followed his gaze.

River looked pensive, which I understood. Sometimes, he was impetuous and didn't think shit through, but he knew as well as I did that this had the potential to blow up in our faces if we thought with our dicks and not our heads.

But even knowing that, he nodded. "We'll see where it goes."

All eyes turned to me. The risks still outweighed the benefits. Even so, I found myself looking at Nova, her eyes wide and her lips slightly parted. "I'm in."

We were already on this path. For better or worse, we'd have to see where it led.

CHAPTER

Twenty-Three

NOVA

DESPITE THE INTENSITY of the decision last night, or perhaps because of it, we'd all gone quietly off to bed. River and Rigby had their first away games over the next few days, and would be gone for five days.

When I woke up the following morning at seven to give Huey his bottle, I went downstairs to catch them before they left for the airport. They were eating a breakfast filled with fruit and protein, while Devan was downing coffee like it was his very life force.

Rigby smiled at me as I stepped into the kitchen, and it made my heart flip-flop. "Morning, Fireball. I'm glad you came down before we had to leave." He stood and stretched, before swaggering toward me. When he reached my space, he leaned down and gave me the sweetest kiss I could ever imagine. It was gentle, yet somehow, I felt it all the way down to my toes. Pulling back, he grinned and then looked down at Huey.

"Morning, little man!" He kissed his chubby little cheek. Someone's alarm went off, and he sighed. "I knew I should have come and woken you up the proper way. Now I won't see you for five whole days, and I'll forget what you taste like," he said with sad puppy dog eyes.

I was pretty sure he didn't mean my lips.

River rose, putting his plate in the sink for the maid service. I still kind of hated that there was a maid service, but it wasn't like I enjoyed doing the dishes, especially not when the guys ate ten times a day, so I let it go.

He whacked Rigby on the back of the head. "Don't be such a simp," he growled, but still, he stopped in front of me.

Before he could kiss me, Devan was there, grabbing Huey. "If you're going to debauch each other before breakfast, I'd rather my nephew wasn't stuck between you."

River flipped him the bird, but he was still looking down at me, his eyes holding mine. Finally, after what seemed like forever, he leaned down and kissed me. Hard. It was a kiss filled with need and self-denial. Pent-up lust. I kissed him back, parting my lips as his tongue pushed into my mouth. I moaned as he gripped my hips, pulling me close. As he bent me slightly backward, his huge hand on my back, I felt like I was being plundered.

When he finally stepped back, I was gasping. He just grinned down at me. "See you in five days." It sounded like the most perverted promise I'd ever heard, and I unashamedly watched his ass as he walked away.

Moments later, both Rigby and River returned, duffle bags slung over their shoulders. They each gave me one last kiss on the cheek, and then they were gone. Pathetically, I kind of missed them already.

I looked up at Devan, because it seemed odd that it was just the two of us. He handed me a coffee sitting beside him, and after I'd taken the first sip, I realized it was made perfectly for me. He'd been paying attention. His left hand held a bottle at the right angle for Huey, who was in his bouncer on the countertop.

He watched me with those dark, assessing eyes that made me feel stripped bare. "What are your plans for the day?"

Swallowing down a gulp of coffee, I dragged my eyes from his face. "Checking in with my clients. Coming off hiatus. Tax season is coming up, and I'm behind already."

He gave me a nod, but didn't say anything. Shit, this was awkward. Was it always going to be this weird?

Kissing Rigby had seemed natural, and even though it had been a shock, kissing River had almost seemed inevitable. But Devan? It was hard to know what he was thinking. He kept his emotions close to his chest, and honestly, I'd been surprised as hell he agreed to Rigby's plan last night.

The silence dragged on, and I sipped my coffee like

this wasn't weird. "What about you? Big plans for the day?"

"I have a board meeting until eleven, and then I'd like to take you for lunch. Huey, too."

I chewed my lip, a nervous habit I'd picked up as a kid. Was it like a date? But we were taking the baby, so it probably wasn't a date. Just two friends having lunch. I was overthinking it.

Devan reached out, his thumb coming to rest just below my bottom lip. He slid it out gently from between my teeth. "The only person who should be sucking on your bottom lip is me." His husky voice sent shivers of need through my body. My lips parted as I sucked in air, my eyes running over his face, trying to decipher what he was thinking. His lips quirked in what could have been a smile. "Wear whatever you like. The place I'd like to take you is quite casual. I have to go or I'll be late."

He leaned forward and kissed my temple, handing me Huey's bottle, and then he was gone too. I listened to the garage door open after a moment, and the low thrum of his car leaving.

Finally, I could breathe. *Holy shit.* I was wet, and all he'd done was kiss me on the temple. Devan felt like the kind of person who would burn you up and then you'd thank him for it as you lay in a puddle of melted remains.

I looked down at Huey, giving him back the bottle. He was such a good-natured kid. I'd really lucked out.

But his uncles were set to give me a fucking heart attack.

"Well, there goes my concentration today, bud. Wanna just sit on the couch and binge watch that new fantasy series about the guy with the big sword?"

Huey kicked his legs. I was taking that as a yes. Then another smell reached my nose. "Maybe after a bath."

Babies were gross.

I didn't know exactly what time "lunch" was, and I kinda hated it when people used that as a time indicator. Was it midday? Was it 2 p.m.? Did I have to sit around for two hours twiddling my thumbs waiting for the correct time?

Which was why I was dressed in a soft purple sundress and sneakers at 11:55. I'd bathed and dressed Huey, answered a few emails, watched a guy with the most perfect jawline beat some monsters up, had a small nap, and packed Huey's diaper bag. I was set and ready to go.

Luckily for me, Devan must have also hated the non-specific nature of lunchtime because at 12:05, I heard the front door open. I had Huey on the couch next to me, playing peek-a-boo to make him giggle, just so it didn't look like I was sitting around waiting for him.

I glanced over my shoulder as he stepped into the room, his face impartial. "Are you ready?"

I nodded, uncurling into a standing position and lifting Huey carefully into my arms.

If I'd been looking anywhere else at that moment, I might have missed the way his eyes flicked down to my legs, then back up to my face. I might have missed the way he swallowed hard. Because in the next moment, his face was back to cool and professional.

But I'd seen. I kept my satisfied grin to myself as we loaded into my car and Devan slid into the driver's seat. We drove along in silence, just the radio playing, but it wasn't awkward like this morning. It was companionable.

I was surprised when he pulled up in front of an old Airstream that backed onto a park with wooden benches. He didn't seem like a food van kind of guy, and that just proved I knew nothing about him.

"The guys and I love this place. Elvira doesn't give a shit that the guys are hockey players, and you'll dream about the food until you come back again."

I looked at the line of people up to the van. The menu said Cubanos and mac'n'cheese, which seemed like an odd combination but still made my stomach rumble. There were several varieties of mac too.

"I usually get the lobster mac. It's like a revelation. But River swears by the Cubano."

We finally got to the end of the line, and I got some broccoli mac and a Cubano. I was never going to be able to eat all of it, but I was going to give it a good try. I was glad there was some stretch to my sundress.

Leading me over to a spare bench, Devan carried Huey's car seat and the drinks, while I balanced all the food. We sat down, and as I watched him fuss with Huey, I couldn't help but think that anyone looking from the outside would think we were a family. That made my heart feel too big in my chest, and I swallowed down the emotion.

He popped the top off my beer and handed it to me. "Do we toast?" I joked weakly, and he smiled back at me. Damn, that smile. It softened his whole face.

"To the beginning of something new."

I clinked the neck of my beer against his can of soda. "To new beginnings."

CHAPTER
Twenty-Four

DEVAN

SHE MADE a soft moan every time she ate some pasta. I mean, I got it, it was really good, but those small noises were torture. I could imagine her making them as I buried myself between her thighs and she rode my face.

My phone dinged beside me, and I glanced down at it quickly. Seeing it was River and not work, I opened it.

River: Landed in New York. How are Nova and Huey?

I looked across the table. Nova was telling Huey that mac'n'cheese was definitely going to be his first food. She was smiling, as was the baby, and the sun was bouncing off her hair until it shone like it glowed. Snapping a quick pic, I sent it through to him. Then I saved it.

The dots at the bottom of the screen that said he was typing appeared and disappeared a few times, and I put my phone back down. "River says hello."

She flushed pink, and I resisted the urge to take another photograph. "Tell him I said hi."

I raised an eyebrow. "Tell him yourself. He'd like to hear from you, I think. They both would."

She cocked her head at me. "Are you really okay with all this? No offense, but you don't seem like the 'sharing is caring' type."

I didn't begrudge her the surprise. I was still kind of shocked I'd so easily agreed. That I'd followed my gut —okay, maybe it was my dick—instead of my head. But if there were more moments like this, then I knew I'd made the right choice, because Nova was something else.

"Rigby made some good points, and I'm not going to lie to you, Nova. I've wanted you since Tucson." I leaned in closer. "I've come more times than I can count to the mental image of you on your knees in front of me."

She gasped, and I worried briefly that I'd gone too far. After all, we'd only made surface level conversation, the type you made on a first or second date. I wasn't going to lie to her, though; the fact I was sexually attracted to her played a role in agreeing to Rigby's insane plan.

When I couldn't sleep last night, I'd done what I did best. I'd researched.Typing "polyamory" into a Google search without the smart filter was not recommended. Not that I didn't watch a few of those clips for "research." But it wasn't porn that I needed. It was advice.

Nearly every blog post, magazine article, and forum thread that I'd seen all listed open communication as the most necessary ingredient in a poly relationship. I'd never entered anything without the view of succeeding, and this relationship, if it happened, wasn't going to be any different. It was how I dominated in business, and it would be how I dominated at this.

I sucked down the rest of my soda. "I don't know how much River has told you about our early lives, but Rigby wasn't wrong when he said it forever altered us. I don't even know who I would be if I'd grown up with two loving parents in middle class suburbia." I shook my head. No point wondering what if now. "Needless to say, my childhood was rough. You should know that now. Both River and I see a therapist for the shit that happened, both before we met and in the foster care system. We're... damaged."

I didn't look at Nova then, couldn't stand the pity I knew would be in her eyes.

"Want to talk about it? I'll show you my damage if you show me yours?"

That made me look up, and I was mildly surprised that there was no sympathy in her expression. I hated pity more than anything. I was a billionaire; I didn't need anyone's pity.

"Maybe later." My voice sounded rough. "When Alana went off to college in Tucson, and River got drafted by the NHL, I found myself alone for the first time in so long. I hated it. Being inside my head was not a healthy place to be. I was working in the mailroom at an investment firm in Saint Paul, and I met a woman. A sweet girl from the admin pool, who filled that gap in my life left by River and Alana moving on with theirs."

Fuck, no one said this communication business would be so uncomfortable.

"We started a relationship, of sorts, and it got pretty hot and heavy over six months. But we both knew that if River or Alana had called, I would have dropped her immediately to go and help them. She knew she was third, or maybe fourth on my list of priorities. I kept her at arm's length, so when I found her in the supply closet with one of the junior accountants, I wasn't really surprised. I didn't really feel anything." He'd been plowing her over a box of toilet paper, which had amused me at the time. "She cried and begged and said it was a mistake, and when that didn't work, she accused me of being a sociopath. Completely shut down, unable to love, no grasp on my emotions. Maybe she was right—"

"She *wasn't* right. You love River and Rigby. You loved Alana. You love Huey. You care about them and their happiness. You aren't a sociopath."

I knew that. My therapist had done all the testing. She'd confirmed what I knew already; I was a damaged kid who turned into a fucked up adult, but I wasn't unfeeling. I'd shut down my emotions so I didn't end up like my father. Feeling nothing was better than hurting the people around me.

I shrugged. "It didn't really matter what she said. She was angry and hurt. I quit my job and moved in with River. We work better together, we always have. His protective instincts helped smooth my distant personality, and my cool head kept him from blowing his career in a barroom brawl. Rigby eventually wormed his way into my affections, because it's impossible not to love that fucker."

Nova threw back her head and laughed. "He's certainly something."

I rolled my eyes. "Yeah. Anyway, he brought the emotions, and he healed more than a therapist could. He gave us unconditional love. That floppy-haired bastard is a gift we don't deserve."

I'd told his mom that when I met her. She'd adopted us much the same way her son had. I wasn't looking forward to the day we had to tell her we were all fucking the same girl.

Nova was silent, her eyes distant, digesting my horror story of a life. If only she knew…

"So you've never done this before? You know, shared a girl?"

"In bed? Yes, we have. Well, River and I have. Is that

what you meant, Nova? Are you wondering what it would be like to be pressed between Rigby and River and me?"

She sucked in a breath so deep, it whistled between her lips. "Yes," she whispered, and I groaned.

Fuck. I had plans to take this slow. But slow wasn't going to be possible.

I changed the subject to something mundane so I didn't have to drive home with a hard-on, but it didn't work. By the time we stepped through the front door of the house, my dick was a bar in my tailored suit pants.

Huey was sound asleep for his afternoon nap, and I was trying not to think of all the ways I could debauch Nova in the forty minutes before he'd wake.

Slow. I needed to go slow.

I looked at my watch. I should've been back at work. I had a video call with a construction company at four. Actually, maybe I'd call Tom and get him to push it back an hour. I'd be home late from work, but I wasn't ready for the afternoon to be over. Besides, Tom would make the calls, because what was the point of a PA if they didn't handle the tedious conversations for you?

Tom answered on the first ring. "Mayson and Cooper. This is Tom."

"Hey, it's me. Can you please—" Whatever words I was going to say cut off as Nova came back downstairs. She had undone the top four buttons of her sundress, and soft blue lingerie peeked out from the edges.

"Sir?" Tom's voice called from the other end of the phone.

"Uh, cancel all my appointments for the rest of the day. I'll see you tomorrow." I hung up and threw my phone somewhere in the direction of the couch. I wanted to make her come to me, to take my normal route of being dominant in the bedroom. But I couldn't. I wanted her too bad. I was a moth, and she was like the sun.

I ate up the distance between us. By the time she hit the bottom step, she was within reaching distance, so I gripped her hips and pulled her to me.

I didn't ask permission to kiss her; I took it. My hands pressed to her spine, I pulled her close and kissed her until I couldn't think of anything but the way her body was curling against mine. I picked her up, my hands under her ass, and strode to the couch. I wanted her on top of me. Under me. I wanted to bend her over the back of the couch until her screams were muffled by the expensive Italian leather.

First things first though, I wanted to taste her lips again. I fell back onto the couch, and she lifted her knees so she was straddling me. She kissed me back, now in control. I wanted to be sure this was what she wanted too. Given the way she was grinding down on my aching cock, she definitely wanted it too.

I pulled back, gasping in air. "This wasn't my intention."

She gave me a cocky smirk. "I know." Then she

kissed me again, her hands running under my shirt and up over my abs. She moaned as she traced the hard lines of my abdominals, and I hissed as she scraped a nail over my nipple.

Fuck. How long had it been since I'd gotten laid? I felt like I was one nipple tweak and a slow grind away from coming in my pants like a teenager. That just wouldn't do. Wrenching my shirt off, I took a moment to be smug about the way her pupils dilated as she took in my body. Made all the hours I spent in the home gym worth it.

I pushed her sundress down her shoulders until it fell off her arms, pooling around her waist. Leaning forward, I kissed my way down that creamy soft skin to the top swell of her breasts. God, they were perfect. Moving my arms around her back, I unclipped her bra, and she tugged it off. I sucked in a breath as her breasts spilled out into my hands.

Jesus fucking Christ. I couldn't wait.

I moved my mouth down so I could take one of those dusky pink nipples between my lips, and she curled against my cock with a moan so loud, I wondered if the neighbors heard.

I needed to take back control, because I was wildly close to losing it altogether. Banding one arm around her spine, I turned us until she was beneath me on the couch, her pretty eyes wide.

"Devan," she breathed, and I was lost.

CHAPTER
Twenty~Five

NOVA

IT HAD TAKEN every ounce of courage I had to walk down those stairs looking like I wanted to be fucked. Which I did. I just didn't think I'd have the ladyballs to do it. I figured a few buttons I could write off as an accident if he just turned away. Anyone with boobs will know that buttons come undone all the time. No biggie, right?

Devan had looked at me like he was stripping me bare on the spot. When he kissed me, pleasure tingled along my veins like electricity. When he took my nipple in his mouth, I was pretty sure I was going to black out from pleasure.

But now, with his big body pressed along mine, his teeth on my shoulder and his gentle thrusts at my core, I was going to go insane before I passed out.

I rolled up against him, our bodies still separated by way too much fabric. "Please," I gasped as I ground my clit against him. I arched my back until my breasts scraped against the light dusting of hair on his chest.

"Ah, Nova, I love the way you beg," he growled, his hand gripping my throat and jaw. "Look at you, all perfectly bright and shiny, like the stars your parents must have named you for, coming to play in my darkness." He tilted my face to his so he could roughly take my mouth again. My mother used to say that still waters ran deep, and fuck, there was so much pent-up passion in Devan, I wasn't sure that I could take it all. "Are you going to be mine, Little Star? Are you going to burn hot just for me?"

I wasn't above begging. "Please, Devan." If he didn't touch me, didn't relieve some of this pressure, I was going to lose my mind.

He curled back up into a kneeling position, and his body loomed over me. He was so fucking beautiful. Sleek lines and golden skin, those dark eyes that were normally so impenetrable now broadcasting his desire like a beacon. "You say stop, we stop. I don't even care if you don't mean it. The word passes your lips, it all ends, okay?"

A part of me that wasn't consumed by lust right at that moment melted at his words. I nodded. "Yes."

Devan climbed off the couch, slipping his now crushed dress pants down his legs. I tried not to be embarrassed by the wet patch now darkening the gray fabric. Actually, I didn't get much time to be embarrassed by anything, because soon Devan was on his knees between my thighs.

Dragging my ass toward the edge of the huge sofa, he hooked his fingers around my underwear and tugged them off, dropping them on the floor somewhere. "Fuck," he breathed, and there was something about his tone that chased away the nerves of the moment. It might have been the reverence, or the way he ran his tongue over his full bottom lip, like he was imagining how I would taste.

He didn't have to imagine for long. Gripping my thighs, he spread me wider, supporting himself with my thighs as he leaned forward and licked along my seam with one long stroke. His tongue flicked across my clit, and I hissed.

Then he started again, stroking through my folds in long, languorous strokes until I was riding his face. Letting go of one thigh, a rough "Keep this here," passing his shiny lips, he thrust two fingers inside of me, curling them up, my body bowing with him as pleasure made me gasp. Then he scraped his teeth over my clit, and I came on a scream.

When I opened my eyes, I realized he was watching me come like it was the most fascinating thing on the planet. My cheeks flushed even redder, but he made no effort to move. "I need you inside me."

"I don't have any condoms," he purred, but he didn't seem annoyed or frustrated. He seemed insanely pleased with himself.

I wiggled my hands into the pocket of my dress, pulling out a small strip of condoms I'd totally pilfered from Rigby's room. I'd apologize later for going through his nightstand.

Devan's grin was devastating. "This is why women go mad for pockets in their dresses?" he growled, climbing back onto the couch with me.

"That, and pocket knives and pretty rocks," I breathed back, my voice shaky.

His dark chuckle spread over my skin like a caress. "I'd believe it." His cock was hard, standing at attention against his lower abdomen. He was long and thick, and honestly, someone should call a dildo company because I'd just found the perfect cock. "Stop looking at my dick like that or I'm only going to last five seconds," he groaned, and I dragged my eyes back up to his face.

He rested back against the couch, his legs spread wide, and he slipped the condom on with ease. Then he reached over and grabbed me, lifting me until I straddled his thighs.

"Ride me, Nova."

I reached down and grabbed his cock, making him hiss. As I lined him up with my core, the noise I made as I sank down onto him was almost animalistic. His hands flexed on my hips, but he let me ease myself down at my own pace. So damn thoughtful.

It was a pity that I didn't want thoughtful. I wanted to be fucked so hard, it would take everything in me just to hang on.

I sank down, down, down until I was fully sheathed around him, my eyes fluttering closed at the stretch and fullness of him. I leaned close to his ear, nipping his lobe a little too hard. "Fuck me hard, Devan."

His growl was primal as he gripped my hips, drawing me up until just the head of his cock remained inside me, then slammed me down. I screamed, and he grunted, but that was all we needed. He fucked me with the intensity of a man who thought this was his last day on Earth, and I fucked him right back. I orgasmed once, gripping his dick until he moaned with me, his fingers biting into my flesh, but he didn't come with me. He wasn't done.

He fucked me through my orgasm and right into the next, then flipped me onto my knees. "You're not the one in charge here, Little Star. I'll fuck you however I want."

Maneuvering me over the back of the couch, he slammed back inside me. He might have wanted to be in control, but I grinned at the fact he was still fucking me hard like I'd asked. My legs felt like jello, and my body was at once pulled taut and completely boneless when he finally came, my name a feral grunt deep in his throat.

We collapsed together, a tangle of limbs and sweat.

I wasn't sure why, but the moment after the first time you have sex with someone is so tense. It's like you're waiting, but for what? For him to leave? To high five? I had no idea what Devan would do, but when he rolled onto his back, pulling me with him until I was draped across his chest, I let my body relax into the moment. I'd overthink this later, when I was wearing my comfy pajamas and on the phone to Chloe.

He wrapped a big arm around me, encasing me in his warmth. "I don't want to move."

I pressed a kiss to his chest, ignoring the pounding of my heart. Sex was one thing, but intimacy was an entirely different beast, one he'd already told me he hadn't mastered. But I needed this intimacy just as badly as I'd needed him. "Then don't. We can stay here."

"What about Huey?" he rumbled beneath my cheek. His voice was a deep vibration that did something to my insides.

I flailed a hand around near his ass, where I'd haphazardly tossed the baby monitor when he kissed me. He let out an *oof*. "I'm pretty sure that thing nearly became an unintentional sex toy."

I lifted the monitor, which showed Huey still sleeping peacefully, swaddled in his wrap. "He's fine. But, uh, I guess you should probably go back to work." I bit my tongue to stop me babbling more out until I seemed desperate and clingy.

I got up the courage to look into his eyes, and what I saw shining back at me threatened to steal the oxygen from my lungs. His eyes were almost molten, his lids hooded.

"Little Star, I'm exactly where I want to be right

now," he murmured, his fingers stroking up and down my spine. He frowned lightly. "Actually…"

My heart stuttered. Fuck, that was quick; he'd already changed his mind.

But I needn't have worried, as he continued, "Let's take this to my bedroom. There are things I want to do to you that involve my bed and way more condoms than you can hold in those little pockets."

I grinned. "Oh yeah?"

His hands gripped my ass and squeezed. "Oh yeah."

CHAPTER

Twenty-Six

RIGBY

I CHECKED my phone once I'd changed out of my gear, the mood in the locker room subdued after our loss. We'd played a damn good game, but they got us in the shootout. It was hard to be too disappointed with that kind of loss, but the goalies always took it the worst.

Ludo came up and slapped my back. "We're going out to drown the loss in beers and puck bunnies. You guys coming?"

I could use a beer, that was for sure, but it wasn't really worth the effort of fighting off the pawing women in the bar. I shook my head. "Nah man, I'm beat. We've still got Tampa Bay and then Florida, and I feel wrecked already."

Ludo shook his head at me. "You're getting old, Rig. Aw well, I'll get more options if your pretty face isn't there stealing all the hot ones."

I rolled my eyes at him, stripping off my gear and giving it to the equipment manager. He was new to the team, and young, but he knew his shit and I could respect that. Finally, I slipped into my post-game suit. I was ready to get back to the hotel. River was stuck doing post-game press, so I'd just meet him back at our room. We bunked together even now, because it was much easier to put up with the habits of a guy I already knew than Ludo's inability to shut the door when he took a piss.

I caught the minibus back to the hotel with all the other players who were straight-laced enough not to party on a game night. Or the ones with wives and families who just wanted to go to bed and call them.

I stopped at the convenience store across the street and picked up a six-pack. Not enough to have a hangover, but definitely enough to help me forget the aching parts of my body. I moved quickly through the lobby and into the elevator, mashing the button for our floor. Pulling out my phone, I sent a message to Nova.

Me: Missed you at the game.

Nova: We watched you on the TV. You guys played great.

I also texted Dev in the group chat I had with him and River.

. . .

Me: Are you being nice?

There were the three bouncing dots of a reply incoming for a moment, and I wondered if he was writing me a novel. In the end it was only a sentence, but man, it was a twist I didn't see coming.

Devan: Nova and I had sex.

Air hissed out of my lungs, and I stared at the phone screen, trying to figure out how I felt about that. The doors opened and closed to my floor while I stood there stunned by the revelation, and I cursed softly.

Me: Well, I guess that counts as being nice.

I didn't really know what to say to that. I hadn't thought they'd get there so fast. They hadn't even spent much time together. If I was being honest with myself, I'd thought I would be the one to make love to her first. She felt the most comfortable with me—or at least I'd thought so. Obviously, I'd been wrong. They must have bonded more than I'd realized while he was packing her up to move from Tucson.

Devan: You okay?

Well, yeah, I'd better be, considering this was meant to be my idea. If I got jealous because they'd fucked, my polyamory solution was going to go down the shitter real quick.

Me: I'm fine. You were good to her? Do I have to give you a Powerpoint presentation on how to fuck a woman like she means something and not like she's a toy?

That was probably a little snarky, but whatever. I pressed the button to go back up to my floor and sucked in some deep, centering breaths through my nose. This wasn't the Middle Ages. It was the twenty-first century, and a woman was worth more than the sum total of men who'd been in her vagina and when. Having sex with Nova was a bonus, but it wasn't the reason I wanted to be with her.

Being a professional athlete came with many boons. The pay was good, the prestige was otherworldly, and the amount of women you could have sex with was limited only by your imagination and stamina. So no, what I wanted with Nova wasn't about sex. It was about so much more.

But I was a big enough man to admit that I was jealous as fuck. My message alert sounded again.

Devan: The day I ask you for advice on how to pleasure a woman will be a cold day in Hell, Engman.

I huffed a laugh, because I could imagine his face as he'd texted that. River would probably still be sitting through press questions, and I wondered what would happen when he heard what Nova and Dev had done. I had to get my own shit together because I wanted this to work, but more than that, I wanted the guys to be happy. This was the first real test.

Me: Well, just remember, you're not trying to stuff the Thanksgiving turkey. Tell Nova I miss her.

He sent me a picture of Nova in his bed, looking over her naked shoulder at him, a soft, contented smile on her face. Her hair was mussed and her lips were swollen—she looked so damn happy. Screw my jealousy. This was what I wanted for all of us.

I closed the group text with the guys and opened my text thread with Nova.

Me: You look so fucking beautiful. I can't wait to see you in five days. Literally counting down the hours.

Nova: You're not mad?

Me: Fuck no. As long as you are happy, I'm happy. Though if Dev is a two-pump chump, I'm more than happy to kick him in the dick for you.

Nova: I'll keep that in mind haha.

I finally made it into my room, pushing through the door and flopping down onto the bed. I didn't even bother waiting until the door was completely closed before pulling off my tie and taking off my jacket and heavily starched shirt. I draped it all over the back of a chair, knowing I'd have to wear it again the night after next.

I placed the beer on the nightstand and cracked one open, leaning against the headboard on the too firm bed. I didn't really want to talk to her about Devan; what was between them was just that—between them. So instead, I texted her about Huey, about the game, about the chocolates she was going to make me. I texted her even though she was in bed with Devan and he probably had her naked body pressed against his.

I was still texting her when River walked in, and I quickly flicked to the other group chat. There was a little note that said *Seen by everyone.* So he knew. But his face was way more impassive than I thought it would be.

I looked up at him expectantly as he threw his bag at the end of the bed and grabbed a beer.

"Good game tonight. Fucking shootout sucked. You know Coach Soukal is going to ride Virtanen's ass for letting that goal bounce off his skate and back into the net."

I winced. I wouldn't want to be our goalie, Virtanen. The kid was tough. He was from Finland, and he didn't take much crap from the press or the fans. But anyone would wither under the sheer disapproval of Coach Soukal.

I narrowed my eyes at River. "You don't want to talk about it?"

"Talk about what?"

I snorted. "You know about what. Don't be an asshole."

"You mean about Nova and Dev? Wasn't that the point of this whole thing? Did you really believe they weren't going to have sex at the first opportunity they had to be alone? Because the opportunities for privacy living with two other dudes and a baby are slim. I'm not surprised they decided to take the step while we were on the road."

He drank half his beer in one gulp and I did the same. "You don't think it was a little quick?"

Flopping down on his own single bed, he just scoffed. "What, did you think they were gonna wait for marriage or something? Get a promise ring? They'll move as fast as they move; no one says you have to move at the same pace."

Who the fuck had inhabited the body of my best friend? "Are you possessed? Where is all this mature shit coming from? Did you get hit too hard into one of the boards?"

He just flipped me the bird. A second later, my phone dinged in the main group chat.

"What? We were just gonna keep talking about her like she isn't in bed with him? May as well add her to the conversation. Besides, you're the one all about the 'sharing is caring' bullshit."

He opened his phone.

River: Mazel tov on the sex. It's a good idea to start with the worst in bed to save disappointment later.

Devan: Fuck off, Cooper

Nova: No comment.

Devan: What do you mean no comment?

· · ·

River laughed and peeled off his suit, hanging it in the closet. He also grabbed my shirt and jacket, hanging them up while he was there. River liked order. He wasn't as bad as Devan when it came to control, but small things slipped through that hinted at what his life had been like in the foster care system. Or maybe even before that.

The need to keep his surroundings immaculately in order was one of those things. My room tended to look like a war zone, and nothing ever ended up back on the hanger. It annoyed the shit out of River; I just said it made me well-adjusted. He said it made me a man-child.

I lifted my phone and snapped a photo of him hanging my shirt and jacket.

Me: You may have Nova, but I still got a bitch. <Picture>

River looked down at his phone, then glared at me. "You're an asshole." But he was smiling. I called that a win. This whole thing was going to be okay.

CHAPTER

Twenty-Seven

NOVA

WHILE THE GUYS WERE AWAY, I was happy, but it didn't seem quite right. Don't get me wrong, falling into bed with Devan every chance I got was absolute bliss. The things that man could do with his tongue would forever be seared in my memory. One day, I would be an old woman on my deathbed, sharing my fondest memories with my nurses, and one of those would be the time Devan finger-banged me so good that I squirted.

I mean, I was horrified in the moment—as horrified as you can be when wrung out by multiple orgasms—but Devan had looked like he'd just won a gold medal or something. It was hard to be embarrassed by some-thing that obviously made him so proud.

River and Rigby would be back this evening, and I was kind of nervous. It was dumb, but Devan and I taken a massive step since they left. Their return was obviously going to affect our relationship. They'd sounded cool about it over the phone, but that was a lot different than seeing it in person.

I'd made dinner, a beef bourguignon that was slowly braising in the oven, as well as some fussy filled chocolates with the stuff that Rigby had bought me. It had been... a pleasure. It had been a long time since a task had given me so much joy. I wondered how long I'd been coasting through life doing what I *should*, just because it was safe, not because that's what I wanted to do?

When had I given up the simple things that made me happy?

Devan was at work, so it was just me and Huey home as I danced around the kitchen, making parmesan bread on a giant fresh baguette I'd picked up from the fancy store in our neighborhood. At least no one thought I was a teenage mother here, because if I was, there would be no way I could afford beef that must've been given acupuncture and positive affirmations before it was slaughtered, since it cost as much as someone's daily wage.

I leaned down and sang an old Bruce Springsteen song to Huey, whipping my hair from side to side just because it made him laugh. The Boss had been my dad's favorite, and he'd always sung his songs to me. I wanted Huey to have a little piece of that, even though he'd never meet the man himself.

Sometimes, when it was early in the morning, and I

couldn't sleep, I thought about how I'd eventually explain this situation to Huey when he was older. What he'd call me. Would he call me Nova? Would he call me Mom? This situation was so fucking hard, and I didn't think it would get any easier as he learned that somehow we were different to other families. I wasn't sure if having three male parental figures would help or hinder that. But I mean, in for a penny, right?

I spun on the tiles in my socks, making Huey kick his legs as Springsteen sang about being born to run. On my second turn, something caught my eye, and I stuttered to a stop. Rigby and River stood in the entryway to the kitchen, their expressions both soft.

"You're back!" I scooped Huey out of the bouncer and sped toward them. I'd missed them. "How long have you been standing there?" I asked with mock disgruntlement.

"Long enough." River reached out and cupped the back of my head, swooping down to kiss me. The caress was filled with an aching feeling, so tender it made my heart break. He pulled back, his nose touching mine. "Missed you," he murmured softly, then grabbed Huey from my arms.

While he made baby noises, Rigby tugged me into his body. He encompassed me so completely in his arms, and I sank against his chest. He kissed the top of my head, then my temples, and then tilted my head back so he could give me a searing kiss that I felt down to my toes.

"You feel so fucking good." Lifting me into his arms, he buried his face into my neck. "If I wasn't starving, and it didn't smell so damn good in here, I'd take you upstairs and show you how much I missed you," he purred.

My whole body flushed hot. He kissed me once more, his tongue pushing between my lips until it was basically a promise of what was to come. Then he pulled away and slid me down his body, one hard muscle at a time.

I wasn't going to survive these men, I knew it, but I was too stupid to care. I wanted what they were offering. I wanted it so bad that I wasn't going to deny myself, like I normally would. I wanted the happiness they promised, and I didn't care about what I *should* do.

I looked at the clock. "Devan should be home soon. Do you want me to put Huey down or…"

River held the baby closer, blowing raspberries on his cheeks. Yeah, that shouldn't have been hot, but it did something primordial to my ovaries. Pretty sure they just exploded. "Nah, I've got it. Let's go get you ready for bed," he said to Huey in a high, sing-song voice that still managed to be gruff.

Rigby grinned, his arms still around me. "I'll make his bottle and bring it up when I drop my shit in my room."

I'd gotten lucky somewhere. It was hard to think that after the year I'd had, but these guys, they made it so much easier than it would have been.

Rigby herded me into the kitchen, and I took a moment to get the bread out of the oven before it turned into a crouton. I also pulled out the beef stew, which was now smelling amazing.

When I spun back around, Rigby was watching me closely. "What?"

"Do you want to go on a date with me tomorrow?" he asked softly, and I nodded immediately.

"Of course. But you know, you don't have to take me on dates." This wasn't a conventional courtship. This wasn't a case of wooing me into something more.

He placed the bottle in the warmer and pulled me closer. "Babe, you deserve dates. You deserve pretty things, and for us to tell you how amazing you are, and anything else your heart desires. You deserve the world, and I intend to give it to you." He kissed my forehead. "But we'll start with a date."

After a few moments, the bottle finished warming, and he grabbed it out. With one last brush of his lips on mine, he grabbed his bags and climbed the stairs shouting, "Shots! Shots! Shots!" like this was a frat house and Huey was about to tap the keg.

I laughed as I finished prepping the salad for dinner, and was still chuckling when Devan strolled in, right on time. He hadn't been staying late at work the last couple of nights. I didn't know if it was because the guys were gone and he didn't want me to be lonely, or if he just liked it better at home. Either way, it was nice.

He shucked off his jacket and tossed his briefcase

onto the hall table. He strode toward me and swept me up into his arms, kissing me like he couldn't wait to get me naked again. Over the last few nights, we'd had a routine: we came home, ate some kind of takeout, and then we'd put Huey to bed. After that, he'd fuck me on every surface available.

It was a good system. But it wouldn't happen tonight, because tonight, we probably needed to have one of those conversations. You know the ones—slightly awkward but entirely necessary.

He pulled back and squeezed me close to his chest. "The guys are home?"

I nodded. "Yeah, they just got in. They're upstairs putting Huey to bed."

He raised an eyebrow. "Did they seem okay?"

"Same as always, but maybe more touchy-feely?"

He hummed an amused sound, unbuttoning the cuffs of his shirt and rolling his sleeves up his forearms. Why was that so damn hot?

"I just bet they are," he growled, kissing me again.

Rigby bounded back down the stairs and grabbed us both in his long-armed reach. "What, starting with dessert first, Dev? Who's a bad boy? You are, yes you are," he simpered in a baby voice. He messed up Dev's perfectly coiffed hair with his knuckles, making Dev swat at him.

"You're a fucking child, Rigby Engman," he grumbled, making me laugh.

Rigby's wide smile conveyed the message that he

didn't give a shit, better than any words could. "Hands off our girl. You've had her for a solid five days, and I'm touch starved."

Devan rolled his eyes, but planted one last quick kiss on my lips and stepped toward the fridge. "Beer?"

Rigby lifted his hand and caught the craft beer flying through the air with ease. Dev passed me mine gently. Sweet jerk.

River came downstairs not long after, and I put dinner on the table. As we all sat down, I knew this was what it could be like every night in a perfect world.

But the world was not perfect.

So once everyone had eaten—the conversation was companionable but mostly about hockey, Huey and the news—I brought up a harder subject. "So, how does this work?"

Rigby shrugged. "Just like this? Though eventually, it stands to reason, there'd be more orgies."

River slapped him in the back of the head, while Dev grunted, "Fucking hell, Engman."

"What?" He pouted. "I don't mind sharing if you don't."

I wasn't sure if I should laugh or be horrified. River just shook his head. "I think that would be up to Nova, don't you?"

I was picturing it then, that scenario that I'd purposefully not let myself imagine. All three of their huge bodies surrounding me, touching me, making me feel good as I made them feel good. The fantasy was one that made me clench my thighs together, but my vagina was a simple creature who didn't think things through. Like, would I actually be enough to satisfy all three men, who were in their prime and so fucking handsome, or was I setting myself up for heartache when they eventually cheated on me?

"This is exclusive, right?"

Devan frowned. "Of course. I can't speak for those two, but I want something stable with someone I can trust."

"But there's only one of me and three of you..." Damn, this was awkward.

"We're men, not baboons. We don't need to have sex every day. I'm happy coming home and holding you in my arms. Intimacy is more than just shoving your dick inside someone." Devan raised a single eyebrow. "Though I'm not going to lie, the sex has been mind-blowing." The look in his eyes told me he was remembering last night—how I'd screamed his name with my knees beside my ears and Devan's cock filling me up in ways I'd never even imagined before now.

"What if one of you gets traded?" I asked River and Rigby, because that was the truth. Hockey wasn't a game where you played on one team for a long time. That was an anomaly, not the norm.

"We both have another year on our contracts, and then I guess we cross that bridge when we come to it. Hopefully we re-sign with the IceCaps, but if we get traded, then we'll make it work," Rigby said softly, but that was easy for him to say. "Don't borrow future trouble, Fireball. Nothing is guaranteed in life, and we shouldn't miss out on today's happiness on the off chance the future isn't what we predicted."

River nodded. "Whatever happens—with this relationship, with the team, with life—you'll always have us. Even if we aren't together anymore, we'll still share Huey. You'll never have to go it alone again."

The lump in my throat grew bigger. "Okay."

Rigby whooped. "On that note, I call dibs. You're mine tonight, Fireball."

River huffed. "That's not fair. We should rock-paper-scissors for it."

"Or let Nova choose," Devan added sarcastically.

But Rigby was already picking me up in his arms. "You guys are just sore losers. You gotta be quicker next time, old man!"

"I'm only eleven months older than you," River yelled behind us, but Rigby was already taking the stairs two at a time, and I couldn't help but laugh.

CHAPTER
Twenty-Eight

RIGBY

WE WERE IN MY ROOM, but now I was nervous. I hadn't been this nervous to have a girl in my room since the ninth grade and Mom said Cindy Kershaw could come over to do homework. That was the first day I ever saw naked breasts, and it cemented my love of boobies for life.

I didn't want this to be awkward, where we both stood around shuffling from foot to foot, so I didn't allow it to be. I just didn't put her down. I shuffled her around so she was clinging to me like a baby koala.

"Hold on! I have to put my stuff away."

My bags were all over the bed, and that just wouldn't do. I had plans. Fantasies. This night didn't have to be perfect, but I wanted it to be so good that she'd never forget, like me and Cindy Kershaw's boobs. This moment would be forever imprinted on both our memories, and I'd rather it wasn't shudder-inducing.

Well, only the good kind of shudders.

"Rigby, put me down!"

I just banded my arm tighter around her waist. "Nope. I haven't seen you all week, and I'm not ready to let you go yet. I'm soaking you in." I snuggled my face into the crook of her neck, kissing it softly through the curtain of her hair. "This is a therapeutic treatment. It's clinically proven that heavy doses of Nova in my arms aids in my recovery from a long week of sports."

I shoved my bags onto the ground and tossed her on the bed. She squealed out a laugh, which made my heart immediately lighter. Fuck, I wanted to hear the sound of her laughter every hour of the day. I almost picked her up and tossed her again just so I could get a repeat hit of serotonin.

Instead, I leaned over, slotting my body between her beautiful thighs. "You want me to be fully recovered, don't you?"

She grinned up at me, and it was like a punch to the gut. "Gotta do my bit for the IceCaps. Go Caps!" she teased.

I'd once asked my dad how long it took him to know Mom was the person he wanted to marry. She was a city girl who'd come to town to visit her college friend. He was a sixth-generation farmer. They shouldn't have worked.

But he'd get this dumb, soft smile on his face and say, "Twenty minutes and thirty-eight seconds." Turns out, he'd been at the bar watching a hockey game on the

TV. She'd sat next to him right as the puck dropped, waiting for her friend to come and grab her to take her back to the family farm. They got to talking. By the time the players slid off the ice at the end of the first period, he knew he wanted to marry the girl beside him. And he did.

I never got tired of hearing that story as a kid, but I'd never been able to imagine just looking at a woman, someone who was barely more than a stranger, and just knowing they were the one. I thought I might get it now, though.

I kissed her softly, but my girl didn't want soft. She curled her whole body around mine and pulled me down, deepening the kiss. I held myself slightly off her so I didn't crush the air from her lungs, but she was doing a great job of stealing my breath all the same.

And for the first time since I was seventeen, I kissed a girl and never wanted to stop. I kissed her over and over until we were both breathing heavily and her lips were swollen and her eyes were hooded and I wanted to do nothing else but kiss her just one more time.

"Baby," I breathed, pulling away so I could look down at her, her hair mussed from where I'd had it wrapped in my fist. "God, you're so fucking beautiful."

She was tugging at my shirt, her hands running over my chest and back. "God, how are you this hard? There's like zero body fat on you. What happens if you get marooned on a desert island? How will you survive?"

"Guess I'll just have to find something to eat?" I teased back. Weirdest foreplay conversation ever, and I kind of loved it. I pushed her shirt up, dragging down the cup of her bra until I could take her nipple in my mouth. Sucking it with increasing pressure, I felt her writhe against me.

Hooray for boobies.

She reached down and gripped my hair. "Are you going to be mine tonight, Rigby? Are you going to be good for me, and give me your cock just how I like it?"

"Yes," I hissed, my dick suddenly painfully hard.

I sucked on her nipples as my hands traveled down her body and between her thighs. She was wet for me, so fucking wet, and I couldn't wait to have her on my cock. But first, she was going to come on my fingers.

I moved from one nipple to the other, back and forth, stroking her G-spot as the ball of my hand ground against her clit. Thrusting up against me, the hold she had on my hair got a little harder as her moans got wilder. She was panting my name when her pretty pussy started fluttering around my fingers, but I wanted her coming so hard I was going to strain my fingers.

Finally, she screamed so loud that I couldn't do anything but grin. Popping off her nipple, I looked up at her.

"God, that's it… Rigby, *fuck*, you stroke my pussy so well," she moaned, and I moaned along with her, my whole body feeling alive. I flipped her over onto her hands and knees, spreading her cheeks and burying my tongue back in her pussy so I could taste her. "*Please,* Rigby," she begged, and I couldn't resist her call anymore. Not without my balls exploding.

I reached over to my oddly depleted condom stash and slid one on. Curling over her back, I nipped her shoulder blade. "You're so fucking beautiful. Your body was made to take my cock." Then I lined up my dick and slammed into her body, making her scream into the pillow. Holding her hips, I thrust into her, and her pretty ass bounced back against me. She felt too fucking good, and I had to think of Coach Toons naked so I didn't blow my load the very second she clenched around me, coming on my cock. I wasn't done. Not yet.

Flipping her onto her back as she shuddered, I pushed back inside her. She was tight around my cock as she wrapped her legs around my waist. "I've been imagining this for so fucking long. I want to see your face as I come inside you the first time."

She stared up at me with eyes that were shining so brightly, and I couldn't believe I'd gotten so damn lucky. I began to move, slower, not wanting to rush this but at the same time, feeling that urgency that told me I needed to come and I needed to come *right now*. But I held back, loving the sound of the whispered praise falling from her lips. Leaning deep into her body, I kissed her as I thrust into her body, her own rising up to mine.

Grabbing one of my pillows, I stuffed it under her

hips and went a little harder, the angle making her mewl. God, I loved the sound of her moans.

"That's it baby, come for me again," I whispered against her cheek. *Please, god, let her come again.* I was about to explode. Grabbing one of her calves, I pushed her leg back and ground down into her in steady, deep strokes.

"Yes, yes, Rigby," she moaned. "You feel so fucking good. Your cock feels *perfect*… Don't stop."

I imagined sticking my dick in an ice fishing hole just to keep myself from coming as her words consumed me. I scraped my teeth over her nipple, and she came, her nails scraping along my back in long lines. The sting made the pleasure tingling at the base of my spine and pulling up my balls even better, as I came in hot spurts. I slammed inside her messily until I was spent, flopping down on top of her, pressing her into my mattress.

"Holy hell, Fireball. That was… I mean, I've never… Fuck," I panted, rolling to the side so she didn't get crushed beneath my weight. Pulling her tightly into my arms as she caught her breath, I didn't want to let her go. Ever.

I wanted to make love to her in every position I could until I knew her inside and out. Until she was singing my praises so damn loud that every person in this house—hell, in this *block*—could hear her.

Feelings fluttered around in my chest that I couldn't give names to just yet, but I knew what they were. It would scare the shit out of her if she knew just how attached I was to her already.

She stroked my hair back from my face, pulling me down for a kiss. "You're amazing, Rigby Engman," she purred, burrowing against my chest. "Now rest up, because after a short nap, I'm going to need to do that all over again."

"Yes, ma'am." I laughed, kissing her so hard, there was no doubt that I was claiming her forever.

We might need time, but I knew my endgame. I just needed everyone to get there with me.

CHAPTER
Twenty~Nine
RIVER

DEVAN and I took our beers out onto the back deck, the baby monitor in my hand. The night was nice, but it was starting to cool down earlier these days and it was already dark. At least it was clear. Dev grabbed the matches, lighting the fire pit that we kept prestacked in the summer.

We were silent for a while, but it was the comfortable silence of two people who'd known each other for so long, it was hard to remember a happy time that didn't involve the other.

I could remember plenty of unhappy times, though. Eating cereal out of boxes for dinner, my arms too skinny, my belly always hungry. My parents passed out or glazed over on the floor. Bruises on my arms, stains on my clothes.

The day I came home from school and found them both dead on the floor from a bad batch of heroin.

There'd been an epidemic of ODs that month as the tainted smack killed off users across the city. The newspaper had been almost happy, despite the loss of life, that there were less users lining the city streets.

They didn't think about kids like me, who had to be placed in a foster home at ten, angry at a world that didn't care that my parents were dead. There'd been no one left in the world who gave a damn about ten-year-old River Cooper. At least, until I found Devan and Alana.

Fuck, I missed her.

"Alana would be laughing her ass off about this, don't you think?"

Devan huffed. "Man, after she got over being jealous that Rigby picked someone who wasn't her. She had the hugest crush on him."

It was understandable. Rigby was everything she'd never had. Stability. Loyalty. Kindness. It was the same reason he'd wiggled his way into our hearts, and maybe if I'd swung that way, I'd have had a crush on him too.

"He never saw her like that." Part of it was out of loyalty to us. We saw her as a little sister, so he saw her as one too. But part of it was that she just wasn't his type, I think. There was something about Alana that was needy, like she was always trying to fill the hole left from her childhood with something. Hobbies, travel, men. But you couldn't stuff a bandaid inside a wound and hope it helped. You needed to heal the wound yourself. Alana had never really learned that lesson, and it would be something I'd regret for the rest of my life—that I hadn't helped her enough.

We were quiet for a little longer, lost in our own thoughts. I didn't think too hard about what Rigby and Nova were doing upstairs. Because I was jealous. Not that she was with Rig, but that she wasn't with me. It was a weird line, and if someone had told me two weeks ago that I'd be sharing a woman with my two best friends, I probably would have punched them in the jaw. But it was working, I think.

"Tell me about how things are going with Nova," I said softly into the night air.

Devan's lips curled into a smile. "She's really some-thing. It hurts me to say this, but I think Rigby was right."

I laughed, because if the trade-off to having Nova was to listen to Rigby gloat about being right forever-more, I could deal with that. "It doesn't weird you out that Rigby is probably up there fucking her right now?"

He chewed his lower lip. "No. I don't think so. I wish it was me, but I don't want to go full primal jealous rage or some shit like that."

I would never say it to my best friend—the person I loved more than anyone in the world, except Huey now—but I was so fucking relieved. Where my parents had been apathetic to my existence, Devan's hadn't been. But not in a good way. His dad had beat him and his mom for as long as he could remember. He'd been violent. Mean. Right up until his mom overdosed on pain pills, and the authorities investigated. Hospital records were checked, and the abuse came to light. Six-year-old Devan went into foster care, and his dad went to prison, where he died of liver failure.

The shit Devan had dealt with in his life made me sick to my fucking stomach, and I knew he tried real hard to not be anything like his old man. He walked away when other men would fight. He was so fucking gentle with women and kids, the elderly. Anyone more vulnerable than him. And he kept a tight lock on his emotions, like he believed deep down that all it'd take was dropping the milk on the kitchen floor one morning to turn him into that raging psychopath.

I knew that Devan would rather cut off both arms than harm anyone. After a ton of therapy, I was fairly sure Devan knew that he wasn't a ticking time bomb of violence too. But the fear remained, for both of us.

Instead of sharing any of those dark fears, I just raised my beer at him. "Same, man. I wish it was me, but I know my time will come."

Devan was still shaking his head. "It's not just the sex, Riv. It's just being with her... it's something else. She's so light and full of joy, despite everything. Being with her just makes me happier. She's like a xanny in human form. I've never felt more, I don't know, content."

Well, fuck. I'd left this hardass alone with a girl for a week and he was about to write an ode in her honor. I didn't tease him about it, though; I was so fucking happy he was content.

"Well, here's to being boyfriends-in-law, I guess."

I'd resisted the urge to steal Nova from Rigby's bed that night, and the next. I didn't want to rush her, and I didn't want her to think that her only worth to us was if we were fucking. My therapist would've been so proud of me.

So instead, I showed her in little ways how glad I was that she was here. I kissed her a lot, because that was quickly becoming an addiction. I made her coffee. Took her for lunch. Held her against me and kissed her temple while we walked Huey around the park. Helped her set up her office space, and watched Huey while she reconnected with her customers and started the huge backlog of requests. She'd come to me when she was ready for more. Until then, I'd wait—no matter how blue my balls were right now.

These couple of days at home between games had been amazing. Sure, we did conditioning every day, hitting up the gym and the trainers, but I was home by lunchtime to spend it with Huey and Nova, and most of the time Rigby too. Dev was back at work, catching up on the meetings he'd put off to spend between Nova's thighs.

And you know what? I was happy. Which was probably a good indication that life was going to kick me in the balls.

So as I was strolling through the park with Huey and Nova, the baby strapped to Nova's chest, I was almost ready for the other shoe to drop. After the last outing with Huey by herself, I could tell Nova was a little more hesitant to go out in public spaces.

That lady still made me righteously angry, especially because IceCaps management had refused to outright ban the bitch when I asked. Corporate said that if we banned every fan who was an asshole, they wouldn't have enough money to pay our salaries.

My agent had told me to let it go. But fuck, it still riled me.

I was carrying a picnic in my backpack, as well as Huey's diaper bag, and was dressed in what I liked to call incognito mode: a cap pulled down low, sunglasses and a plain t-shirt.

"You got any of those fancy little chocolate things in here?" I asked hopefully. That shit had been so freaking good. Nova was beautiful *and* talented.

She raised an eyebrow at me. "Maybe? You'll just have to wait and see."

Just then, a voice behind me made my blood run cold. "River?"

Oh shit. I kept walking, my hand on Nova's spine to propel her forward. Maybe I could pretend I hadn't heard.

"River, wait!" the voice yelled again, and I clenched

my teeth. I looked over at Nova, who was frowning at me, even as her feet slowed to a stop.

Goddammit. I swallowed hard and turned, my face completely neutral. "Hey, Marissa."

The woman in front of me was gorgeous. She had long brown hair that curled artfully down to her waist, but I knew for a fact they were extensions. She had long legs and a fake tan to match her fake boobs. Her smile made people stop and stare. She was a former Miss Arkansas but now worked for some charity or another, not that she actually cared about anyone but herself.

She threw herself into my arms, and I caught her out of habit. I extracted myself as quickly as possible, but she had limbs like tentacles. "I've been trying to reach you for months, River. I wanted to talk to you. I've missed you."

Yeah, I knew that. I'd been avoiding her calls like the plague. I wished I could say her voice was an annoying whine, but it wasn't. It was husky and sexy, and once upon a time it had made me hard just listening to her say nasty shit to me. Now, it had the opposite effect.

"Oh? I changed my number."

It was a lie, but if I told her I'd been dodging her calls, she'd throw a very public tantrum.

She smiled brightly, and once, that smile would have been considered enchanting. Now, it just reminded me of a shark. "Oh, I'll have to get it from you. Luckily, they told me you'd be here. Is this Alana?" She turned to Nova, whose eyes were bouncing between us like she was watching an accident in slow motion.

"No, I'm Nova."

I watched as all the false friendliness fell from Marissa's face, and all that was left was poison. "And who the fuck are you?"

Nova's eyes flew to mine in panic. I shifted, drawing Marissa's eyes back to me. "She's my girlfriend."

Marissa's face scrunched. "*I'm* your girlfriend."

Now it was my turn to look panicked. "No, you aren't. You've never been my girlfriend. What we had was just an arrangement, Marissa. One you signed a contract not to talk about," I reminded her, because she was a vindictive bitch.

"Is she why you left me? I was pregnant with your child!"

Ice ran through my veins. "*What?*" Shock briefly wiped my mind of all coherent thought. Eventually though, my higher function turned back on. "No, you weren't. You have an IUD, and I always wore a condom." I mean, it could happen, but statistically? No fucking way. It was part of our agreement that she'd gotten an IUD—with proof—but still, I'd never gone bare with Marissa. I knew her far too well.

Marissa's top lip curled back over her teeth. "I could have been, but you never would have known because you just cut me off for her." Her eyes dropped to Huey, and her face twisted. "Did you knock her up? Is that why? You could have *talked* to me; I would have accepted your bastard if I still got to keep you."

"Wait a fucking second—" Nova started, but then Marissa's palm was whipping out and connecting with Nova's cheek, her long talons scratching across Nova's cheekbone.

"What the fuck?!" I shouted, stepping in front of Nova and pushing Marissa's shoulder. She stumbled back like she'd been shot.

"Don't fucking touch me!" she screamed. "I'm going to sue you for assault, River Cooper, and you'll *beg* to take me back!"

I stood there in front of Nova, protecting her from this obviously unhinged bitch. "Go away, Marissa. I'm getting a restraining order so expect a visit from the cops, you crazy bitch."

The pure poison leaching from her eyes made me feel like a fool. How had I let it go on so long?

"Run along then, River. Take your little slut and your bastard home. I hope you enjoyed your career, because it's fucking over." She lifted her chin to the left, and I spotted the pap, his camera raised. Then I noticed all the other people with their phones pointed at us.

Fuck, fuck, fuck.

I hustled a shocked Nova back to our car, taking Huey from her shaking hands and putting him back in his car seat. Driving away, I cursed under my breath. This was so fucking bad.

Nova was staring straight ahead, not meeting my eyes.

"Nova…"

I could see the angry red mark of Marissa's hand, the thin lines of blood where that bitch's nails had scratched her. I'd screwed this up already. I knew happiness wasn't meant for me. I'd just forgotten.

I wouldn't forget again.

CHAPTER
Thirty
NOVA

I WAS SITTING in the living room on Rigby's lap, a cold pack being held to my face kind of unnecessarily. But River wouldn't take no for an answer. I was a bit in shock. My heart was still racing, and adrenaline made my skin somehow both cold and tingly, which shouldn't have been possible.

River was in his office on the phone, but I could hear the heavy footfalls of his pacing. Rigby was silent but tense. He was furious. I could tell he was livid—despite the loose way his hands stroked my spine, and the soft words he spoke to me, the sensation of pure outrage poured off him.

Huey had been unsettled, but Rigby had fed him and put him down to sleep in the portable crib we kept in the living room. Other than grumbling, he'd been perfectly fine while I'd stood there like a fucking statue as some lady slapped the shit out of me.

Though she wasn't some lady. She was an ex of River's. Someone who he'd kissed, had sex with, eaten meals with. Someone who thought he was her boyfriend.

I shook my head, and Rigby held me tighter. My phone was going nuts, but I knew it was probably the group chat. "Are you okay, Fireball?" he asked softly.

I nodded. Technically, it was true. I was okay. No one ever died from being slapped. I had some serious regrets about not punching the bitch back, but I told myself I'd had Huey strapped to my chest. In all honesty, though, even without the baby, I probably wouldn't have retaliated unless really necessary. I wasn't a fighter, no matter how disgusted in myself I was right now.

Shrugging, I flopped back against Rigby. "It's not like I ever thought you guys were saints. You've obviously got ex-girlfriends, and statistically, some of them had to be crazy, right?" He huffed a laugh, but it seemed forced.

The front door opened and Devan strode in, his eyes wild. He saw me on the couch and pulled me out of Rigby's arms. Gently gripping my chin, he turned my face to the side and hissed an angry breath between his teeth at the faint mark still there.

"I'm going to sue her so hard, she'll have to live in a cardboard box under a fucking bridge," he seethed. He grabbed my hand—the one still holding the ice pack—and moved it back to my cheek, even though the cold hurt worse than the sting now. "But first, I'm going to beat the shit out of River for being a fucking pussy-blind dumbass."

He stormed off, and I looked over my shoulder at Rigby. "Should you stop them?"

Rigby just shrugged and pulled me back into his lap. "Nope. It'll make them both feel better."

I huffed. "Rigby Engman, you never told me that I'd have to drown in testosterone when you were pitching your polyamory freaking solution." I slid from his lap. "Stay!"

"Yes, ma'am," he teased.

"Good boy." His cheeks flushed, and he looked away. I hadn't been prepared for quite how hot I'd find Rigby's praise kink the other night, but even thinking about it made butterflies alight in my stomach.

Deciding now wasn't the time to be aroused, I walked out of the living room and toward the office space the guys shared. Mostly Devan used it, but sometimes the guys would do video meetings and shit in there. I crept down the hall, not wanting to interrupt River if he was still on the phone. And maybe a little because I wanted to know what they were saying without monitoring their words around me.

"How was I meant to know the bitch was a psycho? The NDA was meant to protect me. Protect us," River grunted.

"You and your fucking need to date crazy-ass bitches was always going to cause us problems in the end. The problem is that she isn't giving a tell-all fucking interview. No, she's setting you up. Setting Nova up."

There was a huge sigh, though I wasn't sure which of them it was coming from. "She said someone told her we'd be there. I don't think Marissa knew ahead of time that I was going to be there. Someone tipped her off."

A chill went down my spine. "You think you have a stalker?" Devan's surprise was evident.

Whatever River said next was too soft for me to hear, but the next bit was clear. "Unless my stalker is a pap, I doubt it. Someone was there, ready with the camera. They knew there was going to be a problem, though how the paparazzi would know about Marissa, know she's fucking crazy, know where I'd be at the park, that's the real question." There was a long pause while they pondered. "You think I should, I don't know, bow out from this thing with Nova? She doesn't need me to drag my fucking issues to her doorstep. She doesn't deserve that."

I bit my lip to prevent myself from gasping. At the same time, I heard Devan's derisive snort. "Nut up, bro. Nova isn't your parents. She isn't going to run away emotionally if shit gets hard. We both know that. You're just worried that she's going to reject you, but I promise you that if you don't give this a chance—give *her* a chance—you'll regret it forever."

"Maybe I should use your nuts. I'll go and ask if Nova can grab them from her purse, since you've obviously lost them somewhere along the way," River teased, and I heard the thump of a fist hitting flesh, along with River's hissed laugh. "I'm scared, man. I feel like I'm already fucking this up and it hasn't even been two weeks."

"Running away now would be a bitch move, Cooper. So suck it up. We'll face this hurdle together, and we aren't going to preempt what Nova wants. If she thinks it's too much, then we'll face that together too."

There was a long silence. "You'd give her up for me?" Another drawn-out silence, and I realized I wasn't even breathing in case I missed the answer.

"I love you, River. More than anyone else in the world. If it was her or you, I'd choose you, but I know that neither of you would make me choose. It's not the kind of people you are."

Hell no, I wouldn't make him give up the only person he considered family. That was, if I was about to abandon him just because he had a crazy ex-girlfriend and a stalker. I decided River had spent enough time in his feelings; I wasn't going to let him keep imagining the worst scenario until he'd talked himself out of a relationship with us.

I snuck back a bit, then stomped down the hall like I was just coming from the living room. I knocked gently on the door jamb. They both turned toward me, Devan giving me a soft smile and River's face a mask of guilt, his eyes looking at the cut on my cheek.

I strode over to him and climbed him like a tree, until he was forced to put his hands under my ass or let me drop to the ground like a lead weight. I gripped both his cheeks in my hand and kissed him hard.

It was a claiming kiss; if someone was watching, other than Devan, they'd know that River Cooper was *mine*. Apparently, the only person second-guessing it was the man himself.

So I told him. "You're mine, River. I'm keeping you, and as long as you hold the baby, I'll bitch fight any ex you have for the honor."

Devan snorted. "No, you wouldn't. You're a lover, not a fighter."

I gave him a death glare. "Fine, I'll give you such a passionate public display of affection that old ladies will blush, ex-girlfriends will see red, and you'll have to protect me from their velociraptor claws."

River shook his head, burying his face in my neck. "I'm so sorry."

"Don't be. Let's just work out how that crazy wench found you and then plug that hole right up, because I'm not buying that she just stumbled across you and created an incident of her own volition."

Dev raised an eyebrow at me, and I briefly wondered if he knew I'd been eavesdropping on them. "I agree with Star. Something seems fishy. Who'd have something to gain from you being embroiled in a PR scandal?"

"Some of the second string, maybe. A rookie or two

who might make my spot. Someone who wants my sponsorships, though I don't know who."

"Or that woman from ASPN," I added.

"Andrea Esperanza," they both groaned simultaneously.

Devan shook his head. "She's a professional sports reporter. Surely she isn't stooping to trying to get shit published in trash newspapers."

River shrugged. "She kind of hates me now."

"She has the means and the motive, just as much as anyone else who hates River. More so maybe, because it's really personal."

River slumped down in the office chair, glaring down at his crotch. "This is your fucking fault." I resisted the urge to laugh. He looked up at Dev. "What do we do?"

"Did you contact the PR department for the IceCaps?" River nodded. "Your lawyer? Tony?" Tony was River and Rigby's sports agent.

River blew out a breath. "Yeah. Tony chewed me out but he's going to keep an eye out, see if he can head any stories off at the pass."

Devan shrugged, grabbing me and pulling me back into his body, like waiting this long to hold me had been a hardship. I rested back into his chest. This was nice. Sure, there was probably always going to be more drama, but there was more support.

"I'll get my lawyers to start the paperwork charging Marissa with assault and getting a restraining order.

The woman obviously needs help, and I'd like it if she didn't get within two hundred yards of Nova and Huey ever again. Then all we can do is wait, and see where this whole clusterfuck lands. Maybe that pap didn't get any good photos?"

I snorted. We weren't *that* lucky.

CHAPTER
Thirty-One

RIVER

THE FOLLOWING DAY, and the one after, was surprisingly calm. I got hauled over to the executive arm so they could grill me about what had happened, but there was no way they could come at me for this. I'd just been walking through the park with my girlfriend. She'd been attacked. We'd done nothing wrong.

But the PR people were grumpy at the best of times, so they mean-mugged me the whole time but eventually agreed. It helped that there was nothing in the papers or even really on the web about the incident. No one had recognised me from their phone footage, obviously, because it wasn't even trending on social media.

It was a fucking relief, but like the chickenshit I was, I avoided taking Nova out in public for a couple more days. Instead, I planned a make-up date. I wanted to show her that my life wasn't all drama, and I had the perfect idea.

Both public and private.

So on Thursday night, between our home games, I took her out. The guys agreed to stay home and look after Huey, so it would just be me and Nova. Watching my best friends kiss her, running their hands all over like they knew what she liked—it made me so fucking jealous. I wanted to know what her skin felt like when I pressed my fingers into the soft roundness of her hips. I wanted to know what it would feel like to have her hair brushing over my shoulders as we kissed naked.

But first, I had to show her that I was in this shit for the long haul, despite the drama that seemed to follow me around like stink on shit.

First step, a proper date. I paced up and down the living room, the guys sitting around with a beer in their hands watching basketball, Huey propped on the couch between them. I lifted my phone and took a photo. Fuck, Rigby had been right. This would work out best for us all, but especially Huey.

Rigby looked behind me and let out a low whistle. I turned, and Nova was there. She looked beautiful. I didn't know shit about makeup, but she was glowing. She had on a sweet little dress that floated around her thighs, a denim jacket and a pair of white sneakers. I'd told her it was casual and damn, my girl came through looking like a wet dream. The perfect girl next door.

I shook myself out of my stupor and strode over, pulling her into my arms. "You look beautiful."

She grinned up at me, and I felt that smile all the

way in my chest. "Thanks. You didn't tell me much about where we were going, so I hope this is okay?"

I nodded. Honestly, the sight of her long, smooth legs had burned out a few of my higher thought processes, at least temporarily. "You're perfect. Are you ready?"

"Uh-huh. Just one second." She walked over to the guys, kissing Huey first, murmuring something softly to him, then leaning in to kiss Rigby and Devan. I could see the heat in the other men's eyes, could see them holding themselves back from deepening the goodbye kiss.

I appreciated those fuckers so much.

When she strolled back over to me, her hips swaying enticingly, I told myself we had to go on a date. I couldn't just take her back up to my room. Then I repeated it until we were in my car, and she was buckled in.

"Where are we going?"

I gave her a cocky smirk. "It's a surprise."

She huffed. "I'm obviously a fan of those."

Man, I just bet. Her whole life for the last few months had been one surprise after another, and not always in the best way. "It's a good surprise, I promise. Not like 'here, this is your baby brother. You have to care for him now' kind of a surprise."

She let out a mirthless laugh. "I'd hope not. I'm not sure I could deal with another accidental half-brother."

I slid my eyes to her quickly, then back to the road.

She never said anything, but she gripped the door handle, or the steering wheel, a little too tightly whenever she drove. She hadn't been in her parents' accident, but there was still some kind of PTSD there. It was understandable. Hopefully, she was working through it with her therapist. I didn't think we were at quite the stage of a relationship where we pointed out each other's trauma.

But I did have a question. "Did you ever consider not taking him?"

She didn't shut me straight down, so that was a good sign for us, right? "It was a shock. And maybe for thirty seconds, I thought maybe he'd be better off with a loving family and not a twenty-four year old who has no idea. But then they said he had a heart condition, and all I could think was, what if he ended up with a family who couldn't afford to give him proper care? What if they didn't love him how I could? How my parents had loved me? I didn't know you guys existed then. The rest of my reasons were selfish," she said, flushing even in the darkness. "I just didn't want to be alone anymore. I wanted one last connection to my dad."

She turned her face away, but I reached over and squeezed her thigh reassuringly. "It's okay. Our reasons were selfish too. But things worked out for the best."

I got the baby and the girl, and if that wasn't fucking perfect, what was?

We made small talk on the drive, the place we were

going well away from the city lights. I found out her favorite foods, color, her first kiss, all that shit you talk about on a first date. We might be doing shit backward, but I still wanted to know Nova inside out.

Thirty minutes later, we made it to where we were going. Our headlights were the only things in the darkness of the country roads west of Ann Arbor. I drove through the gate and into a darkened field.

"Are you going to murder me and bury my body? Because you probably should have done that before the press took pictures of us together. Totally incriminating."

I raised an eyebrow at her. "No more true crime podcasts for you. Fucking hell." Shaking my head, chuckling despite myself, I flashed my headlights. "Normally, there are more people out here, but I bought all the tickets. This is a landing strip for crop dusters by day, and by night…"

As if on cue, the screen at the end of the landing strip lit up. Nova gasped, and I couldn't help but feel insanely pleased with myself.

"It's a drive-in movie theater?" she squeaked out.

"Exactly."

There was one old dude in a pick-up who waved as we drove past. Pulling up where I thought was a good spot right in front, I backed up so the tailgate was facing the screen. Nova's eyes hadn't left it. Out here in the empty darkness, it did seem kind of magical.

I ushered her out of the car and into the rear cargo

area of my SUV. I'd put all the seats down already, and spread out blankets and pillows. "River..." she breathed, and I just kissed her lips softly as I hoisted her into the back of my car, climbing in after her. "What are we watching?"

"*Back To The Future*, both One and Two. And we've also got..." I reached over to the back seat and pulled out a cooler bag with food I'd collected from a restaurant this afternoon. "Gourmet lunchables. Well, the restaurant didn't call them that, but it's basically what it is, right?"

She shook her head, laughing, but looked inside the container I handed her. "This looks delicious."

I reached back into the bag and pulled out two popcorn tubs. "Popcorn and candy mix. And wine."

She shook her head, her smile so wide, it was appling her cheeks. "You've thought of everything."

I linked the Bluetooth of the theater's radio channel to my entertainment system, and the sound of the movie came over the speakers. Pulling Nova toward me, I hugged her close. "I wanted this to be perfect."

She kissed my chest. "It is. It's the most perfect first date I've ever been on."

She went silent as the opening scene of the movie appeared in the darkness, the stars around it like cinema lights. It was fucking perfect, but I wasn't done yet. I fed her little bits of cured meat and oil-dipped bread, as we laughed at the actors on the screen. We drank wine and talked.

And it was fucking blissful.

But nothing was better than lying amongst the pillows, full and content, a little bit buzzed on red wine, watching the movie play in Nova's eyes. Her arm was around my middle, her head pillowed on my bicep, her small hand snaked under my Henley so she could scrape her nails over my abs.

I was about to bust through my zipper, my brain running away with me. I breathed through my nose. I wasn't going to ruin the moment by trying to make a move.

But if *she* made a move…

As if she'd heard my thoughts, her hand slid higher, until those nails were scraping over my nipple. *Fuck.*

"Nova," I warned, my voice rough. And I could swear on the fucking Stanley Cup, she gave me the most devilish grin I'd ever seen and tweaked my fucking nipple.

Oh yeah. It was on.

I growled and rolled on top of her. "What are you doing there, sweetheart?" My lips were inches from hers, and from this position, I could see the raw lust in her eyes.

"Getting to know you?" she whispered, her voice breathy.

"You're getting to know my nipple?" I let out a raspy laugh. "Any other part of me you'd like to get acquainted with?"

"Your lips?" she breathed, and I obliged. Fuck me,

her plush lips tasted like strawberries and they were so soft and plump. I wanted them on my skin, and wrapped around my cock. I kissed her until she was moaning beneath me, then shifted over so I could slide one knee between her thighs.

"Anything else?" I growled against her mouth, my hands skimming down her sides.

"Your fingers."

God, my dick was going to explode, it was so hard. "Where do you want them, baby?"

"Please, River. I want them inside me."

I moved down her body so I could pull the straps of her dress down over her shoulders and breasts. I sucked the soft golden skin, moving further down her body until I could get acquainted with her nipples too. Then I moved my hand over her thighs until I was tracing the lines of her pussy through her panties.

"You want them here, baby?"

"Yes," she panted, grinding up into my fingers. I wanted to tease her more; I wasn't ready for this to be done quite yet. I sucked those pretty nipples and traced through her underwear until she was writhing against my fingers and begging. Her fingers were buried in the short lengths of my hair, and by the time I pushed the lace of her underwear aside and dipped my fingers inside her, she was so fucking deliciously wet. Her body went tense as she clenched around my fingers, my name a whisper on her lips.

I stroked my fingers inside her until she was

coming, her muscles clenching around me and her hand pressing me so tightly to her breast, I might actually suffocate and die. But I wasn't going to move—hell no. I hoped the guys put it on my damn headstone.

"Oh my god," she breathed, and I don't think I'd ever been more proud of anything in my life. My dick was so fucking hard now, my balls aching. She tilted up my chin, dragging me back up her body until she was kissing me like she was branding *me*. Making me hers. Finally, she pulled back, sucking in air. "I want you inside me, River Cooper. Right fucking now."

I wanted to laugh, but the feeling in my chest wasn't humor. I just didn't want to put a finger on exactly what it was. "Anything you want, baby girl, I'll give you." I gripped her underwear and tore the fragile lace at the sides. "Starting with new panties." I released my dick from the meat grinder that was my zipper and pushed my jeans down my thighs. Our first time shouldn't be rushed in the back of the car. Rigby was going to give me shit for fucking up the romance, but I didn't care. It felt right. It felt perfect.

She felt perfect. I played with her clit, reading her body language the way I'd read the body language of an opponent. What made her writhe and pant, what didn't. One day, I was going to know what gave her pleasure as well as I knew what I liked, but I was prepared to play until I knew.

Her legs wrapped around my hips, and she pulled me in tighter until my cock was sliding through the wet folds of her pussy. I groaned. When my cock notched against her entrance, every thought left my brain except the need to be inside. I *needed* to get inside her, or this was going to be an embarrassingly short first time.

"Please," she breathed.

Fuck. Condom. I pulled back, grabbing a condom from my pocket and tearing it open with my teeth. Handling it like it was the most important thing in the world, I slid it on and then slid straight into her. I couldn't help it. I needed her so fucking bad.

I was glad the rest of the drive-in was empty, because the sound she made was pure porn. I thought about Coach. I thought about fucking hockey. I thought about the loss we had last year in the Stanley Cup Play-off. Every shitty thing I could visualize, just to prevent me from thinking about how good her slick little pussy felt around my cock.

Her heels dug into my ass, and she moved against me. "You're so fucking perfect. You feel like fucking heaven on my dick," I grunted at her, ignoring the squeak of the car's suspension as I pounded her into the pillows. I wanted to see her riding me, but I didn't think I could pull the move off in the back of my SUV. Instead, I grabbed one of her legs and bent it back higher, grinding down harder, hitting a spot inside her that was making her grip my cock until I was beginning to see lights in my vision.

She moaned my name on repeat, and I hooked my arm under her other thigh, bending her in half until she was screaming her orgasm. I came with her, taking her lips and groaning into her mouth as my thighs fucking shook with release.

I released her legs and rolled to the side before I crushed her to death. I was panting like I'd just been skating lightning drills, and I couldn't feel my thighs any longer.

She was breathing heavily too, as I gathered her onto my chest. "Holy shit."

"Aw, baby, you know it. That was…"

"Yeah…" she breathed back.

The lightning was striking, sending Marty McFly back to the future, and I had never been so content in my whole damn life. I snuggled down with her, kissing her softly, and we watched the second movie. By the time that movie ended, she was sound asleep in my arms, and I'd lost a little piece of my heart to her.

CHAPTER

Thirty-Two

NOVA

I SAT beside Devan at the IceCaps game, Huey once again snuggled up against his chest. I enjoyed the sight of him effortlessly carrying around an infant. Plus, Huey was probably safer with Devan in case one of River's psycho exes popped out of the woodwork again.

I was definitely getting into this hockey thing now. I was wearing my Cooper jersey, snuggled into Devan's side. We weren't right on the glass today, preferring to sit a bit further up in the stands. I saw Julieta up in the family box and gave her a wave. She'd been blowing up my phone to come over for another girls' night, and my liver had recovered enough—or maybe I'd forgotten the suffering of that hangover enough—that I was totally down.

The IceCaps were up one goal, but Ontario was keeping them on their toes. It was a fast-paced game that was going to give me whiplash with the amount they went up and down the ice.

At the end of the first period, the stadium's jumbotron lit up with the kiss cam, and I laughed as old couples made out like teenagers and friends looked horrified, waving their hands like it wasn't ever going to happen.

Then I saw my face and Devan's, and flushed bright red. My eyes whipped to Devan's, and he laughed at my expression. Reaching up, he cupped my cheek and gave me the lightest brush of a kiss across my lips, everyone hooting and hollering around us like we were doing a live porn show. Lucky, the camera panned away, but Devan kept his lips on mine. He deepened the kiss and then pulled away, his chuckles more a sensation than a sound as the stadium was still rowdy.

He pulled me closer, his arm tight around my shoulders as the guys slid back onto the ice. I fed and burped Huey during the second period, and he was sound asleep against Dev's chest again by the third.

The lady beside me leaned close. "You make a beautiful family," she said kindly, then gave me a wink. "My first husband had that look about him, all mysterious and confident. Best lover I ever had." She sighed happily. Jesus, this woman was pushing seventy-five. "Died in a car crash three years after we married. I still think about him. A love like that? It burns hard and banks hot, if you know what I mean. Some men just imprint themselves on your soul forever."

I nodded, because I wasn't sure what to say to that. "I'm sorry for your loss?"

The old lady waved a hand. "I met Gerald four years later, and the best thing he ever did was embrace the ghost of my ex-husband. Some men, they're threatened by a memory, refuse to let you ever mention their names. But not Gerald. He just made it his mission to love me enough for both Theodore and himself. He's a good man, and sometimes I think it was Theo who sent him to me, you know? We've been married forty-eight years now."

Gah, my heart. I looked past her at an elderly man in an IceCaps trucker hat, who was cheering as the Caps scored another goal. He leaned over and grabbed his wife's cheeks, planting a huge smooch on her lips and literally giving me all the fuzzy feelings. I couldn't imagine being married to a man for so long. They cuddled into each other, and I leaned back against Devan. He kissed my forehead, and we continued watching the game.

The crowd went nuts when we won, though Huey still didn't wake up. We shuffled out with the crowd, and instead of waiting around for the guys, we decided to drive home and meet Rigby and River back at our place.

We stopped to pick up fast food on the way, which we ate on the floor of the living room while drinking beer and watching ASPN highlights. Then Devan made love to me on the couch, the steady hum of the news in the background as I cried out his name.

The guys stumbled in, exhausted, at about 10 p.m. Immediately, Rigby stole me naked off Devan's lap, tugging me upstairs. He fucked me dirty, and the whole time, I told him how good he felt, how much pleasure he brought me while eating me out with crazy enthusiasm. I didn't know praising someone else could feel so fucking good, but every time I told him how good he was fucking me, he doubled his efforts until I was limp with pleasure.

Naked and overheated, I snuggled close to Rigby's chest, despite the warmth radiating from his hard body. I was pretty sure he could be searing my flesh and I'd still try to get closer—that was the hold this man had on me.

"Is it weird for you?" he asked, his fingers trailing over the curve of my shoulder. "Being with us all?"

I chewed my lip, really thinking about his words. The urge to just fob off the question was strong, because overall, it wasn't weird at all. And maybe *that* was what made it weird? But that was confusing, even for me.

"Individually, my relationship with each of you feels right. Even all together, I'm on board with how this relationship is working. Because it *is* working, right? For you guys too?"

He nodded. "I talk with the guys about it all the time. Communication is key; that's what Devan says. And I think the guys like the idea of being tied closer together, though I'm not sure they could get much closer without being naked."

"Do they…?"

Rigby shook his head this time. "Nah, I don't think so. They're close, and they've shared women in the past, but I think that's the only connection between them. They love each other, though—the kind of love that you only get by going through some serious shit together."

Yeah, I got that. Sometimes, when they were doing something together, they moved like they were one person.

"Why do I get the impression you still have doubts?" Rigby asked, tilting my chin up so he could kiss me again.

I shrugged. "I don't know. I feel like I'm cheating on you guys, even though logically, I know that's stupid. What are the guys doing right now? Are they lying alone in their beds, listening to us fuck with steadily growing resentment?"

He laughed. "Well, that's oddly specific, but I see what you mean. You're worried that you won't carve out enough time for each of us, and that's how bad feelings are born?"

"Yes!"

"Okay." Reaching over to the night stand, he grabbed his phone and shot off a text to the group chat. I tried to wiggle up his body to see, but he just moved the phone away. "Nuh-uh. Now it has to be a surprise."

Tossing the phone onto the floor, he moved down

my body. He was trapped between my thighs, his body pinning mine down, and he flicked his tongue across my clit until I forgot about the damn group chat and our conversation and *anything* but his mouth on me.

Two orgasms later—one of which was in the shower —Rigby was toweling me dry, spending a disproportionate amount of time on my boobs. His phone chirped from the bathroom counter. Checking it, he dragged me back into his room and threw one of his shirts over my body. Scooping me up into his arms, he skipped from the room. "Your surprise is ready!"

He headed to the media room, which was one place I'd never spent much time. There was always something to do, and if I wanted to watch TV, I did it down in the living room where Huey's portable playpen was.

When he pushed through the door, I was surprised to see Devan and River there, both in just sweatpants. At their feet was a pile of mattresses and blankets. It looked like a giant nest of bedding, and I was in love.

"We'll work on getting something a bit more permanent for this room, but I thought it might help ease some of those thoughts if we could all be in here together. Still on the same floor as Huey," Rigby told me softly, his arms around my waist. "This way you won't have to worry if the guys are lying there stewing about not being able to hold you."

River raised an eyebrow at his words. "Come on, Tiny. Let's go to bed. I'm fucking exhausted."

I didn't even know where to lie, but Rigby took the

decision out of my hands. Dropping me softly onto the mattresses on the floor, he went and grabbed a bottle of water from the minifridge in the corner. River slid beneath the blankets beside me, Devan bracketing me at the back.

"You're lucky I'm tiny, otherwise this would never work. I need a third side," I grumbled, but Rigby was back, climbing along the bottom of the mattress and hugging my cold feet.

"Just sleep, Star. We're perfectly happy just being close to you," Devan murmured.

I snuggled further into River's chest, while Rigby put on a movie, the volume down low. This was nice. I was warm and happy. When was the last time I could've said that? Not with my ex; although he was lovely, he never made me feel even a fraction of what these guys made me feel.

Rigby gripped my calf, his soft snores humming through the room before the movie had even begun. River laughed, kissing my forehead, and before I knew it, I was asleep, cradled in the arms of my boyfriends.

Plural.

CHAPTER
Thirty-Three

DEVAN

"SIR?"

Tom's voice seemed hesitant, and that always meant bad news. Did the Marcello merger get rejected in the final hour?

"What is it?" I strode into my office, flipping through my messages. There seemed to be a lot, mostly from associates, and most of them nondescript. The hell was going on? "Did our stock crash overnight and I missed it?"

Tom shook his head. "No, sir. Have you seen the news?"

I'd lingered in bed for as long as possible this morning, my morning wood nestled against Nova's ass. It was the best way to wake up. I'd sprinted through my morning routine, which would normally have included watching the Finance channel.

"Not this morning."

Tom winced as he handed me his tablet. "You might want to check it out, sir."

Grabbing the tablet, I looked down at the news article Tom had pulled up on the screen.

Puck Bunny Princess.
How having sexual relations with one woman is the new form of team bonding.

Star defenseman River Cooper has embraced a new technique of building a rapport with his team—sharing a booty call. Publicly linked with Cooper and fan favorite forward Rigby Engman, is this woman the new queen of the Ann Arbor IceCaps, or just another indicator of the misogynistic culture permeating the IceCaps locker room? The mystery woman has also been seen with eligible bachelor and IceCaps sponsor Devan Mayson, so it seems the Caps are happy to make sure everyone feels like they are a part of the team. She has even been linked with married Captain Clint Vanmussen, having been seen leaving his home in the early hours of the morning. This whole situation flies directly in the face of the team's supposed "family first" values…

I looked up at Tom. "Is this a company tablet?"

He nodded, stepping to the side and shutting the door. He'd been with me long enough to know what came next. I threw the fucking thing against the wall.

"God fucking *dammit!*" I yelled. Why couldn't I just get to be fucking happy? I swiped everything off the desk, throwing a full temper tantrum. When I straightened, heaving in breaths, Tom looked almost frightened.

Fuck. I'd lost control.

"I'm sorry, Tom." I softened my voice. "Can you get the lawyers on the phone, and then probably the public relations team. Cancel all my other appointments, and reschedule the ones that can't be emails." With a nod, he left as fast as he possibly could.

I needed to call the guys. I grabbed my phone, but it rang before I even managed to unlock it, Rigby's face flashing on the screen.

"I saw it," I said instead of a greeting. "Has Nova seen it?"

The low growl of Rigby's voice told me more than his words that he was pissed. "I don't fucking know. She was still cocooned in bed when we left for training. But she's not going to magically miss this. She's going to find out. River and I are getting dragged to the owner's office now."

"What are you going to say?"

Another low curse from Rigby. "The fucking truth. That we're in a committed relationship, that it's none of their fucking business, and everything printed in that article is a fucking lie that can be corroborated by at least thirty other people. Who the fuck would do this, man?"

I wished I'd looked at the byline before smashing the tablet. "I don't care. I'm going to destroy them, and I'm going to fucking enjoy it."

There was a loud shout and the sound of something heavy hitting the wall. River.

"Tell him to not punch the wall. He needs his fucking hands. We'll get this figured out as soon as possible. And then whoever printed that bullshit will pay—I promise you that."

I needed to get this shit over and done with before Nova turned on the news. She wasn't a news lover, so I might have a little time to nip this in the bud. But I wasn't betting that I'd be that lucky.

Tom called an emergency meeting with the lawyers and the PR department inhumanly fast. He must have made them sprint from their executive offices. I was gonna give that kid a raise.

I sat around a small conference table, a printed copy of the article in front of me. The byline wasn't a name I knew, which was surprising. But the photos in the article were incriminating, and proof that someone had been following Nova for a lot longer than that pap in the park last week.

Her hand on Rigby's through the glass—though me and Huey were conveniently cut from the picture—us on the kiss cam, River with his arm around her at the park. Even Nova standing in the doorway of Muss's house, from an angle where you couldn't see Julieta beside him.

I pushed the article into the middle of the table before I gave into the urge to tear it to pieces. "I want this squashed. Gone. And I want you to find the reporter and sue the fuck out of them—and the newspaper. Anyone who had *anything* to do with this bullshit." I looked at Chantelle from PR. "Put out a press release."

"What do you want it to say exactly?" she asked, eyeing me warily.

"That my relationships are no one's fucking business would be a start," I growled.

My lawyer, Malik, was young, and honestly a bit of a shark, but I liked him like that. "With all due respect, sir, I can only sue them for slander, or damage to the company's reputation, if the statements made aren't actually true."

"She's not a fucking whore!"

Malik raised a hand. "What you do in your relationships is none of our damn business. I really hate this tabloid shit. But if you're all in a relationship with this woman, then we don't have much of a leg to stand on."

"She isn't fucking Clint Vanmussen."

Malik shook his head. "It very carefully didn't suggest that she was. Only that she was seen leaving his house in the early hours."

I slammed my hands on the table. "We were all fucking there that night. This is such a goddamn clusterfuck." I looked around the table. "Fix this. I don't care who you have to bribe or threaten, *nothing* like this gets printed again. Buy the company and fire the fuckers if you have to. I'll be at home."

I strode out of the conference room and back into my office, grabbing my shit. I needed to go home. We'd only just settled shit with Nova, and if this got to her before we did…

Giving Tom a barrage of instructions on the way out the door, I stared down the people who tried to get into the elevator with me. I needed a fucking moment, and the less people who saw me the better. I was so close to losing my cool, to becoming someone I hated. I had to get my shit under control before I saw Nova. The thought of her reading that vile poison and being hurt by it made me irrationally angry.

Walking to my parking spot, I climbed into the Porsche and slammed my palm on the steering wheel. "Fuck! Fuck, fuck, *fuck!*"

I tried to call Nova, but it was just ringing out. I also tried the guys, but their phones just went to voicemail. Tom had tried to get the sponsor rep for the team to come to my emergency meeting, but apparently they'd declined, which was a fucking problem. This was going to blow up in all our faces.

I weaved through traffic, the radio on low. But when I heard the word IceCaps, I turned it up.

"And the big news coming out of the hockey world this morning is the little love nest the team is turning into. One girl for the whole team? We had a word for that back in high school, but I don't think I can say it on air," one radio presenter laughed.

"Hey, I'm a huge IceCaps fan, and if this is the way the team wants to bond to keep their winning streak going, then I'm all for it. They can have sex with her all the way to the Stanley Cup finals for all I care, as long as we get there," a second guy said.

"I don't know, guys," the female presenter declared. "Did you see Devan Mayson, eligible bachelor extraordinaire, with a baby strapped to his chest? I think there's more to this than meets the eye."

"Probably a mystery bag baby," the first guy chuckled. "Don't know whose it is until it's out of the womb."

They all laughed, and I slammed the stereo to mute a little too hard. *Goddammit!*

I pulled up into the driveway and was out of the driver's side the second I had it in park. I burst through the front door, out of breath. As I moved down the hall, I could hear the television on.

My heart sank.

I stepped into the room, and Nova was there, standing so still she was like a wild animal in the path of a predator. She had Huey clutched to her chest, as if she was protecting him from whatever she was seeing.

Playing on the morning show were pictures of us, flashing through in a reel, while the presenters made jokes about how lucky she was, about Huey's paternity, and made thinly veiled references to her being a whore.

I jumped over the back of the couch and turned it

off. Spinning back around, I looked around at Nova's pale, shocked face. "Nova…"

She passed me Huey and then turned, fleeing up the stairs like she could run from this shitshow. I wished that were possible for us all.

CHAPTER
Thirty-Four
NOVA

MY PHONE WAS a constant buzz on the couch, but I didn't want to look at it. Didn't want to answer it and talk to people. I'd masochistically Googled the guys' names after seeing the segment on the morning show, and that article had been the first thing to appear. I could have almost taken that. It was a shock, but it wasn't totally unexpected. But the hateful comments underneath tore at my insides until I was a bleeding mess.

Puck pussy. I mean, points for alliteration, and it was much better than the other less imaginative slurs people were posting beneath the article—which was now being featured on at least three gossip news sites.

Whore. Slut. Clearly no self-esteem to allow myself to be passed around like the Stanley Cup. Some people were telling me that I should just die. It was worse than awful.

Today, I'd woken up feeling amazing. Now, every-thing was in a fucking shambles.

Devan had knocked on my door several times, but I didn't answer. Chloe's name had flashed across my phone screen, but I ignored that too.

When Julieta's name popped up, cold dread washed across my skin. I had to answer this. She had to know that I would never ever do that. Taking a deep breath, I pressed the answer button. "Julieta? I swear its all fucking lies. I would never—"

"I'm going to stop you right there, Nova. Of course you fucking wouldn't. Clint wouldn't, either. I know that. Hell, the whole world knows that, if they'd actu-ally think with their brains. I'm not ringing because I believe that fucking drivel they're spewing. I'm ringing to see how my friend is."

I let out a choked sob. Fuck being stoic. "I'm so sorry you guys got dragged into this."

"Enough, stop apologizing for shit that clearly isn't your fault. Now, what can I do? Do you want me to babysit Huey for the day while you guys put out fires?"

The wave of thankfulness I had for this woman—who was still a new friend, who could have easily stayed away and I wouldn't have blamed her one bit—was monumental. "Thanks, Julieta. I don't know what we're doing about this yet, but I might take you up on that soon."

"Girl, you can come and hide in my bunker, eat cheese and watch romcoms until this whole thing blows over if you want." We laughed together, mine edged with tears. "I mean it, though. If you and Huey need a place to stay, for whatever reason, you're always welcome here. If this whole thing—whatever it is you've got going on over there in Hotel Hunks-A-Plenty—goes pear-shaped, you've got me and Muss. No questions asked."

I swallowed the lump in my throat. "Thank you."

"Anytime. You're a good person. Don't let this bull-shit get you down. Now tell me what's going on with your roommates, because I'm dying to know."

I laughed again and spilled the whole story. From the night we left her house until now. It was therapeutic to get it off my chest. Even though it wasn't really a secret, we'd still kind of kept it under wraps. Obviously for good reason.

I spoke to Julieta for close to forty-five minutes, and by the time I hung up, I felt somewhat better about the fact the world thought I was a fame whore. I emerged from the bedroom and found Devan in the media room, amongst all the mattresses where we'd been so happy not twelve hours earlier. Huey was with him.

He saw me and straightened into a sitting position. "Are you okay?"

I shook my head, because no, I wasn't. He stood, keeping one eye on Huey as he walked over to me. He stopped a foot away, holding his arms out, offering me solace but not forcing me to take it. His eyes were guarded, his whole body tense.

I hesitated, but only briefly. I stepped into the strong circle of his arms, burying my face in his chest. This whole thing might blow up in our faces, so I was going to be selfish and take the consolation where I could.

"Want me to buy the newspaper and burn down the building?" he whispered into my hair, and I laughed, a choked, bitter sound.

"Yes." I very much wanted some old-school revenge on the people who'd so callously decided my life, my reputation, and the reputations of the guys meant nothing. Because why? They were public figures and therefore it was open season? Fuckers. Still, I sighed. "No. You're too pretty for prison."

He chuckled softly. "I'm really not." His words were loaded, and normally I'd chase down the secrets that darkened his tone, but not today. Today, I just wanted to bask in the feel of his hand sliding up and down my back. "It'll blow over, Nova. Or it won't. I don't give a fuck what anyone says. None of us do. It's going to be okay in the end—you just have to be strong and ignore the toxic shit being spewed by people who don't know us."

I knew he was right. Julieta had said much the same thing, but it wasn't Devan, or River or Rigby being called the most vile things. It wasn't them being torn apart: their looks, their life choices… everything.

. . .

Devan's phone kept buzzing. He'd check it briefly, then go back to cuddling me and Huey. We were watching Disney movies in the media room, ignoring the world. I finally answered my own texts, of which thirty were from Chloe. I felt slightly guilty that I hadn't talked to her in ages, and even though we were closer in distance, we hadn't been talking as much.

I realized belatedly it was because, other than my parents, she'd been the only constant in my life for so long. I'd relied on her so heavily all my life, but now I had the guys, and they were sharing the emotional load of being my friend. Still, her last text said *Getting in the car now. You better answer your door, bitch.* I had to laugh. It was only from ten minutes ago, so I called her back, turning down the volume on the surround sound.

She answered on the second ring. "Are you okay?" she asked immediately, and I felt guilty about how frantic she sounded.

"I'm fine, Chlo. A little in shock, but I'm okay. You don't have to come."

I could tell she was in the car, but when I heard the faint, rhythmic click of her indicator, I knew she was pulling over. There was a moment of silence. "What's going on, Nova? I haven't heard from you in ages, and I let it go because I knew you were settling into parenthood and a new city. But the first I hear of my best friend in a month is on a gossip page on social media? Should I be worried?"

I sighed heavily. She was right. I'd been a shitty

friend. "No, I was happy." I caught myself. "I *am* happy. This is just a weird speedbump." My eyes met Devan's, and he picked up Huey, miming feeding him. I nodded and watched him leave, my heart doing this weird little flip thing. "So fucking happy, Chloe. But sometimes, I'm not sure I'm meant to be happy."

Chloe gave a derisive snort. "Stop that shit right there. You deserve happiness more than anyone else I know. But you're going to have to start at the beginning. Are you actually dating four fucking hockey players?"

I frowned at the reminder that Muss and Julieta were being dragged into this shit. "Only two hockey players. And Devan Mayson. Huey's uncles."

Chloe made a strangled noise. "You're fucking Devan motherfucking Mayson? Billionaire Devan Mayson? *Forbes* 'Thirty under Thirty', bachelor of the year, Devan damn Mayson? And you didn't think to tell me, *your best friend of twenty-three years*?"

I cringed. "It's a new thing."

"Not so fucking new if the world is looking at pictures of you gazing lovingly at each other." She sounded kind of mad, and a fresh wave of guilt hit me.

So I explained everything again, for the second time that morning. Chloe sat quietly and listened, and unlike with Julieta, I spared no details. She gasped when I told her about Rigby going down on me in the kitchen, and River kissing me, and the bitch from ASPN catching us.

When I got to the part with Rigby's proposal of polyamory, she screeched. "Oh my freaking god! I am happy for you right now, but also insanely fucking jealous. They all agreed?" I made a humming affirmative noise. "And now you're being dicked down by three extremely fucking attractive men on the regular? Wait, I'm pulling up Rigby Engman's player profile. I already Googled River Cooper when you told me he contested for Huey's guardianship, so I knew who I had to put a hit on if he made you sad." I chuckled; she would, too. "Oh. My. God. He looks like sunshine, if sunshine was a buff human with a fucking ass sculpted from stone. Girl, if I was there, I'd high five you so hard right now…"

I laughed, because she wasn't wrong. There was just something about Rigby. Sometimes even just seeing him walk into the room made me happy.

"I'm really lucky."

"Bitch, yeah you are. So I want you to get up off the damn couch where I know you're moping and feeling inadequate. I want you to go find the closest one of them fine specimens, and have 'fuck you' sex to all those repressed, sports-loving, inbred incels and jealous hos who think they have the right, the *audacity*, to judge my best friend and her ménage of lovers."

I huffed out another laugh. "It's been too long, Chlo. I've missed you."

"Damn right, you have. I'm coming to visit so you can set me up with… hang on… Number 12. That man is fire."

I made a tsking noise. "The player profiles aren't a catalog for cock," I teased, and she just snorted.

"Whatever. What's the point of having a bestie with insider access if I don't use the opportunity to hit on some players and give them the cardio workout of their career?" We both laughed, until the sound trailed off. "I mean it, Nova. I've missed you. Don't keep me out of the loop so long next time, okay? I've always got your back, always. I love you."

"Love you too."

"Well, strap on your lady balls and stop giving people who don't know you the ability to hurt you. Talk soon, okay?"

I made promises to call her again in a couple of days. After she hung up, I did what she said. I womaned up and went in search of one of the men who made me so fucking happy.

We'd get through this shit. Together.

CHAPTER
Thirty-Five

RIGBY

HARVEY MONDERRA WAS rich as hell. He owned the majority of the IceCaps, and the better part of the west side of Detroit. He didn't take shit, he protected his investments, and right now, he was pissed as hell.

He was scrolling through a file the public relations team had given him on a tablet, and hadn't said a word to us, even though we'd been sitting here for at least fifteen minutes. Even Muss—who didn't even need to be here because he'd done nothing, literally nothing at all—was starting to look a little panicked. He almost looked like he was wondering if he'd sleep-walked his way to Nova's bed and just didn't remember. That was the Harvey Monderra effect.

Finally, Harvey put down the tablet and looked at Caitlyn from PR. "How bad?"

"Memberships are down immediately, and we've had at least six requests for statements—four from the

tabloid departments of nationally syndicated newspapers. It wouldn't have been so bad if we didn't have the
Hefferman scandal less than five years ago."

I winced. That shit was bad. Isaac Hefferman had
gotten picked up by the cops soliciting prostitutes for
blowjobs in the back of his Bugatti. It got rough, and the
guy ended up losing his contract, being forced to retire.

I gulped. Surely, that wasn't what was about to
happen here, right?

River made an angry noise in the back of his throat.
"We aren't fucking hookers in dirty back alleys. I'm—I
mean, *we're* in a committed relationship with Nova. It's
no one's fucking business who we date, and whether
we date three women or one."

River was angry. Like he'd jumped past seeing red
and gone straight to seeing incandescent white. I
bumped his knee with mine, trying to get him to calm
down without giving away he was about to blow his
shit like Vesuvius.

"Muss has nothing to do with this; we were literally
at his house for dinner. All of us. If that doesn't tell you
the level of reporting, then nothing will," I told Caitlyn
from PR, and she shrugged.

"The truth doesn't matter. Just the optics."

Muss leaned forward. "That's fucking bullshit. So
how are we, as players, meant to protect against blatant
fabrication by the media? You want us to become
fucking monks? Recluses except for team-approved
outings?"

Caitlyn gave him a cool look. "It would make my job easier."

Harvey looked at Muss. "I believe you. Go to training." He turned his gaze to us as I went to stand. "Not you."

I gulped again, but tried to keep my face impassive. I reminded myself we weren't doing anything wrong. We weren't breaking any laws, clauses in our contract, nothing. We were in a committed relationship, even if it was unconventional.

Harvey stroked his jaw, looking between us. "The IceCaps have always been the family club. You can bring your six-year-old daughter and know she's going to enjoy a good hockey game without the fighting and the drunk assholes. We've spent a lot of time and money cultivating the image that we are community focused. Toy drives, family events, peewee training and mentorships. Millions of dollars in marketing. And you guys come along and decide to all fuck the one girl like she's group property?"

River was out of his seat with a roar. "You don't fucking talk about her like that. I won't hear *any* fucker talk about her like that. Not you, not the press—*no one*."

I jumped up before he could do something dumb, like hit the owner of the team that literally had us locked down in airtight contracts for the next year. I got in front of him, the big bastard. Fucking enforcers.

"Calm the hell down," I hissed. "The last thing we need is you getting a fucking assault charge and ruining your career forever." I shoved his shoulder until he paced to the other side of the room.

I sat back down, turning my body slightly so I could keep one eye on him. "With all due respect, Mr. Monderra, you don't know shit about our relationship with Nova. And you don't need to know. There's nothing in our contracts that dictates who we can and can't date."

"There is a clause about doing your best to maintain the reputation of the club," Caitlyn countered.

I slid my eyes to her and curled my lip. "That would be relevant if we were out fucking hookers, or puck bunnies, or someone else's wife. But we are all consenting adults, going into a relationship with full transparency, and just because it doesn't look how *you* feel it should, doesn't make it any less valid. If you want to make those kind of dictations, it won't be long until you're the owner of a team of desperate rejects who have nowhere else to go, because anyone with any skill will fuck off to some other team who isn't meddling in their relationships, telling them what to do."

Monderra looked at me, his eyes narrowed. He knew I'd walk if I didn't like what he said next. I might float around as a free agent for a while, but someone would pick me up eventually, scandal be damned.

Finally, he nodded. "Keep your noses clean and out of the papers until after the playoffs, or you're out."

River scoffed. "Good luck winning the Cup without us."

Monderra looked at him, his face a mask. "None of you are irreplaceable—remember that."

I stood, hustling River out the door before he got us both benched for the rest of the season. When I reached the threshold, I looked between Monderra and Caitlyn. "None of us asked for this. Our privacy was invaded. Our lives are under a fucking microscope. We could have gone our whole career without this ever being a problem. Maybe you should ask who wants to see the IceCaps getting screwed over in the court of public opinion, rather than trying to micromanage our relationships."

I shut the door softly behind me and caught up to River, who was striding down the hallway like he'd happily rip the head off the next person who looked at him funny. We made it to the locker room, and luckily, most of the guys were out on the ice at practice. We'd missed most of it anyway, so fuck it, we could just go home.

Everyone with any brains vacated the room when River stormed in, picking up a hamper of dirty towels and throwing the whole thing at the opposite wall. "FUCK!"

I winced as it hit with a crash, and that wince stayed a permanent fixture as Coach Toons appeared in the doorway. He looked concerned, which was never a good sign. "What did the boss say?"

River stomped to his locker, pulling out his gear and stuffing it in his duffel bag. I shook my head and looked back at Toons. "He basically put us on probation."

Toons slid a hand down his face with an exasperated sigh. "Fucking players. Can't keep your dicks out of the limelight."

River turned on the spot and glared. "You got something to say, old man?"

Toons raised an eyebrow. "Watch your fucking mouth, Cooper. I legitimately don't give a fuck who you sleep with. In fact, I wish more of you would date one girl, because then I'd only have to worry about one tell-all story in the fucking tabloids, instead of Ludo's fuck buddies gushing how big his dick is in the damn gossip column every other week. That shit is a nightmare." He looked between us, shaking his head. "If you get benched because of this shit, I'll do what I can. I know it seems unfair, but if you could keep your shit out of the public eye for just a little longer, I'd appreciate it."

I grunted out a noncommittal noise. I wasn't hiding Nova away like she was a fucking dirty little secret. But I wasn't going to push her into the public eye, either.

Toons shook his head. "Go home. Sort shit out. I expect to see you back here tomorrow for the game." He strolled out of the dressing room. "Don't forget to train," he yelled back, and I shook my head.

Packing up my shit, I grabbed my phone. River's was in pieces inside my bag. He'd thrown it at the wall after someone had made a joke and Ludo, who'd been uncharacteristically solemn, had shown him an article. He'd doom-scrolled through his own phone, finding all the articles, and then tossed the expensive piece of hardware at the wall.

Let's just say, the jokes stopped after that.

My phone had dozens of voicemails, including a message from my mom and one from my dad—which must have meant they were worried, because he hated phones—but hundreds of text messages.

When I opened the message thread from Dev, I resisted the urge to do the same thing River had done.

She saw. She's locked herself in her room.

He'd sent the message over two hours ago. Fuck. This was bad. Would she run? Would I blame her if she did?

The answer was that I didn't know. So I herded River out of the rink, out to the car and we hightailed it back to the house. Seeing there were paparazzi around our gate, I resisted the urge to give them the finger. Fuck, didn't they have anything better to do? We weren't big news. We might've been pro athletes, but we were small-time.

Apparently, it must have been a slow news week because they all snapped photos as we drove through the gate. River snarled, his hand on the door handle like he was personally going to go out there and take his frustrations out on every single one of them.

"Stop. You're just giving them what they want." I did skid the tires a little so rocks flew up in their faces and at their precious camera equipment, though. Hazard of being a vulture, right?

I threw the car in park right in front of the door, climbing out quickly and keeping my face averted. They weren't going to get any cheap shots now.

Striding into the living room, it was empty, though the television was on. I quickly turned it off before something we didn't want to see came on and then we'd be stuck with another broken piece of tech when River inevitably put his fist through it.

A small noise from the kitchen had me sprinting toward the room, but when we rounded the corner, it was Devan. He looked rough. Huey was cradled to his chest, a bottle between his lips even as his eyes fluttered with sleep.

"Where is she?"

"Upstairs in the media room. She's on the phone with her friend Chloe." He put the baby over his shoulder, burping him gently. River turned, heading up the stairs before I could stop him. Dev and I watched him go, and I had a bad feeling in my gut.

"How's she taking it?"

Devan shook his head, his lips pressed tight and his jaw tense like he didn't want to be the bearer of bad news. Dread settled on my chest, and I resisted the urge to chase after River, to kiss Nova and hold her in my arms until she knew all this bullshit was just that. Shit. We were what mattered, not the opinions of the rest of the world.

"The lawyers?"

Devan let out a long, defeated sigh. "Nothing they can do. They sent cease and desist letters on our behalf, on her behalf—hell, I even did it on Muss's behalf. They're refusing to print a retraction. I'll sue the bastards until they're bankrupt for defamation of character if I have to. Someone is gonna pay for this, Rigby."

Huey was asleep over Devan's shoulder, and I reached up, taking him and settling him in my arms. I looked down at the sleeping baby, so blissfully unaware of the turmoil of his guardians.

I'd read every single one of those articles. Dissected every word like they would give me a hint as to who wrote them. But the only thing I got was the certain feeling that shit was going to get way worse before it got better. If it got better at all.

Holding Huey, I wondered if our time with him, and with Nova, wasn't running out.

CHAPTER
Thirty-Six
RIVER

I'D WALKED up to Nova, scooped her up and taken her to my bed for the rest of the day. I held her to my chest for hours, neither of us saying much. I kissed her, trying to convey the swirling emotions that were happening in my head and in my chest. I couldn't even face the idea of losing her over something as dumb as this. She seemed better than I thought, but there was a distance between us that hadn't been there when I'd climbed out of bed this morning.

We could get past this. There would be no other option.

We lost ourselves in mindless television, and eventually moved back downstairs for lunch. We all sat around, talking about anything but the obvious elephant in the room. The neighbors messaged to say that the photographers had swelled around the middle of the afternoon, but were starting to slowly dissipate when they realized we weren't going to leave the house and that no one was going to have an epic public meltdown. We were one-day news, there and gone, so it was hardly worth camping in front of our gates.

We went to bed that night, pretending the day hadn't happened. But if my childhood had taught me anything, it was that pretending only helped for so long. The bad shit still happened, even if you hid under your blankets and plugged your ears.

But sometime overnight, Nova's identity was discovered. And with that, someone who knew her father, who knew the whole story about Huey and Alana, decided to profit off her pain. If I ever found out who this "source close to Ms. Stone" was, I was going to tear them limb from limb.

All the progress we'd made yesterday disappeared as soon as the phones started ringing again, until I locked them all in a drawer and refused to answer them. Close-ups of Huey appeared, zoomed from photos of Nova and us, next to headlines of "Like Father, Like Daughter?" and "Heart of Stone."

I wanted to smash shit. I couldn't hide with her in my arms today, either. It was a fucking game day. PR had told us to leave Nova at home because they didn't want that bullshit in the stadium, and while I agreed, I hated that she might feel like a dirty little secret.

My agent was blowing up my phone, and Rigby's, but I was ignoring it. I wasn't interested in whatever bullshit he had to say.

Julieta appeared after school drop-off, completely unannounced. She was already at the gate before we even knew she'd arrived. Muss's youngest daughter flipped off the reporters outside the gates as they drove in, and honestly, I was gonna buy that kid a pony for her birthday. She might only be four, but she had Julieta's attitude.

Julieta unloaded an entire cooler of shit that looked like an epic girls' night in, and sent us all off with promises that she'd look after Nova and Huey until Devan got back after work this afternoon. Not that Nova needed someone to care for her; she was so fucking tough. But I could see the damage the words on the screen were doing to her. She was curling in on herself protectively as her family's reputation was dragged through the mud on national television.

I was skating around the rink, doing some last-minute drills. Muss slid up beside me, his face a mask of concern. "You haven't been texting back. We were worried about you."

I raised an eyebrow at him. "Julieta said as much when she turned up."

Muss snorted a laugh. "I would have warned you that there was no stopping Hurricane Julieta, if you'd answered your phone. We've got your back, man. You know that. With the team, with the media—whatever you need."

"You're a good man, Clint," I said roughly. Honestly, for so long, the only people I could rely on were Dev and Rigby. We always took care of Alana, not the other way around. But Clint gave his support over and over again, without ever expecting anything in return.

He slapped my shoulder hard. "So are you, Cooper. Don't let this shit get to you." With that, we skated off the ice and in to see the trainers.

The crowd at tonight's game were wild. Corporate could say what it wanted, but the stories hadn't done anything to the crowd numbers. In fact, there were more women in the crowd than ever, some holding signs that said things like "Are you looking for a fifth?" and "I want to visit the Eiffel Tower" which Ludo explained meant they wanted to be spit-roasted while the guys gave each other a high five.

Fuck me. Ludo was enjoying it, though. That kid was a fucking peacock, and was busy skating the boards and flirting with girls in oversized jerseys. I just shook my head. Somehow public relations would make that my fault too. Like there hadn't been horny puck bunnies in this sport for decades.

As I skated out, there were hoots and cat-calls from the supporters of the other team, and I ignored them. I'd channel this shit into the game, and then they could suck my dick when I trounced their shitty fucking team into the ice.

The puck was dropped, and I fell back to my line. The game was fast and furious, and I could see the

Penguins defense fucking with Rigby, but he skated around them easily. He was fucking glorious on the ice. He'd always been a natural, like he'd been born with a stick in his hand and skates on his feet.

The guy had him on the boards, and whatever he was saying had Rigby throwing off his gloves and throwing hands. I skated up to them as another player swooped in as well.

"I'm going to fuck your little whore too, Engman. Think she likes all player cock or is she only into you pussies?" the guy taunted near his ear, and I saw red. I barreled into him, his helmet flying off and my fists pounding into the mouthy fuck's face until the referees were in there, trying to drag me off.

Muss was beside me soon enough, fucking up some other player, until everyone on the ice was getting into it. The referees wisely got the fuck out of the way, and even Perrier came up and was laying into the Penguins goalie.

Toons was trying to keep the rest of the team on the bench, and I hoped they stayed. I was probably already fucked, but it was a ten-game match penalty if you left the bench to join in. The crowd were screaming like monkeys at the zoo, and I was throwing punches as someone else laid a hit into my temple, making the room spin.

"You fucking pussy piece of shit," someone grunted at me, but I couldn't see who it was from the blood running down my eyebrow and into my eye.

Finally, the referees dragged away the guy on top of me, and I grimaced with satisfaction that he was bleeding just as much as me. Muss grabbed Rigby from the refs, shoving him toward the bench, where the trainer was waiting to patch us up.

I noted Ludo had a bruise blooming on his cheek as well. I lifted my chin at him, and he grinned. "Can't let you guys have all the fun."

Except he said it just a little too loudly.

"Fun?" Toons said softly, ominously. "Fun... He thinks this is fucking fun? Get your ass in here, Ludo, before I beat the shit out of you myself."

The referees slid over to the bench and unsurprisingly put both me and Rigby in the box. I'd been slightly worried that it was going to end in a match ban, but fuck them. No one talked about Nova like that. *No one.*

The game continued, but we were all out for blood now. It was hard and dirty on both sides. Third period came around, and the original defenseman was on Rigby's line again. Fucking asshole. He was getting in Rigby's face, saying shit that the refs couldn't hear. Finally, whatever he was saying got too much for Rigby, and he spun, lifting his stick high and nailing the fucker in the face when he went for the puck.

It could have been an accident, even when they replayed the tapes. They'd both been skating fast, Rigby had turned hard and got the other guy in the face just below his fucking helmet. Straight in the teeth. His mouthguard went flying, and there was blood on his chin.

It could have been an accident—if it wasn't Rigby, who had better stick control than any person I'd ever met.

Ref called a game misconduct penalty, and Rigby got sent off. Muss argued with the ref that it was a minor penalty, just an accident, but he wasn't hearing it. One of the rookie IceCap players got subbed in and game-play resumed, but out of the corner of my eye, I watched Rigby head toward the locker room.

The player he checked was now missing a tooth and on the bench, but it didn't stop him smirking at me. *That fucker better hope I don't catch him in the parking lot, because he's going to be missing a lot more teeth.*

In the end, we scraped by with a win in the last five minutes, and the crowd was still going nuts. It was more like a blood sport than a hockey game, and with one look at Toons's face, I knew we were in deep shit. I was going to be chewed out by him and Monderra and probably the media.

Let them. Some things were worth fighting for, and Nova was one of them.

All press requests for Rigby or I were denied, and we were sent home in disgrace. Toons said that Monderra wanted to see us the following day, and that was without the possibility of NHL sanctions.

We got home to find it silent. Dev was on the couch,

still in his suit pants and dress shirt, a scotch in his hand. He looked us over, and I knew we looked rough.

"Did she see?" Rigby asked roughly. Dev nodded, and my normally happy friend made a wounded noise. "I'm going to bed."

We both watched him go. My heart hurting, I went to the wet bar in the corner, unlocking the cabinet and pouring myself a drink. Slumping down beside Dev, I let my shoulders curl inward as I buried my head in my hands. "This is bad."

Dev hummed his agreement. There were no two ways about it. It was bad for our relationship. Bad for our career. It was just… bad.

The clock had hit zero, and now we were playing on borrowed time.

CHAPTER

Thirty-Seven

NOVA

I'D ALREADY HAD the worst day of my life. Nothing would touch that moment. But this week was shaping up to be a real contender for the worst week of my life. Almost all my clients had ditched me when they'd made the connection between me and the girl they saw on the news. Except for the romance authors—I think they just saw me as inspiration. I'd take it, as long as it meant they stuck around.

The guys were at home, because the team had given them a three-match ban. Sidelining them for three games at the beginning of the season sent a serious message to them, and to their teammates, as well as to the NHL. They were taking this misconduct seriously. I overheard River saying he was worried that they'd pull their contracts at the end of the season, throwing them back into free agency.

I'd done that. I'd been greedy, and this was the

result. Sure, I hadn't thrown a punch, but it was my honor that they'd been defending, like there was any place for that bullshit in modern society. I was the reason their contracts were in peril, all because I couldn't keep my legs closed.

Magazines and newspaper outlets were hounding me for soundbites and interviews, like I could add anything to the sordid story they'd concocted about me, about my family. Devan kept promising that this would all blow over, but somehow it had gone viral, our unconventional romance, and it felt like it was never going to go away. I needed to get out of this before I was in too deep.

You're already in too deep, that little voice in my head taunted. But I wasn't. I wasn't in love with them. I could get out now with my heart reasonably intact.

That little voice gave a derisive snort at my delusional thoughts, but I refused to listen. Which was why, as the guys were at Rigby's Player Safety hearing, I packed a bag. One for me. One for Huey.

River had said he'd probably get a four-match ban without pay for unsportsmanlike conduct, and another fine for high-sticking. That was thousands of dollars, and I knew it looked bad on his record. Hockey might be brutal, and fighting might not be as frowned on as it was in other sports, but they weren't going to turn a blind eye. This thing we had was killing his dream, but he was too stubborn to quit. I'd be responsible for us all.

I tried not to cry as I loaded our bags into the back of

the car that Devan had given me. I'd have to give it back eventually; it didn't feel right taking things from them when I couldn't give them what they actually wanted. Or maybe they'd be relieved that I was gone. They could go back to their carefree lives.

I wouldn't keep them from Huey. We could share custody of him, because he might be a baby but he loved those men. He'd lost enough people in his short life.

I was going to stay at Julieta's for a couple of nights until I found somewhere for me and Huey to stay, or if I couldn't find a place to rent, I'd go and stay with Chloe. I could go home, back to Tucson, but the idea of leaving was a physical ache in my soul. Hurrying to click Huey into his car seat, I left the place I'd considered a home as fast as I could. Pulling dark glasses over my eyes, I peeled out of the driveway and away from the photographers that I knew were still there, lurking in the bushes.

As tears streamed down my face, I told myself this was for the best. A small hurt now to prevent a bigger hurt later. This was for the best for all of us. There was no way what we were trying to create would have worked. There were too many outside pressures. The very idea was foolish and utopian. It could never work in the real world.

I repeated that thought process until I drove up to Julieta's house, stepping out of my car and into the tiny woman's strong arms.

And then I cried.

I'd left them a note, but it hadn't helped. They blew up my phone until I turned it off. I'd asked Clint about Rigby, and he said the NHL had given him a three-match ban without pay, which was apparently pretty expensive.

I felt fucking awful. I knew it wasn't my fault, because Rigby was a grown man who made his own decisions, but he was also fiercely loyal. If I hadn't reacted so damn bad, we could have laughed this shit off and gotten over it. But no, I had to be all sensitive.

On the third day of me being gone, during which I searched for real estate in Ann Arbor with growing despair, River appeared on Julieta and Clint's doorstep. I hid in the kitchen like a fucking chickenshit.

"You've got to let me see her, Muss."

I felt bad for Clint and Julieta. I needed to get out of their hair before I permanently ruined their friendship with the guys.

Julieta's soft voice was saying something that I couldn't quite pick up. Clint's was easier to hear. "She doesn't want to see you, man, and I'm not going to make her. Give her time. You can't force this."

I turned and fled from the kitchen, back up to the room I was sharing with Huey. The Vanmussens had been amazing, but I'd moped around enough. I had to sack up and get my life on track. I had a baby now. I couldn't drag my feet around, feeling sorry for myself. I either committed to my decisions or I went back.

The problem was, my heart desperately wanted to be back there. Because if I'd learned anything over the last day or so, it was that my head might tell me it was too soon for the L word, but my heart had other ideas.

Pulling out my phone, I ignored all the messages from Rigby, because I knew my resolve wasn't strong enough to hear his pleas and not fold like a paper swan. I opened up a new message to Devan.

Me: I'll drop Huey around tomorrow. You guys can keep him for a few hours, or I can pick him up in the evening. Let me know.

It was read almost immediately. Then there was nothing. No reply. No little dots to tell me he was thinking about replying. Nothing.

I messaged a real estate agent, who promised to meet me at a crappy little apartment on the other side of town tomorrow at eleven. It was only one bedroom, but it was within my means and it would do as a start. Huey and I didn't need a lot of space just yet. We could look at something bigger later.

Finally, an hour after I messaged Devan, his reply dinged through my phone. I opened my phone quickly, my heart in my throat.

.   .   .

Devan: 9. We'll have him all day.

That was it. And I knew then, that it was over, at least with Dev. Everything we'd had was done, and I knew I should be glad about that. It was what I'd wanted.

But why did my heart feel like it was being smashed to smithereens?

I went to bed early, being polite to Julieta and Clint, who watched me with worried eyes. They told me again that I was welcome as long as I wanted, Clint joking that Huey was curing Julieta of her baby fever without them actually having to have another baby.

I laughed along with them, but the sound was brittle. Feigning tiredness, I went to bed, where I tossed and turned for hours before the sun peeked above the horizon again.

Like the traitor my body was, I went to sleep then, not waking until my alarm went off at eight. Huey was awake, swaddled in his cot, and he smiled up at me. I chewed on my lip as I smiled back at my baby.

"We're going to see your uncles today. Do you miss them?" I asked, as I undressed him and changed his diaper. "I miss them, so fucking much. But this is for the best, kiddo. And you deserve the best, not having to be that kid that has three dads and whose mom is considered the Whore of Ann Arbor."

Someone knocked on the door, and I turned to see Clint standing there with Huey's bottle. "Heard you moving around up here and thought Slugger might need his breakfast." Lifting Huey into my arms, I took the bottle from Clint, testing it on my wrist.

"Thanks," I said with a smile that felt too forced to be real. "I'm going to check out an apartment today at eleven."

Clint didn't sigh, but I could almost feel his exasperation. "You're welcome here forever if you want, Nova. The kids love you. Julieta appreciates the company. You don't need to rush into anything irreversible." I made a noncommittal noise, and this time, he did sigh. "All right, but I'm coming with you to make sure some sleazy real estate dude-bro doesn't rip you off. It'll give me an excuse not to go to church with Julieta and her family. Her great-aunt thinks I don't know she still calls me 'The White Philanderer' after all these years. Julieta thinks it's hilarious."

I snorted a laugh. "I'd like that. Thank you."

I helped Julieta get the kids ready for church, braiding their youngest daughter's hair while Julieta chased the boys around yelling, "Where are your good shoes?" and swearing underneath her breath in Spanish.

Finally, Julieta cursed Clint once more under her breath, climbing into her SUV, and Clint hopped into the passenger seat of mine. We drove Huey over to the guys' place, and with every mile closer we got, the more my heart pounded in my chest until I was a total mess.

I could tell Clint wanted to say something, but he kept his mouth resolutely closed. I pressed the gate opener still attached to my dash, then pulled into the driveway. I looked over at Clint, hoping I looked more together than I felt right now.

Climbing out, I grabbed Huey out of the car seat. Devan appeared in the doorway, his face an impenetrable mask of neutrality. Walking toward him was like walking to the gallows, and I couldn't even look him in the eye.

Handing him Huey, I stared at his chest. "I'll be back around four to pick him up."

"Why are you with Vanmussen?" Devan's cool voice had me looking up at him. Did he think there was truth to the rumors I was sleeping with the guys' team captain?

"He's coming to look at an apartment with me. Throw some credibility behind my application."

Devan made a noise in his throat, and my eyes flashed to his. We were caught in a weird stare-off until he swallowed hard, spinning around and walking back into the house. In the doorway behind him was Rigby, his face dragged down with sadness.

Devan shook his head at his friend. "Leave it. She made her choice."

Rigby took a step forward. "Nova," he called softly, like his heart was fucking breaking.

Just like mine was. "I'm sorry."

I hightailed it off the front porch and back into the car, speeding out of the driveway and down the road several blocks before pulling off onto the shoulder. Then I broke down in huge, wracking sobs.

"I'm… sorry…" I said in disjointed hiccups to Clint, who rubbed my back soothingly.

"Fuck, it's okay, Nova. Come sit on the passenger side. I need a fucking beer, and its only 9 a.m. Lucky I know just the bar for day drinking."

And that was how we both ended up catching an Uber to the open house at eleven, half-drunk on mimosas—hold the orange juice, please—and signing the contract to my very first apartment less than an hour later. Turns out the agent was an IceCaps fan and willing to skip formalities for season tickets in the VIP seats.

Julieta chewed us both out like we were naughty teenagers when she picked us up from the real estate office after lunch, which just made me laugh. Somehow, my laughter just made her look more worried, but she told me she was happy I'd found a place, though she'd miss me.

It was one more step on the path to independence, and I hated every minute of it.

CHAPTER
Thirty-Eight
DEVAN

IT HAD BEEN two weeks since Nova left. Muss had been feeding us insider knowledge up until three days ago when Nova and Huey moved into their own apartment. He hadn't told us her address, but thankfully Nova had. She'd trusted us with the knowledge, believing we would respect her wishes and not turn up on her doorstep at 10 p.m., begging her to come back. I was pretty sure she had too much faith in us.

Or at least in Rigby, who I'd caught every night for the last three days, standing in the foyer, staring at the door with his car keys in his hand. But eventually, he'd put them back down and retreated back to his room. He'd barely been out of it since Nova left. He trained. He slept. He ate what he was contractually obligated to eat. That was it.

He was hardly speaking to us unless Huey was here. He was pining, and it was truly a pathetic look on a man who was twenty-five and had once gotten more pussy than the other two of us combined.

I'd have told him that, if I wasn't pining for her to come back too. But I'd never say so. I was used to rejection; this shut-down feeling was almost my default now. Instead, I threw myself into work. Twelve, sometimes fourteen-hour days, so I didn't have to return home and hear the deathly silence that had fallen over the place. I didn't realize how much noise one woman and a baby made until it was gone.

The silence created an echo chamber for the thoughts in my head and the pain in my chest. The one that screamed we hadn't been worth it. Worth the fight. Worth standing together against everyone else.

Someone knocked on my door, and I swallowed the internal groan as Elise stepped through. I didn't have the mental fortitude to deal with this shit right now.

"I'm just heading home, Mr. Mayson."

"See you tomorrow," I grunted out, willing her to turn and leave.

"If I may say so, sir…" She purred the word *sir*, like it would do anything for me. It didn't. "You seem really tense."

I just stared at her, willing her to leave. But apparently, she took my silence as encouragement. She put her hands on her blouse and started unbuttoning down along the front.

I flicked the switch on my computer that set the security cameras to record. Everyone signed a contract when they first started to say that they gave permission to be recorded by security cameras. Kept things honest and safe, and protected me for situations like this. I wasn't a fool.

"You need to go home, Miss Quigmire."

Her fingers didn't stop unbuttoning though, and she was wearing some kind of lingerie beneath. She'd definitely planned this. "I think we could both relieve some stress, some of this tension between us," she cooed, slipping her blouse off. She was definitely attractive—I wasn't blind—but she was an employee, and I had no interest in *any* woman right now. Well, any woman except the one who'd been very clear she didn't want me.

"You need to leave, or I'll be forced to fire you. Fraternization is frowned upon." I leaned back in my chair, staring at the ceiling.

"Consider this my two weeks' notice then," she said saucily, clearly thinking I was just playing hard to get.

Fuck.

I stood up. "Resignation accepted—don't worry about the two weeks' notice. Clear out your desk as you leave."

"What?" she gasped.

I picked up my phone and called the security extension. "Jeff, can you come up to the fourth floor and escort out a former employee? Thanks."

Elise was still standing there, gaping at me.

"I don't know how to make this any fucking clearer.

I don't want you and your fucking desperate attempts to... what? Get on my dick? Do you think your vagina will be so fucking magical that I'll wife you up?" She was beautiful. She'd probably wielded that beauty like a weapon her whole life. "Leave."

Her face flushed. "Fuck you, Devan Mayson."

"Not in your wildest damn dreams," I growled.

"I'm going to sue the shit out of you for wrongful dismissal. I'm going to tell everyone you seduced me and then fired me. Who wouldn't believe me now, you fucking pervert? Is that why you don't want me? Can't get it up without your buddies watching?"

My face remained motionless, not giving her any of the reaction she so desperately wanted. "Go ahead. This room has a security camera. You signed an NDA. I'll ensure you have to move countries to work in finance again." I gave her a cruel smirk. "At this point, destroying a conniving cunt like you might actually get me hard. Well done. Now get the fuck out of my building."

She turned and strode out of my office, screeching threats, and I slumped back in my chair. Fuck, when did this get so tedious?

Jeff appeared, and didn't even say a word. He tilted his head toward Elise, who sounded like she was trashing the place. I wouldn't have put it past Jeff to have been watching the whole thing on the security feed.

Standing, I quickly sent a copy of the footage to my

lawyers for safekeeping, and then headed to the elevator. I wanted out of here.

A call came through my car stereo speakers on the way home. The private investigator I'd put on the task of finding who the fuck wrote those articles and who was basically stalking us for a story. I'd also put her on watching Nova, to make sure she was okay. Safe.

"What have you found?" I said without niceties. I wasn't paying her for niceties.

"Well, good evening to you too, Mr. Mayson," Daria sniped back. Her voice was sickly saccharine, but I had no doubt Daria would cut off my balls rather than try to seduce me. She was from the old days, before we were billionaires and professional sports people. Before Rigby.

River and I had met her at a bar, when I was trying to pick up the same girl as her. Fair to say, the girl rejected us both, but she'd become a useful contact over the years. She had a nice boyfriend now, but she still argued she could fuck my girlfriends if she wanted.

Luckily, I'd never had girlfriends to test the theory until now.

"Sorry, Daria. It's been a trying day."

She snorted. "Whatever. Like I care if you're a snippy asshole. Just letting you know your girl is fine. She took the baby on a stroll around the block. She looks like shit, but the baby seems happy and healthy." If Daria had an opinion about the fact that I was basically getting her to stalk my ex-girlfriend, she kept it to herself. "On to more important topics. I might have something on your little problem from the other week. Unless you want to let sleeping dogs lie, now that the buzz around your little ménage—quadage?—has calmed down."

I sucked in a breath. "Tell me."

"I had a little peek through the windows of your girl Esperanza's windows, and the bitch is lowkey obsessed with River Cooper. Like, there's an entire wall of press pictures and team photographs. I'm pretty sure I even saw a used condom in there, man. Full Fatal Attraction style."

All the air left my lungs. "Did you get pictures?"

Daria snorted a derisive sound, "Are you doubting my skills, Mayson?"

Fuck, finally some good news. "Do you think she leaked the photos and shit to the other journalists?"

There was silence down the end of the line, some shuffling noises. "Yeah, I think that's a fair call. I was able to get in with one of the copy editors of the Tribune at a bar, and he told me that one of the junior interns presented the story, and they ran it. It took me three whiskey-doubles and his pawing hands to get that info, Mayson, so you bet your ass I'm charging this shit to your account."

"You're worth every penny, Daria. Every fucking dollar. Chase down the leads. I need to pin this on Esperanza with all the evidence I can. Half the female fans of the IceCaps have pictures of River on their walls.

I need something concrete so I can prove harassment and get her thrown out of the sports world, at the least. Out of journalism altogether, if I can."

Daria was scrawling notes; I could hear the pencil sliding across the page. "I'm on it." She paused slightly. "What are you going to do about Nova Stone?"

I swallowed the lump in my throat. "She made her choice, Daria. I'm going to respect it."

I expected Daria to make some smartass comment, but she just sighed heavily. "I think you're making a mistake, Devan. Now isn't the time to play the martyr. Now is the time to play the White Knight. She looks fucking miserable, and honestly, I'm going to go home and ask Xander if we can adopt her or something, because this shit is heartbreaking." She made a frustrated sound in the back of her throat. "I know you're technically my boss, but as a friend, I'm telling you now —fight for her, you chickenshit, or you guys will regret it for the rest of your life. She loves you. It's written all over her fucking heartbroken face. Do something."

Then she hung up in my ear, but her words spun around and around in my head for the rest of the night. Even after I repeatedly tell myself I was doing the right thing.

Was I respecting her wishes? Or was I just protecting myself, like the chickenshit Daria said I was?

CHAPTER
Thirty-Nine
NOVA

I RAN the receipt numbers through my online accounting system for one of my long-time clients, while Huey grizzled beside me. "Two more minutes, baby boy, and then we'll have some dinner."

I turned on the mobile that spun around the top of his rocker, which kept him momentarily mesmerized.

My phone pinged again, my cash-sharing app telling me that River had put in another two thousand dollars for Huey's upkeep. I opened the app and sent the money back. I could look after Huey. And I had no idea what he thought Huey needed that required two grand in a day! I sent him a picture of Huey mesmerized by the bees on his mobile as proof of life.

I worked for another ten minutes, until Huey started grumbling again, and then it was time to stop. Picking him up, I walked into the small kitchen and grabbed his bottle from the fridge, setting it into the bottle warmer. Grabbing a frozen meal from the freezer for me, I shoved it into the microwave and bounced Huey on my shoulder.

He was grumpy today, and I had a feeling he was just picking up my mood. Or maybe he was teething? His gums seemed slightly red, and he was protesting a bit, gnawing on his pacifier. I'd take him to the drugstore tomorrow and see what the pharmacist said.

As if to cement my decision, he started to wail a little. "Hey, hey, I'm sorry, sweetheart. Just a few more minutes, okay? And tomorrow, I'll get you a nice cool teething ring. You can gnaw on it like a tiny piranha until you feel better, would that be okay?" I bounced him more, rocking side to side, hoping to settle him.

His bottle was finally warm, and I was just lifting it to his lips when someone knocked at the door. Fuck, the walls in this place were paper thin; it was probably the neighbors complaining.

I figured it was karma, considering they had loud sex all fucking night. I'd actually swapped my room and the living room, because we shared a wall and it had been keeping Huey—and me—up all night.

But when I opened the door, it wasn't the neighbor. It was a middle-aged woman, with soft, graying-blonde hair and crow's feet around her eyes. She was a fraction taller than me and had extremely blue eyes.

"Hi? Can I help you?" I shifted Huey slightly back

further into the house, just in case this lady was a wack-adoodle. She looked nice, and my gut said she was safe, but you could never be totally sure.

"You must be Nova. And this must be Huey." She looked adoringly at the baby in my arms. "I'm Lorraine Engman, Rigby's mother."

My mouth fell open. Now she'd said it, I could see the similarities in their faces, though obviously Rigby was a broader, more masculine version of the woman in my doorway. "Oh, hi."

Fuck, what the hell did I say to this woman? *Hi, nice to meet you. Sorry I dragged your son's career down the toilet and then broke his heart?*

Probably not.

"Sorry to drop in unannounced like this. I just wanted to meet you."

I shook my head, chasing away the shock. My mother would've been appalled by my lack of manners. "I'm sorry—please come inside. I was just feeding Huey."

The woman gave me a bright smile, so like her son's. "Thank you."

Even though it had been worth it for some sleep, the problem with swapping the bedroom and the living room was that the main area now opened onto my bedroom. Lorraine's eyes traveled over the room quickly before averting her gaze. At least I always kept it tidy.

I directed her into the living room, with the couch and television, light pouring through the big windows that had attracted me to this poky little apartment in the first place. "Can I get you something to drink?"

Lorraine shook her head. "No, sit. It's fine. Finish feeding your son. Brother? Rigby was a bit hazy on how you were choosing to raise him, as a sibling or like your child until he was older."

Man, that was a good question, but not one I wanted to discuss with a complete stranger, despite the fact she was giving me warm fuzzy feelings—so like her own son.

I sat down, shaking my head softly as Huey drank deeply, unaware of my turmoil. "Did Rigby send you? Because I'm—"

Lorraine held up a hand, cutting me off. "Gosh no. If Rigby knew I was here, he'd give me an hour-long lecture like he was the parent and I was the child. No, he's off his suspension for tonight's game, so my husband and I came down to give the boys some extra support. Well, my husband did, anyway. I still haven't quite gotten used to watching the physicality of hockey, even after fifteen years. He's still my baby, and you never get over that protective urge to go mama bear on anyone who hurts them, professional sportsman or not."

Yeah, I could understand that.

"Devan gave me your address. I just wanted to check on you, I guess. Rigby spoke a lot about you, and

I know my boy. When he said you'd broken up…" She sighed. "Tell me if I'm overstepping. I know what happened to your mama, and if our roles were reversed, I'd want to know that someone was checking in on my boy if his heart was hurting, and making sure he was okay."

Gah. Tears sprang to my eyes. "I can see where Rigby gets his empathy from."

Lorraine waved a hand. "He might have his father's size, but he got my heart. His father has the emotional intelligence of a cactus, but he was never shy about showing his love to our boys and me. Rigby's brothers are the same. Just can't say the words, not like Rigby. It's probably because he's the baby."

"Did he tell you about…" I couldn't work out how to ask this woman if Rigby told her about his polyamory proposal.

She grinned. "About the unconventional relationship you found yourselves in? Of course. That boy can't keep a secret from me. He's an open book, always has been. I used to worry that some girl would come along and take advantage of that. Destroy the sweetness in him. I was glad when he found River, and then Devan —they temper his openness. They wouldn't let him get hurt, and he trusts them. They trust him too, I think. They make quite a good team, so I wasn't too surprised when he told me that the three of them were dating the one woman. You." She shook her head. "Nasty business with the press, though."

I nodded slowly. There was nothing more to say about that. Huey finished his bottle, and I placed him over my shoulder, burping him softly until he fell asleep. Lorraine seemed content to just watch me as I put him down in the crib I'd borrowed from the Vanmussens and moved back into the room.

"So are you?" Lorraine asked softly.

"Am I what?"

"Okay?"

I bit my bottom lip and shook my head. Then I burst into tears. Lorraine bundled me into her arms and held me as I gave up on holding myself together. I let myself feel every ounce of hurt and pain, let myself grieve for my own parents who I couldn't turn to anymore when things got tough. I hadn't really grieved them yet, not properly. At first, I'd been numb. And then I had Huey. And I couldn't let myself feel sadness for my father— the man who'd loved me unconditionally for as long as I could remember—when I was in deep with the men who hated him.

So I cried on the shoulder of this stranger, letting her comfort wash over me. She held me and told me that eventually, everything would feel right in the world again. That I would be the most brilliant mother, and I'd have a wonderful partner who would make sure I was never alone. She said all the things you'd want a mother to say, and not once did she mention any future with Rigby. She didn't put any pressure on me, the woman who'd broken her son's heart, to get back together with him.

Instead, she told me that only I knew what was best for me. Rocking me softly, she let me sob my little heart out until her shoulder was soaked with my tears. "Did you love them, sweet girl?"

I nodded. I wouldn't hurt like this if I hadn't loved them. It was ridiculous, and problematic, but my heart didn't care. "I refuse to make them choose between the careers they love and me."

Lorraine pulled back a little, wiping the tears from my cheeks. "But would you make them choose? Would you go back with the ultimatum that they *had* to choose between you and hockey?"

I frowned. "Of course not."

"Then you aren't the one making their life difficult, Nova Stone. You aren't the one making them choose between love and their careers. That's on Monderra and the NHL. That's on those shitty human beings who masquerade as reporters. You just have to decide if loving them is worth the scrutiny and the ill feelings you'll inevitably get from the world. You have to decide if you're strong enough to stand beside them and tell the world to go to Hell if they don't like it. You don't have to sacrifice your happiness for theirs, because in the end, no one is happy at all."

She stood, kissing the top of my head. "Whatever you choose, whether you're with my son or not, you're always welcome with me and Larry. Come and visit with Huey. We mothers have to stick together." I gave her another watery smile. "And just know, if you do decide that being with them is worth the hardships and the hurdles, we'll stand right behind you, supporting the four of you."

She squeezed my shoulder and left, leaving me reeling and confused all over again.

CHAPTER

Forty

RIGBY

THE FIRST GAME BACK, I played like I had something to prove. But now, we were playing five away games in a row and I was just fucking tired. I went out with the guys after our third win in a row, and drank one beer while River got hammered. He'd been doing that a lot recently. Getting wasted after every game, until I had to drag his ass back to the hotel. He'd almost gotten in a fight in Chicago at some dive bar when someone had a go about Nova. He was volatile, and honestly, I was worried about him.

As Ludo and I struggled under his weight, getting him into the elevator back up to our rooms after the game with San Jose, I knew this shit had to stop.

Ludo grunted as River tipped to the side. "Fuck, this guy is heavy. How the hell does he push himself around the ice without a pack of goddamn sled dogs?"

I huffed a laugh. "Quads of steel?" Fishing our room

key out of my pocket, I opened the door, thankful that we were only three rooms down from the elevator.

Ludo was still grumbling under his breath. "Needs to lay off the fucking protein."

We shuffled River inside and let him fall face first onto the bed. Better this way if he puked in his sleep. Ludo and I stared down at him, this man who'd seemed so in control, so stoic for all the years I'd known him, but was now crumbling like an ancient fortress in front of my eyes.

Shaking his head, Ludo turned to stare at me. "I'm worried about him. So is Muss."

I nodded, because Muss had told me. So had Coach Toons. Like I had any control over the big fucker and his locked-down feelings.

"Me too."

Ludo cocked his head at me. "Just so you know, the team is behind you. Me and Muss, we'll go to bat for you if the team is the only reason you're… you know, not pursuing things with your girl. They shouldn't get that kind of say in our personal lives."

I really looked at Ludo, the fun-loving manwhore I'd consider a friend. "I appreciate it, man. But it's not that easy. They aren't obligated to keep us, any more than they're obligated to keep you. The only person who they wouldn't break a contract with is Muss, and that's only because there'd be a fucking riot among the fans."

Shaking his head, Ludo huffed. "It *is* that easy. You love her, right?"

"Yeah, of course."

"And I'm going to assume that the big guy down there snoring like a freight train loves her too?"

I looked down at the mess of a man, who was once my mostly emotionally stable best friend. "Yeah, I think that's safe to say."

Ludo rolled his hands, like he was trying to get me to the point he was making, but I actually had no idea. He huffed. "If you blew out your knee tomorrow, and your career was over, would you be happy with the decision to give her up? In ten years, when you're fucking washed up and feel like you've been hit by a truck every morning when you roll out of bed, will you be happy with your decision then?"

I was shaking my head before he'd even finished. "It wasn't my decision, man—it was hers. I can't make her want to stay."

Ludo threw his hands in the air. "And they say *you're* the emotionally un-stunted one."

"Who says that?"

"Doesn't matter. What I'm trying to say is she gave you up so *you* didn't have to give up your dream. Your shiny, fancy job. She didn't make the decision because she hates your guts and the sight of your shriveled dick makes her want to gag. From everything you said, she left so you didn't have to stop playing hockey. So you didn't spiral down a one-way trip to fucking indefinite suspension." He frowned at me like a disappointed parent, and that would have been hilarious from my younger teammate if his words weren't like a punch in the chest. "That tells me she is a good woman. It tells me she loves you. So how about you pull your fists from your asses, and go and tell her that she's worth growing the balls you need to ignore the bullshit sledging from other teams. She's worth playing so good that the team would be crazy to give you up over some fucking bad press." Ludo snarled. "Bad press is one thing, but winning games is more important. You have a losing team, you aren't going to be making any fucking money either."

I stared. "Who the fuck are you and what have you done with Andrei Ludokov?"

Ludo winced. "Don't use my full name, man. Gives me flashbacks to my mom beating me with her shoe every time she caught me climbing back in my bedroom window in the mornings." He grinned. "I dunno, man. I love women. And I love a good love story almost as much as I love fucking. Almost." His grin was one I was more than familiar with. Ludo headed for the door, still shaking his head. "Tell the big guy he owes me one. These Chi-Town girls are fucking wild, and I was well on my way to a threesome when we had to pull his ass out of the bar."

He swaggered out, and just before he disappeared, I called out for him. "Ludo?"

He leaned back in the room. "What?"

"You're a fucking good friend. I love you, man, even if you are a manwhore."

My teammate laughed and flipped me the finger. "You're saying 'I love you' to the wrong person, fuck-head. Get some damn sleep."

With that, he was gone.

I pulled off River's shoes and sank down onto my bed. Ludo was right—not something I ever thought I'd say. Nova was what I wanted. Now. In ten years. In fifty years. She was it for me.

I climbed into bed and started to come up with a plan to win her back.

We won our final away game, but the mood in the car as we drove back to the house was still somber. River was hungover as hell, so I was driving again.

"Ludo's worried about you," I told him over the sound of the country song on the radio. That's how you knew shit had gotten bad; River had resorted to listening to music about how sad a man's life could be without a good dog and a good woman. In that order.

River just grunted, staring out the window. "Ludo can mind his own business."

I huffed. "Fine, I'm worried about you too. You're hitting the bottle too hard, and it's affecting your game."

"Fuck off, Rigby."

Fuck off? Was this asshole serious? I pulled over onto the shoulder of the freeway, ignoring the blast of a car horn behind me. "Listen to me, River fucking

Cooper. I love you. I love you more than the idea of winning the Stanley Cup. I love you more than hockey, full stop. You're my brother. My best friend. And when I see you spiraling into an addiction like you're trying to recreate history, you better fucking *believe* I'm going to call you out on it."

"You don't know—"

I cut him off. "I don't need to have fucking experienced it to know that you wouldn't want to do that to your own kids. To Huey. To us. Six months ago, you'd have been holed up at the therapists every day, rather than succumbing to the call of the fucking bottle. Come back to us, man, before it's too fucking late." I checked the mirrors and pulled back into traffic, and then flicked him one last irritated look. "I'm going to get them back, River, so get your shit together or I'll make them happy without you. You have one shot at this kind of happiness. Don't blow it by letting your demons win."

He was silent the whole way back to the house, and as soon as I slowed to a stop, he was out of the car and slamming into the house. I'd pissed him off, but I'd do it a hundred more times if it shook him out of his spiral.

I grabbed our bags out of the back, walking slowly into the house. My body ached after a hard hit in Chicago, and I was just fucking exhausted. Dropping our shit in the foyer, I dragged my feet into the kitchen. I needed a beer, despite my spiel in the car. I shuffled my ass out to the hot tub and stripped down to my underwear. Climbing in, I settled in front of a jet so it could pound the aching muscles in my spine.

Tomorrow, Operation Get Nova Back would begin. I just needed to know if the guys were with me or if I was going solo. The idea of giving up my best friends for the girl I loved definitely hurt, but the idea of her never being mine again hurt more.

The patio door opened, and Devan strolled out. He looked tired, his shirt unbuttoned, and he'd lost his suit jacket already. His hair was rumpled, as if he'd been running his fingers through it constantly.

"You look like shit," I told him, noting the beer in his hand too. Maybe it wasn't just River using alcohol as a crutch. Maybe we were all doing it, to a lesser extent.

He tipped his bottle at me. "Cheers, brother. Appreciate the compliment."

I lifted my chin. "Get in. You look like you could use the soak."

He didn't argue, stripping down and climbing in. We'd gotten a huge hot tub, because none of us found sitting too close to each other in the hot water particularly appealing.

"I just told River, and now I'm telling you. I'm going to get Nova back. You can either help me or get out of the way. I love her, man. I'm sick of hurting both of us like this, for what? Fucking hockey? I'm so damn rich now, I could retire and live comfortably for decades. I have you to thank for that, and I know it. But she's worth more to me than anything." I leaned forward, so I could meet his eyes. "I want you guys with me. She loves you too, and I am one hundred percent fucking certain you guys love her. Sack up and help me get her back."

"Are you done?" he huffed. I nodded, and he was silent for a long time, then met my gaze. "What's your plan?"

I grinned. "First, we clean up River, and then…"

We discussed how to win back our girl long into the night, and for the first time since Nova left, I slept soundly.

CHAPTER
Forty-One
NOVA

I'D SETTLED INTO A ROUTINE. I'd wake up, feed Huey, take him for a walk in the morning sun, and then come home to work while he napped. When he woke up for lunch, I'd play with him for a little while longer, go to the store to buy some kind of instant meal for my dinner, and then he'd play or nap or watch the colorful baby shows while I worked some more. Then I'd feed him, bath him and put him to bed, and that was when I did the bulk of my daily work.

I'd struggle to bed about midnight, and be up at six in the morning to do it all over again. It wasn't the most healthy routine, really, but there was happiness in predictability. At least, that's what I told myself.

So when Julieta called and insisted that she had a babysitter and I was coming out with her, I wanted to argue. But she was pretty insistent. Julieta was a force of nature when she wanted to be. So I messaged the guys and asked if they'd watch Huey for the night, all the while feeling guilty as hell that I was abandoning my baby as soon as it was inconvenient to look after him. Of course the guys agreed.

Julieta said I was being ridiculous with the guilt thing. I was fucking twenty-four, not fifty-three, and did I think she was a bad parent for wanting a night out with her husband and her brand new bestie?

Of course not, and I realized Julieta had talked me into a corner. She should have been a lawyer. So that was the reason I was dressed in my only clubbing dress, with heels that were probably too high. My face was painted for the first time in months, and I kind of looked hot. Maybe I could find a nice guy to kiss tonight, but not take home.

Devan had said to drop Huey off when I was ready, and honestly, I felt more nervous rocking up to their house dressed like this than I did about going out for the first time in months. I stopped in front of the house and tugged at the hem of my dress. Unclipping Huey's seat, I walked up to the door like I was walking up to the gallows: heart pounding, palms sweaty, my breathing so loud I could hear it echoing in my ears.

As I knocked, the door opened almost immediately. Then I frowned. Rigby's mom's smiling face greeted me. "Nova! It's so good to see you, sweetheart." She dragged me into a hug, and I patted her back one-handed. I was kind of embarrassed to see her dressed like a hoochie, as my grandmother would say before she died. She stepped back. "Oh, don't you just look smoking hot."

"Mrs. Engman, it's nice to see you again."

She made a tsking noise. "Lorraine. You must call me Lorraine. Mrs. Engman is my mother-in-law, and that woman is a dragon of epic proportions. Don't tell Larry I said that," she whispered conspiratorially. "Boys, Nova's here," she yelled over her shoulder, reaching for Huey's car seat. "Let me take the handsome boy. Hello, sweet thing!"

A man that could only be Rigby's dad appeared around the corner. He grinned at me, thrusting out his hand. "Larry Engman. You must be Nova. I've heard a lot about you."

I winced. I just bet he had. I stood awkwardly in the doorway. "Are you guys down for a visit?"

Larry nodded, dropping into a squat in front of Huey's seat with a groan. "Look at you! Such a big strong boy already." Huey seemed immediately enamored with Larry, kicking his legs. "Look at those hockey legs. See that, Lorraine? Next generation is here. We should give Rigby his old mini's gear for Huey."

Lorraine looked at me and rolled her eyes. "I think we might let him get to the crawling stage before we put skates on him, don't you think?"

Watching them dote on Huey was making feelings well in my chest that would definitely result in me destroying my eye make-up. "I have to get going. Can you let the guys know I'll pick him up tomorrow morning?"

Lorraine looked over my shoulder. "You can tell them yourself."

I looked over my shoulder, and all the guys were standing there, looking mouthwatering. Rigby was rocking the mountain man look in dark blue jeans, white sneakers and a check shirt that clung to his pecs and biceps like it wanted to be part of him. Devan was wearing dark, tight chinos, and a rust-colored button-down that seemed to make his skin even more deliciously golden. River was wearing black jeans that seemed to scream for mercy around those hockey thighs, and a white shirt that was loose and cool, but stretched across the places that mattered.

In short, they looked fucking delicious.

Rigby grinned at me. "Your mouth is hanging open, Fireball."

Hearing his nickname for me had the dual effect of knocking me out of my blatant perusal, and making my heart ache. I shook my head. "Sorry, I didn't know you guys were going out. I'm happy to stay in and mind Huey. I must have gotten our wires crossed about which night it was."

I'd message Julieta in the car and beg off. It would be a relief after seeing the guys looking like that. They were obviously hitting up the clubs, and looking like that, probably going home with some pretty girls they didn't have to share.

There was a long silence between us until Lorraine huffed. "We're here to babysit, Nova." My head whipped between her and the guys.

Rigby was nodding. "We're going out with you, but if we don't hurry up, Julieta will pregame too hard and we won't make it to the club at all." They bundled me out the door, and before I knew it, I was in the back seat of River's SUV.

"I didn't realize you guys were coming too," I said, trying not to think about how good they smelled.

River didn't start the car. We just sat in the driveway as Rigby turned to me. "Nova Stone. We were dumb to let you go. Dumb to care what other people thought. Dumb to let some corporate shark in a suit tell us who we could and couldn't love. This? This is special. Worth fighting for."

I was dumbfounded. My mouth kept opening and closing, but nothing came out.

Rigby reached over and grabbed my hand. "Tonight, we're going to go out. We're going to dance, and have fun, and fuck what everyone else says. The only people who matter are in this car."

"And your parents," I whispered.

Rigby laughed. "And my parents. But my mom has already mentally adopted you after she met you once, and my dad is thrilled to have a grandson already. I think he's bored in retirement and wants someone to dote on. Huey's it."

I swung my eyes to the front seat. River was

watching my face in the mirror, his expression shuttered. Devan was twisted in the passenger seat, watching me over his shoulder.

"You all feel this way?" I couldn't do this without them. I loved Rigby, but if I felt bad about being a sledgehammer to their careers, I definitely couldn't live with breaking up their friendship.

Devan let out an incredulous snort. "It's taking everything in me not to climb over there and show you how much I missed you. God, Star, you look so fucking beautiful tonight. These last few weeks have been…"

"Hell," River finished for him. Even dressed up, River looked rough. Dark circles under his eyes, the lines of his face pulled down. "It's been hell without you. Please…" He trailed off, but he didn't need to beg.

I sucked in a deep breath. "We'll try it slow, okay? I'm not moving back in—"

"Yet," Devan added.

I raised an eyebrow at him. "Yet. But I've missed you guys so much too. It's been so shitty."

Rigby grinned, pulling me into his lap and kissing me hard. "We'll take it whatever pace you like, Fireball. We're in this for the long haul." He kissed me again, and kept kissing me like he was making up for lost time.

River started the car, and we drove into the center of Ann Arbor to a popular nightclub, parking a few blocks away. I stepped out of the car and straight into Devan's arms. He kissed me too, backing me up against the car door. I was glad my dress wasn't white. He didn't say anything, but he didn't need to; the desperation of his lips on mine said enough.

"I've missed the scent of you," he murmured against my neck after a moment. "Your smell on my pillows haunted me until it faded, and then I just missed you even more."

I ran my hands through his hair. "I know."

I was dragged from his arms and into River's. He picked me up, his arms tightly banding around my waist, his face burying into my shoulder as he just breathed me in. He was muttering things against my skin that I couldn't hear, but the desperation in his touch, the way he was holding me like his life depended on it, told me everything I needed to know. The guys were watching him with worried eyes, and I knew I'd have to talk to them about it later.

"It's okay, River. I'm here now. We'll deal with all this shit together. As a team." He squeezed me tighter, his arms shaking, and I tapped his shoulder. "Come on, big guy—I need to breathe." He finally let me slip to the ground, and I looked up into his face. His eyes were shiny, making me feel awful all over again.

Leaning down, he kissed me reverently. "Please don't leave again."

Stroking his hair back from his head, I smiled up at him. "I won't, not if I can help it."

That would have to be enough.

River tucked me tightly beneath his arm, and we

walked toward the club. "So what's the plan?" I asked him.

"No plan. We're going to live our lives how we want, and if other people have a problem with it, they can go fuck themselves. I'm going to show my girl a good time, drink, dance, and party with our friends. It has nothing to do with anyone else."

CHAPTER
Forty-Two
RIVER

NOVA MOVED on the dance floor like she was made to dance. Her arms were looped around Rigby's neck as they bounced around to the DJ's tunes amid the mass of other human bodies. Fuck, she was so beautiful, and I didn't miss the eyes of the other men around her as she danced with complete abandon.

They wouldn't get close, though; I knew that. She only had eyes for Rigby right then, as the song changed to something with a slower, more sexual beat. He ground down against her, and it was so fucking erotic, with his hands on her ass and his thigh pressed between hers so there wasn't an inch of their body not touching. They may as well have been fucking on the dance floor.

My lips quirked as I turned my eyes away from the intimate scene. If Rigby kept working his magic, we'd all be going home with her tonight, and I'd worship her body in a different kind of dance. Devan was talking to Julieta, who was sweaty and smiling widely after stepping off the dance floor herself.

Muss nudged my shoulder with his. "You guys really have no jealousy? Engman is down there basically being pornographic with your girl, and you don't care?"

We were sitting in the VIP section—the good side, not the side they gave to any person off the street. Ludo was on Muss's other side, sipping straight vodka like a psychopath.

I just shrugged. "Not if it's Rigby. But that other fucker who's trying to sneak up behind to sandwich her between them is about to lose a limb," I growled, watching some shitty clubgoer trying to move in on Nova, his eyes trained on her ass. I looked at Devan, but he was already halfway down the stairs. We all watched as he cut his way through the dancers, getting up in the face of the guy who was now only a foot away. I couldn't tell what he was saying, but the guy held up his hands and moved away quickly. Devan situated himself behind Nova, and she looked over her shoulder and smiled at him. He kissed her shoulder, and they danced with her between them.

Turning back to Muss and Ludo, I saw they were both looking at me like I was crazy. And maybe from the outside it was. But to me, it was just right.

I shrugged again. "I hate dancing," I said, like that

explained everything. And to me, it did. I hated it, but Rigby moved like he was born to it. Even Devan didn't mind it, if he found the right partner. So if my girl wanted to dance, she had two dance partners who'd keep her on the floor until her feet ached.

When we got home, I'd do my dancing horizontally on a bed. Or maybe against the wall. Or in the shower. It made sense to me.

Julieta slapped me on the shoulder. "I see the perks," she teased with a wink, which made Muss grunt.

"Don't go getting any ideas, woman. I'm way too much of a caveman to share."

Julieta rolled her eyes. "Are you kidding? Like I need another man to take care of. It would be a constant cacophony of 'Honey, have you seen my socks? J, have you seen my keys? Does this cut look infected?'" She mimicked Muss's voice so good, I choked on my Coke. "No thank you. One man is enough for me. I'm too old for that shit."

Muss grabbed her, tugging her onto his lap. "Julieta, you're as fucking energetic as the Energizer Bunny and you know it." Pulling her close, he whispered something in her ear that made her laugh and bite her bottom lip.

"Gross," Ludo grunted. "It's like watching your parents dirty talk."

I laughed and went back to talking about work with Ludo, while Muss took Julieta back to the dance floor and moved like they were on their way to making baby number four.

Finally, Nova and the other guys reappeared, and she flopped down in my lap. A few hairs were sticking to the sweat on her brow, and I pushed them away, one hand wrapping around her waist to pull her tightly to my chest.

"You looked fucking beautiful out there," I growled into her ear, and was rewarded with goosebumps dancing across the skin of her arms. I ran my nose up the side of her cheek, my teeth nipping at her jaw.

I knew this night would result in more gossip column news, but I didn't care. Muss and Ludo, as well as Julieta, were here to show that our relationship had the support of the team. We were all together to show that we were a united front.

I wasn't giving in easily this time. As much as I'd wanted to punch Rigby in the mouth the other day, he'd been right. I'd given up and fallen into a dangerous hole that could have spiraled into something major. But the booze had numbed the pain of her loss for just a little while.

I didn't believe that having parents who were addicts automatically meant I was more prone to substance addiction, but it wasn't a theory I wanted to test. I wouldn't do that to Huey, and I wouldn't do it to Nova. I was going dry for a little while, long enough that I wasn't leaning on it as a lifeline anymore.

I wanted to prove to myself that I could kick it, just

as much as I wanted to prove it to the guys. The only addiction I wanted was giving my girl orgasms.

Actually… "You look hot. You want to go and cool down in the bathroom?" I whispered in her ear, my tone pitched low. "Maybe I could help?" I ground my hardening dick against her tight little ass. God, I loved that ass.

She turned toward me, her lips turned up in a smile. "Sure, but I think you'll have to show me the way."

Ludo rolled his eyes at me, but Rigby was grinning wide, like he was sending me off with my prom date or something. I slapped the back of his head and led my girl out of the VIP area toward the bathrooms at the back. Luckily, this section had private bathrooms, so we wouldn't have to wait in line with sixteen other people.

I dragged her into the men's bathroom, and into the cubicle right at the very end. The bathrooms in this club had little shelves above the cisterns, though I wasn't sure what men needed them for. I knew women put their handbags on them, but what were we meant to put on there? Our beers? If you're taking a beer into a fucking public bathroom, you probably need to be ejected from the damn club.

Luckily for me, I had something perfectly valuable to rest on that little shelf, and it put her at the perfect height for me to eat her out. I pushed her dress up her hips and found a not-so-tiny pair of panties. "Holy hell, these things go on forever," I grunted, as I kept pushing her dress further up until I finally came to a stop a few inches below the underside of her tits.

She slapped my hand, but she was smiling. "This dress is too tight for panty lines. It was either this or no panties, and honestly, I didn't realize I was coming out with you guys tonight. Hooking up wasn't in my plans, so I didn't think anyone would see them."

I growled at the idea of her coming out with no underwear on, and some other guy rubbing up against her like Rigby had been, feeling that tight little pussy that was meant only for us. Peeling them down, I stuffed them in my pocket, and then she was gloriously bare before me. My mouth watered, and I groaned. I straddled the toilet seat, and she was perfectly the right height for me to bury my face between her thighs.

But first, I was going to savor the moment, because I hadn't thought I'd ever get to be here again. I ran my tongue up her left thigh, and she let out a tiny moan.

"Uh-uh, baby. You're going to have to be quiet or we're going to get kicked out of the club. No sound, or I stop." I flicked my tongue up her wet slit, and she slapped a hand over her mouth to stifle the moan. "Mmm, good girl."

She moaned again, getting wetter. "Now I know why Rigby enjoys that so much," she breathed.

"Mmm, enjoys what?"

"He's got a praise kink."

I raised my eyebrows at her. Well, that was interesting. But I didn't want her thinking of Rigby at this moment, just me. "Quiet now, baby, I've got to get reacquainted with this delicious pussy."

I wouldn't say I was an expert at eating a girl out, but I knew the basics and made up for it with enthusiasm. And from the mewling noises Nova was making, and the way she was grinding against my face, enthusiasm was working. I sucked on her clit, thrusting two fingers inside her, and she rode me hard. Her hand was all but wedged inside her mouth now, and the other hand was tangled in my hair, holding me where she wanted me. I wanted nothing more than to stand up and fuck her against the wall, but this wasn't the time or the place. No, first she'd come on my tongue, and then we'd get the hell out of here.

Pulling back, I looked at her beautiful fucking face, her head thrown back as my fingers curled inside her. "Come for me, Nova. I want to taste you gushing on my tongue."

With that, I sucked her clit firmly between my lips. She slapped both hands over her mouth and screamed her release into them. She slumped back against the wall, and I laid my cheek on her thigh.

There was a soft round of applause from outside the cubicle. "Holy shit, dude! I don't know who you are, but I swear to fucking god, I nearly came from that. Well done." The words were slurred, and moments later, the door opened and closed.

I looked up at Nova's shocked face. Neither of us had heard anyone enter the bathrooms. "Whoops?"

Her lips twitched, and that turned into a giggle, then full-blown laughter. She pulled me up her body and kissed me, despite the fact I still had her release smeared across my face. Helping her off the bench— and onto those heels that made me have all sorts of bad thoughts—I held her steady until she got her land legs back. I tugged down her dress, but didn't give her back her underwear. They bulged in my pocket, and I briefly considered framing them. They were amazing, and so was my girl.

I wanted to tell her I loved her right then and there. Wanted to tell her that I'd been lost without her, and that I wanted her back home, in my bed, in my life. I wanted us to be a family. But I held my tongue. The bathroom of a nightclub wasn't the place for grand declarations of love—and honestly, we weren't there yet. I wanted her to come back to us, get comfortable with us again. I didn't want her to think of my love as some kind of shackle that I was trying to tie her to me with.

I ran my fingers along the crease of her bare ass, unable to resist pushing it up and cupping those cheeks again. God, I was addicted to this woman. Maybe I could make her come on my hand one more time before we left this cubicle?

The door opened and closed again, someone standing at the urinal taking a piss longer than that of a racehorse, and we both laughed silently until he left. Without washing his hands. Fuck, people were gross.

"Come on, baby. Let's get the guys and go home. I have a few more things I want to do to show you just how much I fucking missed you."

Her eyes got soft, and she leaned in to kiss me again. "Let's go."

CHAPTER
Forty-Three

NOVA

WE GOT a rideshare back to my apartment, the guys not arguing about coming back to my place instead of going home, where Rigby's parents were watching Huey. Lorraine and Larry might like me, but that didn't mean they'd approve of what was about to happen.

We stumbled out of the car and into my apartment. River grabbed my keys, as Devan grabbed me, pushing me against the wall beside my door. He kissed me hard, his hands snaking up the backs of my thighs to my ass, his groan reverberating in my mouth when he realized I wasn't wearing any underwear.

"Fuck…" he breathed, lifting one of my thighs until his fingers could brush my exposed pussy. I sucked in a gasp, and he groaned again. "Open the damn door, Cooper. I'm overdue to be inside our girl."

Our girl. I wasn't sure I'd ever get used to that.

River pushed the door open, and Devan picked me

up, stepping me into the tiny apartment. I'd never been more glad that I'd moved the bed into the living room. Half a dozen long strides later, and Devan was dropping me to my feet so he could unzip the tight bodice of my dress. He stripped me out of my lingerie, until I was naked before him.

"Rigby? A little birdy told me that you liked to please our girl. Get on the fucking bed so she can ride your face."

Already naked, Rigby raised an eyebrow, but he flopped down onto the bed, his grin wide and deliriously happy. He made grabby hands, and I squealed as River lifted me up and slid me down over Rigby's face.

"Ride him, baby. Show him how much you've missed his tongue between your thighs," Devan whispered in my ear, and I was helpless to resist. Rigby's hands were on my hips, dragging me over his face, his tongue plunging inside me as his nose hit my clit.

Holy shit.

I murmured things that probably made no sense, telling him how I missed him, how no one tonguefucked me like he did. The whole time, Devan and River stood beside me, also naked, stroking their already hard cocks.

I orgasmed hard, coming over Rigby's face, but he didn't stop, lapping up my release and flicking his tongue over my sensitive clit. Finally, someone took pity on his need to breathe, and I was lifted back onto the bed.

River pushed me backward until his huge body was wedged between my thighs, and his cock was grinding against my aching folds. I slid my hands up his back until I could bury them in his hair, and he kissed me like he'd never get the chance to do it again. It was a kiss full of both heartache and relief, so fucking tender it almost brought tears to my eyes. As his cock notched against my entrance, he pulled back, and I whimpered a little. I wanted him inside me.

I rolled my body upwards, pushing him just inside, and he growled down at me. Rolling us until I was on top, he looked up at me with more love than anyone could express with words. Hell, maybe I wasn't ready for the words. But as I sank down on his cock, I knew he could read the same thing in my eyes. Well, until they rolled back in my head.

Devan appeared beside the bed, grabbing my chin and turning my face toward him and his thick cock. "Suck me, Nova. Show me how much you missed me."

I didn't argue, and River took control, holding my hips and slamming up into me as I slid Devan's cock between my lips, sliding him deeper until he was hitting the back of my throat. He held my face in his hands, thrusting shallowly in and out of my mouth, groaning deeply every time I moaned around his dick.

"Fuck, this is like watching the best porn ever," Rigby breathed from where he was still spread on the bed beside us, his hand stroking furiously.

Devan slid his eyes to him and smirked. "One day,

we'll work you up to taking all three of us at once—
would you like that, baby?" His fingers stroked my
cheeks roughly. "All of us inside you, fucking you
together until you're just sweaty, overheated flesh we
can use for our enjoyment?"

I moaned around his cock, and his own eyes rolled
back. "Rigby, be a good boy and play with her ass. Get
her used to where we'll be one day."

Rigby curled up onto his knees, his eyes hooded
with pleasure. Leaning over, he kissed my spine as
his hands ran down the curve of my ass and in
between my thighs. His fingers were so close to
River's cock as it slid in and out of my body, and
the man below me gasped as Rigby pushed a finger
inside my pussy, stretching me, even as River
moved in and out. Then he pushed in another one.
He was stroking us both, and River frowned, like he
wasn't sure if it was okay to like the feel of Rigby's
fingers against his cock or not. He didn't stop;
instead, he went deeper, grinding me down on them
both.

"Fuck..." Rigby breathed. "You're soaking my
hand." But he pulled his wet fingers and slid them up
the crease of my ass until they circled my hole.

Devan still gripped my chin, forcing me to look up
at him. "Relax, baby. Let Rig in." At his words, one of
Rigby's fingers slid into my ass, stroking the thin walls
between him and River's cock. I screamed around
Devan's, and his eyes squeezed shut. Then Rigby added

another finger, moving them in and out of me in time with River's thrusts.

I moved off Devan's dick, looking over my shoulder. "I want Rigby inside me."

The collective groan around the room made me feel powerful. I could bring these three men to their knees.

Devan looked down at me, his brows low over his eyes. "You sure?" I nodded. "You got lube in this drawer?" he asked, sifting through my nightstand. He pulled out the Pink Rocket with a grin. "We'll play with this another time." He finally found the lube and threw it over to Rigby. Whatever he saw on my sunshine boy's face made him pause. "Gentle, man. This is important."

Whatever silent conversation happened afterwards didn't bother me, because River had lifted his head so he was sucking on my nipple, his cock just inside me, moving my body in shallow thrusts.

Lube poured down my ass, and River pulled out, making me whimper. But not for long. The head of Rigby's cock was there, pressing tightly against my back entrance, and he was panting over my spine. He was positioned between River's thighs, and if any of them worried about his knees being so close to River's balls, they didn't say anything.

"Breathe out and relax, baby," River grunted, as my nails flexed into his chest and Rigby pushed past the resistance of my ass. I threw my head back, moaning at the sensation, and he thrust gently, getting me used to it.

I wanted more. "River…" I whined, but he was already there, tapping his cock gently on my clit—making Rigby curse—before sliding back inside my willing body.

Holy shit, I was so full. So fucking full that I didn't think I could breathe, let alone move. But it didn't matter, because the guys moved me between them, shallow thrusting so there was a constant brush of their cocks inside me.

I came hard, and they grunted in unison, but they weren't done. "Fuck, it feels like you're fucking me too," River growled at Rigby, and I smirked at the idea.

Devan was staring down at me, his eyes flicking to where my body was being used, then back to my face. "Are you ready for one more?" I nodded, and he slipped back into my mouth, just as Rigby's hand came around my hip to find my clit.

Our bodies were a tangle of limbs. I'd never imagined this would happen, even when we'd agreed to be poly. I'd never really thought about orgies or how this would work, but I would never forget this moment for the rest of my life.

Rigby slapped my ass, and I screamed out my orgasm, one sensation too many tipping me over. I clamped down on them both, and the tightness had Rigby coming with me, River not too far behind him. Finally, Devan pulled out of my throat and came all over my chest, panting. I collapsed onto River's chest, whimpering as Rigby pulled out.

River was next, and I moaned at the empty feeling in my body. Every one of my muscles felt wrung out.

River kissed my face, over my cheeks, the sweat from my temple. "You are everything, Nova Stone," he whispered softly against my cheek. I held him tighter. "But Devan's spunk is all over my chest and yours, so I think we should probably shower."

I laughed, letting him pick me up and carry me to the shower. We both barely fit into the tiny cubicle, and there wasn't a whole lot of room to move. But he cleaned me up gently, then washed himself down, before carrying my towel-wrapped body back into the bedroom.

Rigby was lying spread-eagled on the bed, snoring gently, his dick out. Devan rolled his eyes as he walked back into the room. "Not sure I'm going to enjoy the 'staring at other men's cocks' part of this relationship."

They'd stripped off the bed while we were showering, and there were now fresh sheets on there. We had been a little bit juicy, I guess.

"Really? I think that might be my favorite part," I told him, crawling onto the bed beside him, River squeezing his body in beside mine.

"I bet it is, you little pervert," Dev whispered. Pulling me tightly to his chest, he held me close. "Don't leave again. I'm not sure any of us could take it."

I kissed his overheated skin, still salty with sweat. "I promise."

CHAPTER

Forty-Four

DEVAN

TOM SMILED at me as he handed me my morning coffee. "If I may say so, sir, you look happier today."

I grinned. "You may not say so."

He raised an eyebrow. "Well, I just did, so I guess you better fire me then."

I huffed, and the kid continued to smirk. Ballsy little fucker.

"Just letting you know that Daria—your, uh, consultant—has a 10 a.m. meeting with you."

I looked back down at my spreadsheet. "Thanks, Tom." I'd give him a good bonus this year. He'd weathered this bullshit like a champion, and I believed in rewarding loyalty and commitment.

It had been a week since our very public outing as a quad, and as expected, it had kicked off most of the gossip and bullshit again. We weren't blindsided by it this time, though. We rode it out. I threatened to pull the company's sponsorship from the IceCaps, which wasn't a whole lot of money to someone like Monderra, but his board of directors saw it differently. The guys stood their ground against the coaches and the exec team, and their teammates backed them up, under the urging of Ludo and Muss.

We didn't open our phones, or social media, or even turn on the television for a week. We just enjoyed each other's company, and that of Rigby's parents, for the full week. Every night, one of us would return with Nova to her apartment, and make love to her all night.

I was so fucking happy; tonight was my turn, and I had so many things planned. I was going to woo the hell out of Nova Stone.

I got the brief report from my public relations team, whose job it was to keep me apprised of the general vibe of the drama and let me know if I needed to step in. The lawyers had been working overtime sending cease and desist letters. In my opinion, the amount of extra money I was spending in overtime and billing hours was money well spent. It was an investment in happiness, and they were the best kinds of investments.

My time got lost in numbers and bottom lines, and all too soon, my 10 a.m. appointment was here. Daria strolled in, waggling her eyebrows at Tom as if she'd personally love to devour him like a black widow spider.

"Stop eye-fucking my personal assistant, Daria, and

come in. Tom, can you grab Daria a drink? Water? Soda? Coffee?"

"Double-shot espresso. Black. Like my heart," she cooed at him, and he visibly gulped before nodding and scurrying away. Yeah, Tom had some self-preservation skills.

"Don't scare the poor kid," I chastised, though it amused the hell out of me. Daria was an interesting character. She was Middle Eastern, I think, her skin golden like warm sand but her hair a wild halo of curls that she didn't even try to tame. Nope, like her, she didn't try and make it anything else. You either accepted her how she was, or you got the fuck out of the way. I could respect that.

And arguably, she was beautiful. In another time, she might have been a fertility idol, all wild hourglass curves, pouty lips, and soft freckles across her nose. She wasn't the socially accepted standard of beauty, but I'd once seen a man trip over a barstool when she bent down to tie up the laces on her Doc Martins, allowing the thigh-high split of her long, tight black skirt to show a little more thigh than intended.

She was the kind of beauty that both men and women were drawn to, and she blessed both with her attention. When she'd said she could steal my girlfriend, I had no doubt she could. It took a special kind of man to handle everything Daria had to offer, but she attracted those bisexual women like moths to a bunsen burner.

Daria was still watching Tom walk away. "A little shake-up every now and then is good for the soul, Devan Mayson—which you should know."

Despite Daria's obvious attractiveness, and the amount of time we'd known each other, we'd never been more than friendly. We saw through each other's bullshit, and it made us respected acquaintances, if not friends. I'd used her PI services a few times over the years whenever I thought I was being screwed over, or to investigate the guys' fuck buddies, but that's all it had ever been. Although I had no doubt that a night with Daria would change a man, I was happy how I was.

Tom reappeared with her double espresso, looking a little dazed. Today she was in a long, blood-red skirt and a band t-shirt that was more rips than actual shirt, as well as a leather jacket covered in zips.

She smiled up at him, all teeth. "Thank you, Tad."

"It's Tom," he said in a voice an octave too high, and I swear to god, Daria's eyes got predatory.

"How about you come home with me and I'll call you whatever you like, babycakes?" Tom's eyes went wide, and I took pity on the poor bastard.

"Daria!"

She huffed and turned back toward me, and I gave her a stern frown. Tom took the opportunity to escape. "What would Xander say?" Her boyfriend was huge. Like, fucking massive. I wasn't sure what he did for a living, but I figured it might involve eating billy goats under a bridge.

Daria grinned shamelessly. "I didn't say I wasn't going to share."

Shaking my head, I waved a hand at her notebook. "Tell me what you found instead of harassing my employees."

Suddenly, Daria was all business. "I talked to the photographer Esperanza always has with her, and there's no loyalty or love lost there. He thinks she's a piranha who wants to chew his balls off. So I don't think he was your early, camera-happy stalker. But I wouldn't put it past Esperanza herself to have done the dirty work and just handed off the info to some poor, unfortunate intern. I'm working on connecting with the intern herself, and maybe I can get some concrete evidence. At least, enough to get Esperanza fired from her position."

I scowled, because it wasn't enough. I hated that this crazy bitch was still running around as a possible threat to my new-found happiness. "I'll pay you double if you can get it done in the next week."

Daria grinned. "Consider it done, Mr. Mayson." I rolled my eyes at her, and she slouched back in her chair. "So, I see that you're back with your girl. About fucking time. I thought you guys were going to be little bitches about it forever. Honestly, I was waiting for you to pay me, and then I was going to swoop in like a fairy godmother and take her for myself. Xander was even on board. You know he's a sucker for a damsel in distress, and he certainly doesn't get the opportunity with me."

"Mine," I growled at her, and she had the audacity to laugh in my face.

"Yeah, yeah. I know. Anyone with eyes can see she's happy now. Just keep it that way—she's a nice girl."

"How would you know? It was meant to be a no-contact assignment."

Daria grinned. "Well, it just so happens that the apartment next door came up for rent, and Xander and I needed a place. So we moved in next door, because all the better to surveil her with, right? She's never once complained to the super about the noise, and Xander and me? We get noisy."

I screwed up my nose at the thought. Daria was beautiful, but Xander was a monster. I honestly wondered how he didn't split Daria in half like a fucking watermelon. Maybe there was justice in the world, and he wasn't in proportion. But judging by the shit-eating grin that seemed to permanently be etched on Daria's face, I wouldn't bet on it.

I thought back to how Nova had her bed in the living room instead of the bedroom, because she said her neighbors had incredibly loud sex every night. "For fuck's sake, Daria." Then I remembered last Saturday. "Oh *shit*."

The woman cackled like a damn witch. She held up her hand in front of me. "High five for the orgy the other night. That shit sounded fire. Who doesn't like a good orgy if it's done well? And given the fucking cacophony coming from next door, you were doing it *real* well."

I blushed bright fucking red, which just made her laugh harder, and I flipped her the bird.

Just then, her phone pinged. She pulled it from her pocket, still chuckling. As she looked down at the screen, I saw the mirth slide from her face until her forehead was creased in concern.

"What's wrong?"

She was already striding out the door, her old-school doctor's bag that she used as a briefcase already in her hand. "Get your shit. Andrea Esperanza is outside Nova's door right now."

My whole body went cold. "*What?*"

"Move it, Mayson. We'll take your car." I sprinted out of the room after her, ignoring Tom's startled expression. I ran to the elevator, Daria already there, holding it open.

"How do you know she's there?"

Daria rolled her eyes. "Cameras, obviously. Don't be a dumbass." She pulled up the video feed of Andrea Esperanza at Nova's door. I couldn't hear what they were saying, but Andrea was waving her hands about.

Then Nova let her inside.

The place where Huey was sleeping.

I hadn't told Nova of my suspicions about Andrea, because I couldn't prove anything; all I had was a gut feeling. I was such a fucking *idiot*. The woman that

River loved, that he'd very publicly claimed, had just invited his stalker into her home.

"*Fuck!* I'm calling 911."

"I'll call Xander. We'll see who gets there first." I didn't care who got there first, as long as my woman wasn't alone with that psycho. My heart thrummed, and the minutes seemed to drag, even though I was going over the speed limit. At this point, I didn't even care if we got pulled over by the cops. I'd just lead them right to Nova's doorstep and pray we weren't too late.

CHAPTER
Forty-Five
NOVA

I HAD that one client who was always a disorganized mess. Every year, she posted me a box of her receipts and twelve months of bank statements, and told me to work it out. I always did, because she didn't kick up a fuss about my fee and she always paid promptly. Plus, she was lovely. Disorganized chaos, but lovely.

Someone knocked on the door, and I pushed back from the desk. Casting a look over at Huey, I saw he was out for the count. Milk drunk. His little lip moved, and honestly, I was head over heels in love with that kid.

The person at the door knocked again, and I hurried from the living room, shutting the door so whoever it was didn't wake him. I cast a quick look around, happy to see that my house didn't look too much like it had been tossed by ninjas.

Wrenching the door open, I was surprised to see

Andrea Esperanza. "If you want an exclusive comment, I promise you that you won't like what I have to say," I hissed at her.

Andrea rolled her eyes. "Please. I'm a serious sports journalist. I don't give a fuck who's sticking their dick in you."

Yeah, sure bitch. "What can I do for you then?"

"I've got information about who was taking those photos and releasing them to the public." I narrowed my eyes at her, and she threw her hands in the air. "Look, I don't give a fuck about you. But River Cooper is a damn good player, and he's on track to be one of the best. I don't want you to ruin his chances by being a literal ball and chain. Plus, she freaks even me out, and I don't want him permanently maimed by some kind of bunny-boiling psychopath." She looked to the left and right. "Can we talk about this somewhere less fucking public, or are you so self-absorbed you don't give a shit about River and Rigby's careers?"

Gritting my teeth, I let her into the apartment. She walked around with a single eyebrow raised. "I knew this was a shitty neighborhood, but I thought the inside of the place might be nicer, considering the net worth of the men you're fucking."

Damn, I really hated this chick. "Get on with it, Andrea. Who's the woman? And how did you get your information?"

Andrea spun around, her nose screwed up. "God, it must be delightful to be this stupid and still beguile some of the most eligible bachelors in the state. Hell, in the country. You must be one hell of a good lay."

Fear trickled down my spine, although she hadn't said anything more toxic than what she'd been saying in the hallway. No, there was something about the way she'd said it. Softer but somehow more monotone.

"I think you should leave. Any information you have you can give to Devan's lawyers."

Then she pulled out a gun.

Every part of me froze. My bones. My skin. My heart. Andrea pointed that gun at my chest, and I stumbled back toward the door.

She waved the gun. "Don't fucking move."

My heart started back up, but every thump was a single name. *Huey. Huey. Huey.* I willed him to stay asleep. Prayed to my parents to keep him quiet and safe. Maybe she'd forgotten he existed. Maybe she thought he was with the guys.

Andrea gestured with the gun. "Toward the bed, whorebag. This only works if you're on your back, but that should be your natural position, right?"

I moved, my hands out in front of me. I tried to think about the self-defense classes my mom had made me take in high school. I'd complained, of course. I'd told her I was smart—I wasn't going to be walking around late at night, or in shitty neighborhoods, or going on dates with psychopaths. She'd said most men were good, but some were bad, and the problem was that sometimes they were indistinguishable from each other until it was too late. So it was better to know how to protect yourself.

She probably never thought I was going to be attacked by deranged journalists, though.

I moved toward the bed, because that moved her focus away from the room where Huey lay sleeping. Sitting on the edge of the bed, I watched her, barely blinking. "Why are you doing this? I don't understand."

Andrea snorted, her eyes so wide I could see the whites around her irises. "He was meant to be mine. He *was* mine until you came along. Sure, he had Marissa— that dumb bitch—but I knew they just had an arrangement. He was a professional, and he respected my career too much to out us as a couple. She was just a ruse."

Woah. Crazy town had arrived. I wasn't stupid enough to provoke her, though. "You're ready now?" I said softly, like her spiel was completely legit. "I have Devan and Rigby. If you say River is yours, then he's yours." *Over my fucking dead body.*

Andrea narrowed her eyes. "Oh, you think you can just give me what's already mine and I'll thank you? Fuck off. The only way he'll truly get over you is if you're dead. Dead as your shitty parents. Dead as his shitty parents. We'll raise his nephew together. I'll be an amazing mother. Where is he?"

My breathing became ragged. "Huey isn't here. He's with Rigby today."

"I think you're a fucking liar. Let's check, shall we?

Maybe it would be best if we ruin your whole family line. I mean, every time he looks at that bastard, he's going to think of you, right? I'm going to pin this on Devan, because I've always hated that fucker. Thinks he's so much better than everyone else. Like he isn't a petty fucking criminal." She laughed. "Honestly, you've set this up for me perfectly. A crime of passion. He couldn't stand the fact that his best friends were fucking you too. It's a tale as old as time."

She started toward the other room, and I panicked. "Wait!"

But she ignored me. Keeping her gun trained on me, she was almost at the door to the room where Huey was sleeping. It was now or never.

I ripped the lamp from the side table and threw it at her head. I wasn't an athlete, so she ducked it easily. But that meant taking her eyes off me. I dived for her stomach, taking her down to the ground, but she still had hold on the gun. Grabbing the arm holding the gun, I wrestled it up and then bit her hard on the fleshy part of her bicep.

"Argh! You fucking bitch!" But she loosened her hold on the gun, although a shot went off and hit the window with a cracking sound. Yanking the gun away and tossing it behind us, praying it went under the bed and into the hands of the dust bunnies, I wasn't focused enough to dodge the headbutt that came right at my face. I reared back, my vision going white then black, before she was on top of me again. Her forearm was now pressing down on my throat, cutting off the oxygen. She wasn't big, but she was fucking crazy.

I went for her eyes, turning my head so she didn't crush my windpipe, but I knew I only had a few seconds before I passed out and was done for. I got a hand to her face and a thumb in her eyeball, making her pull back a little and giving me some airflow, but not enough to get her off of me.

I was fucked. So fucked.

I kicked my legs and lifted my hips, trying to get back on top, but she was back to pressing down on my windpipe. I continued to struggle, because I wasn't leaving Huey alone with this psycho. I couldn't.

Blackness danced at the edges of my vision when Andrea suddenly went rigid, falling to the side. Standing above us was an absolute giant of a man. Like, he must have been seven feet tall and built like a barn. He was holding a taser, which was crackling loudly.

Who the fuck was this guy? I panted as I drew oxygen back into my lungs, knowing I should get away because if I couldn't win a fight against Andrea, I stood no chance against this behemoth.

He smiled down at me, giving a groaning Andrea a glare. "Let's give her another zappy-zap, what do you say?"

I was panting loudly, shock and adrenaline coursing through my veins and making my heart feel like it was about to explode. The big guy leaned down and zapped

Andrea again, the buzzing sound deafening in the room.

Finally, he stood back up, thrusting his hand toward me. "Hi, I'm Xander. Your next-door neighbor."

A part of me relaxed, and I reached up to put my hand in his. Jesus, his hand engulfed mine like I was a child. I'd never met a man so big before. I wonder if he was proportionate.

"The noise makes sense now." I slapped a hand over my mouth. I was definitely in shock.

The behemoth didn't take offense, just tilted back his head and laughed.

I looked past him at the door. "Huey!" I breathed. I looked down at Andrea, then back at Xander.

He waved a hand. "Go get the little one. I've got this."

I raced to the other room, and there was Huey, still sound asleep, swaddled tightly. I picked him up, careful not to wake him, and held him to my chest. All the fear came rushing back, and I sucked in lungfuls of air.

"Nova!"

Devan's voice from the living room had me running back out of the room, straight into his arms. He squashed me and Huey in his grip, waking up the baby, who grumbled and then started to whimper.

"You're okay. You're okay," he whispered, his hands running all over my back. I pulled back a little, gently bouncing Huey, but I stayed wedged to Devan's side.

He rubbed his hands all over my back. "This is my fault," he murmured. "All my fault."

I thought I'd be a tear-fueled mess, but right now, I felt nothing. The cops came in next, followed by the paramedics. One of them guided me away, and I handed Huey to Devan.

"Hey there, my name is June. I'm just going to get you cleaned up." That was when I realized I was bleeding. There was blood on my hands, and my face was sticky. There was blood on Huey's sleeping sack. Panic hit me again, and I reached for Huey.

"There's blood on that. Take it off him," I yelled at Devan, who didn't tell me to calm down; he just did what I asked. He threw the suit away, and then Huey was just Huey again.

"Look back at me, Miss Stone. I need to check out your face." The paramedic held my face firmly as she checked me over. "Your nose seems to be broken, but everything else looks okay. Did you lose consciousness at any point?"

I shook my head. "No."

"You have bruising on your neck."

"She tried to choke me," I said through the lump in my throat. Now that the medic had mentioned it, it kind of hurt to talk or swallow.

She looked over my head. "She probably should go to the hospital and check if there's any serious damage, but she doesn't look like she has a concussion."

Devan nodded. "We'll take her."

"Dev…" I just wanted to go home. Not here. Back to the home I shared with the guys, where I was happy.

"I'm not taking any chances with you. This was all my fucking fault. I knew Andrea was a problem, but I kept that shit to myself until I had proof." He looked tortured.

Andrea was in cuffs by the door, and there were even more cops. They dragged her out, kicking and screaming like a banshee, until it took two of them to basically pick her up and carry her out of my apartment.

One of the remaining cops strode up to me. "Miss Stone, how are you doing?" His eyes seemed soft.

"I think I'm in shock," I whispered back. I ticked all the boxes for it.

"I think you might be. Can you tell me what happened?"

I felt Devan's eyes burning into me as I recounted everything, all the things Andrea had said—about me, about Huey, about the gun and the struggle. He wrote it all down, not interrupting unless he wanted me to clarify something. I told him the gun was under the bed.

The crime scene guys turned up, and one of them took photos of my injuries, their manner calm and gentle.

They were still talking to the big guy who saved me, Xander, but beside him was a short woman with killer curves and wild hair. She was talking animatedly to the cops, showing them something on her phone. The big guy had his hand on her spine protectively, and I had to assume she was his girlfriend, my other neighbor.

Their size difference was… alarming.

"How does he not split her in half?" I whispered to no one in particular, causing the cop beside me to make a choking noise.

Devan let out a snort. "Can I take her out of here?"

The cop nodded. "She'll need to come down to the station and give an official statement sometime in the next twelve hours or so, but she can go home now. We'll be here for a few more hours."

"Come on, Star. I'm taking you to the hospital to get checked out, and then we're going home."

I went with him willingly. I didn't ever want to come back here if I could help it.

CHAPTER
Forty-Six
RIVER

THE CALL I'd received from Devan that day was the worst one of my fucking life. Firstly, because I'd completely missed it while we'd been out on the ice training, and secondly, because if anything had happened to Nova and Huey... I shuddered even thinking about it.

I didn't let either of them out of my sight for a week. Nova was putting up a good front, but she'd whimper and cry out in her sleep. We all ended up sleeping in the media room, and Rigby had dragged Huey's crib in there too.

The press had a field day with the story. We were already newsworthy, so throw in a psycho stalker and a hostage situation, and we were nationally syndicated news. I heard from Ludo, whose sister was a marine biologist in Australia, that we'd even made the news over there.

We weren't just an attention-grabbing headline, though; we were people. What they'd found in Andrea's apartment had been terrifying. Pictures of me everywhere, like a fucking shrine. She had a body pillow with my damn player photo on it. Old condoms and sweat-covered towels. Jerseys and photoshopped pictures of us together. Compromising photos of her with me, but my face photoshopped on.

I had no idea what she'd been planning to do with those ones, but they scared the hell out of me.

She wasn't granted bail and was put in a psychiatric treatment facility while she awaited trial for attempted murder. I hated that Nova would have to go through that. Hated that she'd have to relive those moments again.

And through all this, we were expected to play as normal. Nova had promised she was okay, and Devan was working from home, putting his VP in charge of anything that didn't need his direct input. That made it partially better, but I hated that I couldn't be there for her, and I knew Rigby felt the same.

We had a meeting with Monderra, and honestly, if I didn't like what was said in the meeting, I was this close to telling him to fuck right off. I had no patience for his money-making bullshit when my girlfriend had almost died at the hands of a fucking sports reporter.

Turns out ASPN had received multiple complaints from cameramen and photographers assigned to her, about her obsessiveness about the IceCaps and me in particular. They'd ignored the complaints because she was pretty and the viewers liked her.

Ted, her cameraman, had personally come and apologized to me. The guy looked rough, his face etched with guilt. "I'm sorry, man. I knew she was off, and I reported her to HR, but I should have warned you specifically. I didn't think she'd do that shit, you know?"

Yeah, I got it. Destroy my career in the media, sure, but no one expected her to be a gun-wielding maniac. I didn't blame Ted, but I sure as shit blamed ASPN. Devan was having his lawyer sue the company on Nova's behalf. It wouldn't make up for the mental damage, but it would give those fuckers a bit of accountability.

I met Rigby in front of the elevators. We'd both been summoned, apparently.

"You think he's gonna trade us?"

I shrugged. "He'd be a fool to do it now that we're in with a chance at the playoffs. He'd wait and spring it on us after the season was done." He wouldn't want us to put in a half-assed effort, like we ever would. I loved my team too much to punish them for Monderra's bureaucratic bullshit.

We were led into the conference room by the receptionist, and Monderra was already there with the team lawyers, as well as Monderra's daughter. I'd heard he was training her to take over, but she looked like she wanted to be anywhere but here. The lawyers all looked stony-faced.

Ah shit. This wasn't good. My agent, Tony, was there too, and I raised an eyebrow at him. He shrugged, like he didn't know what was going on either.

Didn't matter. Even with the mess that my private life had been, I'd played fucking well this season. There was no doubt I was an asset to a team, and if it wasn't the IceCaps, I'd find someone else who'd take us. Me and Rigby. It would be tough, but we were good enough that someone would commit to us both, even if we had to take a bit of a pay cut. It was worth it to keep our family together.

"Thanks for coming, boys. I know you weren't expecting this, and I appreciate you taking the time."

Well, I hadn't expected polite Monderra. That shit made me even more suspicious.

He continued, "My daughter has informed me that I have handled this situation all wrong." The girl in question raised an eyebrow at us. "She tells me that my expectation for the relationships of my players is… What is it you said?"

"Archaic and out of touch with most of today's societal expectations, unless you're a middle-aged white man who has all the benefits of society and expects everyone to conform to your belief system since you hold a position of power over others."

Rigby sucked in a breath, and Tony snort-laughed, then badly tried to cover it up.

Monderra gave baby Monderra a haughty look. "Indeed. So I apologize, personally. What happened to your girlfriend is horrifying to me, as a father and a husband." He gave the girl a soft look. before turning back to us, now all business. "As such, I'd like to extend your contracts for another year and promise you the full support of the team in your unconventional relation- ship." Baby Monderra sighed and rolled her eyes, but I just grinned.

"We appreciate the offer, Mr. Monderra. We'll have our agent and the lawyers look over the contracts," Rigby answered, and I nodded.

I stared Monderra down. "I love the IceCaps. But I love my family more."

He nodded. "I understand."

The lawyers and Tony went over the specifics of the deal, negotiating among themselves, while I zoned out. I liked our agent, and it benefited him to get the best deal possible for us. I would have kept the same deal as always just to stay in this place, with my friends and a home where Nova and Huey were settled, but I didn't tell him that.

Once we were finally free of the meeting, Rigby and I got the hell out of there.

"What do you think? Is Monderra giving us blood money so we don't out him after this disaster?" Rigby asked as I negotiated the traffic.

I shrugged. "Probably. But I'd prefer Nova to be

secure and happy where she is then take revenge on the fucking old bastard for the way he handled shit."

Rigby grinned. "Did you see the way Tony was eyeing the tiny Monderra? I can't even remember her name."

Yeah, our agent was definitely more than a little interested in the owner's daughter, but he knew better than to compromise his work ethics, especially if she was really going to be running the IceCaps one day. Monderra had the right idea, because if he couldn't get the members and fans on board with us all being in a relationship with one woman, then Baby Monderra was going to struggle when she took over, being a female team owner in a world of good old boys.

It was coming up to the Christmas break, and I was excited for Huey's first Christmas. *Our* first Christmas. "I think we should ask Nova to marry us."

Rigby turned to me, his mouth hanging open. "You don't think it's a little soon?"

I shrugged. "We don't ever have to have a ceremony, but I think a physical sign that we're in this relationship for good, all three of us, would cement our bond."

Rigby frowned, chewing his lip as he thought it over. Finally, he nodded. "I think I'd like that. I want her to know that we're serious." He looked at me as I pulled up into the driveway, ignoring the paparazzi still camping at the gate. "If it's okay with you and Devan, I think I'd like to give her my grandmother's engagement ring. I know you guys could afford a Mt. Rushmore-sized rock, but it would mean a lot to me."

He looked so unsure in that moment, like I'd throw a tantrum about that shit. I pulled him into a man hug across the center console. "I think that would be perfect. I think she'd like that too." I swallowed hard. "I never said this, man, but thank you. Thank you for being my friend. Thank you for pushing me and Devan out of our comfort zone and giving us the opportunity to find someone we could love this much." He opened his mouth to protest, but I shook my head. "Nah, man. We both know we wouldn't be where we are today without you. I love you."

Rigby grinned at me, thumping me hard on the back. "I love you too, man. Obviously." He grabbed his door handle. "Let's go inside before the paps get a picture of us hugging and then run a story we were tongue-kissing and having a torrid affair."

I snorted. "You'd be so fucking lucky, man."

We hurried into the house. If someone had told me six months ago it was because I was eager to see a woman and not a cold beer, I'd have laughed. The house was quiet, though.

"Hey, where is everyone?" I called. I'd never tell anyone but my therapist, but every time I came home and the house was empty, I still wondered if she'd decided to leave because it was too much. I knew better now, but it didn't stop the fear that they'd leave one day.

"Out back in the hot tub," Nova called back, and Rigby slapped me on the back with a grin.

"First one there gets Nova on his lap."

I grabbed him by the shirt and yanked him back. I was going to get the girl—but then I'd give him a turn, because that's how families worked.

Epilogue
NOVA

EIGHT MONTHS LATER

"SO, I feel like everyone thinks they know your story, but do they really?"

The interviewer sat across from us in the living room, her face perfectly made up and her phone recording on the coffee table between us. Huey was in the playpen with his favorite IceCaps toy, flinging it around happily.

We'd agreed to a single interview, and the money would go to the American Stroke Association in Alana's memory. We'd decided, after a lot of begging on their behalf, that it would be the best way to put the whole narrative to rest, and also shed some light on the ideals behind a poly lifestyle. To explain that it wasn't one size fits all, despite the crap being spouted in the newspapers again this week. Apparently, we'd inspired the sports world to evolve from the ground up, but that didn't mean that the world was taking it smoothly.

I smiled at the interviewer. "As outsiders, no one ever knows the real story, do they? Unless you are living it, it's always just rumors and conjecture."

River snorted beside me. He was still super pissed with the whole media storm that had gone down when we first got together. I couldn't blame him.

The interviewer didn't seem to take offense, though. To her credit, she focused on me instead of fawning all over the guys. "That's very true. Some have discredited your relationship as a media stunt, others as an attack on religion, but more than a few people have argued that polyamorous groupings are the way of the future, especially as the world gets more and more difficult to navigate on even a dual income. Working class families are in a similar position as the single mother of a decade ago. Struggling to make ends meet. The working poor."

I shrugged. "I couldn't even begin to comment on that. I've never been in that position, but I understand that a lot of families live below the poverty line. I wouldn't suggest polyamory as a financial strategy, though. It takes a lot of hard work to balance the needs of four adults and a child."

The interviewer smiled. "And one on the way."

I grinned at her, stroking my stomach. I was only just starting to show, but it had recently become head-line news. That was another reason we'd decided to give this interview.

"Yeah. At least there's always someone about to do night feedings," I joked, and the interviewer laughed along with me.

"Any idea who the father is?" she asked, making Devan scowl.

I patted his thigh gently. "Of course I do. It's Devan," I said softly. "And Rigby and River. They're all the father. The exact paternity isn't something we need or want to know unless there's a medically necessary reason for it."

She nodded. "Understandable." She looked at her notes, and then turned her attention to Rigby. "Some people are saying polyamory is the key to winning the Stanley Cup. Congratulations again, guys. As a lifelong IceCaps fan, I couldn't be happier for the win."

Rigby grinned, and damn, the man was disarming. The poor interviewer looked like she'd been struck by lightning. "We had a lot to win for, and we're stoked that we could bring the Cup home to Ann Arbor. It's easier to focus on hockey when we aren't constantly being hounded."

The interviewer got serious. "Andrea Esperanza was sentenced last week, receiving a life sentence with a twenty-year non-parole period for the attempted murder of yourself, and the conspiracy to murder your infant. Do you find comfort knowing she is behind bars?"

I hated talking about Andrea, but I knew with her recent sentencing, it was going to be a question that came up in this interview. "Miss Esperanza was extremely unwell, and I hope she gets the help she needs while incarcerated."

The interviewer's eyes were soft with understanding. "So, can you tell me how your story started?

I grinned, looking between my guys. This story I didn't mind telling, because although it had a tragic beginning, it had a happy ending.

"It started, I guess, with a knock at the door…"

Acknowledgments

This book took a village to create, more so than normal. As an Australian, I like ice hockey, but there's nothing quite like living and breathing the sport. So I needed help, and my amazing readers provided. Honestly, you guys are the best.

Firstly, I have to thank Pascal Morency for answering all my inane hockey questions, from training and travel, right through to the Stanley Cup playoffs. It was super informative and he was so patient, so if the hockey scenes in this book feel authentic, you can thank Pascal for that! If you find any errors though, that's on me and my terrible note taking. "I'll remember that" is the biggest lie I tell myself daily.

Secondly, I have to thank Amy Jo Schuster and Robert McSweeney, who went out on a limb for me to make sure this book was the best it could possible be. You guys are wonderful and I can't thank you enough.

Lastly, massive shout out to Nicole and Stephanie, who double checked that even with all that help, I still didn't mangle the scenes. I appreciate your speed and your kind words. Thank you!

About the Author

Grace McGinty is eclectic. She has worked as a chocolatier, a librarian, a forensic accountant and finally a writer. Like her professional career, the genres she writes are also eclectic. She writes romance, reverse harem romance, fantasy, contemporary young adult and new adult books.

She lives in rural Australia with her crazy family, an entire menagerie of pets, and will one day be crushed by the giant piles of books that litter every room.

Head over to www.gracemcginty.com and join my mailing list for sneak previews into what she is working on and to stay up-to-date with new releases and giveaways!

Want more delicious sports romance? Check out 8 SECONDS TO FLY - a contemporary bull rider reverse harem romance.

8 SECONDS TO FLY

A STANDALONE COWBOY ROMANCE

GRACE MCGINTY

www.ingramcontent.com/pod-product-compliance
Lightning Source LLC
Chambersburg PA
CBHW050113120726
47904CB00004B/1328